THE VOICES OF THE DEAD

Then there was the grandfather clock of unbelievable size and beauty, all in red lacquer, with raised arabesques traced in gold – where on earth did he find that, and when, we wondered, as we listened to its dainty chimes, the silvery notes striking the hour. Even Nitti, the watchmaker, who was called in to see if the clock had suffered any damage in transit, to balance it correctly and synchronize the movement, was open-mouthed, said he'd never seen one like it in all his life, it must be terribly old. Because the clocks he was used to, with their chased jacaranda cabinets, were made by local joiners, only the movement came from abroad. People came from far away to listen to the clock, feast their eyes on it (the more daring would even timidly touch with their fingertips, as if deciphering an inscription on stone, the arabesques with their oriental patterns), charm their ears with the silvery tone of its dainty chimes, that same music which later, when the clock had stopped, was to strike the hours of our remorse.

AUTRAN DOURADO was born in Minas Gerais, Brazil, in 1926. From the age of fourteen he lived in the state capital, Belo Horizonte, where he attended high school and university. In 1954 he went to Rio de Janeiro as press secretary to Juscelino Kubitschek, the future president of Brazil, and he has lived there ever since. Since 1947 he has published novels and short stories, most of them set in his home state of Minas Gerais. *Uma vida em segredo* (1964) was published in English translation, *A Hidden Life*, in New York in 1967. *Ópera dos mortos* (The Voices of the Dead) was published in Brazil in 1967.

THE VOICES OF
THE DEAD

Autran Dourado

Translated from the Portuguese
by John M. Parker

THE VOICES OF THE DEAD
ISBN 0 600 20779 X

Translated from the Portuguese *Ópera dos Mortos*
First published in Great Britain 1980
by Peter Owen Ltd
This paperback edition 1983
Copyright © 1967 by Autran Dourado
English translation Copyright © 1980 by
John M. Parker

UNESCO COLLECTION OF
REPRESENTATIVE WORKS
BRAZILIAN SERIES
This book has been accepted in the Brazilian
Series of the Translations Collection of the United
Nations Educational, Scientific and Cultural
Organization (UNESCO).

Zenith books (Hamlyn Paperbacks) are published
by
The Hamlyn Publishing Group Ltd.,
Astronaut House,
Feltham, Middlesex, England.

Made and printed in Great Britain by
Hazell Watson & Viney Ltd
Aylesbury, Bucks

To my parents

To Fátima and Andrew

To the many Brazilian friends to whom I owe so much

(Translator)

INTRODUCTION

Autran Dourado (Waldomiro Freitas Autran Dourado) was born and brought up in the politically and culturally important state of Minas Gerais. From the age of fourteen he lived in the state capital, Belo Horizonte, where he attended high school and university. In 1954 he accompanied the future president of Brazil, Juscelino Kubitschek, to Rio de Janeiro as press secretary. He has continued to live in Rio, but remains faithful to his background and his novels and stories have, with occasional exceptions, been set in his home state; more specifically in the small towns where he spent his childhood and which he has synthesized in the literary community of Duas Pontes.

Born in 1926, Dourado belongs to the generation of writers in Brazil who began to publish at the end of the Second World War – perhaps more significantly for them the end, also, of the dictatorial regime of Getúlio Vargas – turning their backs on the regionalist social-realist fiction dominant in the 'thirties and early 'forties, avoiding overt political orientation and following rather the introspective fiction of the same period, with its roots in Symbolism and the spiritual revival of the 1920s. While they concerned themselves with man as an individual and with predominantly spiritual and philosophical aspects, it would be wrong to suppose that they ignored social reality. However, their vision was a historical one worked out in terms of myth, eschewing the more immediate socio-economic realities in order to insert Brazil into what might be called the anthropological tradition of western Christian culture.

It is only in these terms that one can refer to Autran Dourado as a regionalist writer, including him in what is beginning to be known as the 'new regionalism' in Brazil, to distinguish it from its immediate predecessor, the 'novel of the North-east' practised by such well-known figures as Jorge Amado, José Lins do Rego and Graciliano Ramos (whose *São Bernardo* has also been published in English translation by Peter Owen in Britain and Taplinger in the USA). There can be no doubt that Dourado's works are steeped in the atmosphere of what we might call 'old Minas': the gloomy baroque of the eighteenth-century churches and the Aleijadinho's sculptures, the sluggish un-eventful monotony of life in the sleepy little towns of the interior, where gossip seems to be the main activity, yet which can be the scene of tragedies of almost Aeschylean proportions. This has been the case more specifically since the publication, in 1964, of the short novel *Uma vida em segredo* (English translation *A Hidden Life*, New York, 1967), which was acclaimed as a minor masterpiece by Brazilian critics. Although Dourado began to publish back in 1947, his early works reveal Existentialist tendencies which he subsequently abandoned and during the 1950s he seems to have been more concerned with the practice of character study, via a series of short stories. He returned to novel writing with *A barca dos homens* ('The Ship of Men', 1961) – translated into French, Spanish and German – a book which marks the beginning of his maturity as a writer of fiction. Always a careful writer, Dourado has usually allowed three or four years to elapse between the publication of each of his works of fiction. *Uma vida em segredo* was followed by *Ópera dos mortos*, the novel here

8

translated as *The Voices of the Dead,* in 1967, since when it has gone through six editions. In 1970 Dourado gave us the superb *O risco do bordado* – an English version of the title might be 'The Pattern in the Carpet' – in which the narrator returns to the scene of his adolescence to seek, in family and other relationships, explanations for an apparently fated past. *Os sinos da agonia* ('The Death Knoll') appeared in 1974, raising the intensity of tragic passion already achieved in *Ópera dos mortos* to an often unbearable temperature, in a tale of incest and murder evoking the classical stories of Phaedra and Medea, set in eighteenth-century Minas Gerais, when Brazil was still a colony of Portugal. *Novelário de Donga Novais* ('Donga Novais' Story Book') came out in 1976, reminding us, delightfully, that humour has been a frequent feature of recent Latin American fiction and showing us some of the more respectable members of the Duas Pontes community in quite unsuspected postures. Dourado's most recently published work of fiction was a volume of four novellas, *Armas & Corações* ('Weapons & Hearts'), published in 1978, which concentrates on the use of point of view and suspense in the telling of a story, while continuing to emphasize suffering as an essential feature of man's life on earth. (As I compose this introduction, news reaches me of another volume, shortly to appear with the title *As imaginações pecaminosas* ('Sinful Minds').)

Dourado is a writer for whom, true to his baroque leanings, death and the erotic are closely connected. The use of the word 'baroque' is not an idle label in Dourado's case. The author himself has acknowledged it on more than one occasion and his enormous admiration for the Spanish baroque master Francisco de Quevedo is only one of many symptoms. *Ópera dos mortos* is a novel whose baroque nature starts with its very title, not only in the

9

different meanings attributed to it by Dourado himself – seven, at least – but in the central reference to the opera, followed by the operatic form in which the novel is cast. The opening section calls attention specifically to the baroque nature of the architecture of the manor house, which is itself the key to the book : as the past speaks through the building, so the voices of the dead control the destinies of Dona Rosalina and José Feliciano, *vulgo* Joey Bird. The narrator is part chorus, the collective consciousness of the town, but overflows this classical function to become an involved party, which explains why he sometimes includes himself in the general first person plural, while on other occasions the members of the local community are 'they' and he clearly dissociates himself, siding with the inhabitants of the manor house. He has, undoubtedly, identified with them in the process of trying to understand their mystery. It is not my intention to provide a reading of the novel, but certain features do seem to require some explanation. One of them is the constant interweaving of dialogue, narrative and stream-of-consciousness, which leads to the author deliberately omitting quotation marks. It is also responsible for sudden switches of tense, which may seem to offend tense sequence, but which in fact point to deliberate fusions of narrator-time and character-time. Time, of course, constitutes one of the most important symbolic elements of the novel, constantly stressed in the many references to the stopping of the clocks and particularly in the re-enactment of two such scenes, not to mention the climax of the novel, when the last clock is stopped and Rosalina metaphorically joins the ranks of the dead, thus closing the cycle. The manor house is evidently a region of death – the references to its lack of movement are frequent, almost as if it were an underworld, with Quiquina as the Cerberus barring the entrance to strangers. There are many possible myth readings of *Ópera dos mortos*; perhaps, as with the novel's title, no individual one is intended or favoured – certainly, neither Joey Bird nor the narrator succeed in deciphering the enigma. Similarly, the Cota family is extinguished without having made its peace with the local community and at the level of Brazilian history this may be interpreted as the end of an era without a logical continuation.

A few comments on the translation. My intention has been to convey Dourado's mode of writing without falling into an unnatural, foreign-sounding English. Particularly, I have tried to ensure the correct linguistic register. This offers certain difficulties, because of the fluctuating position of the narrator and because of the way he mingles his speech with that of the characters. The general tone of the novel is high, yet one of the main characters (Joey Bird) is obviously semi-literate, at best. The 'incorrect' forms I have used occasionally in his speech are intended as a reminder, but have deliberately not been overdone in order to avoid lowering the tone of the text. With regard to names, I have translated those which *mean* something and would be meaningless left in the Portuguese; in a few cases I have substituted English forms for less important names which might make reading the text more difficult. My hope is no doubt that of most translators : not to have betrayed the original too often and to give the English-speaking reader a version capable of conveying some of the qualities of a very fine novel.

Coimbra. January, 1980   John M. Parker

Translator's notes are indicated by superior figures in the text and may be found at the end of the book.

'The Lord who owns the oracle at
Delphi neither speaks nor hides his
meaning but indicates it by a sign.'

HERACLITUS
Fragment 93

To Otto Lara Resende

I

The Manor

If you want to know the story, first look yonder:

In that house over there, the one with all the windows with coloured transoms, lived Rosalina. A house of the gentry, at least that's how they used to see themselves. It still preserves its stately, aristocratic bearing, the manorial air that time hasn't altogether worn away. The paint of the windows and the door is faded with age, the plaster has fallen away in places like great sores to reveal the stones, bricks and laths of its flesh and bones, made to last a lifetime. Some of the window panes are broken, but that was done by the local kids when they were up to mischief and came to pester Rosalina (not with malice aforethought, just lads with nought better to do with themselves), and she hiding behind the curtains and drapes. The handrails of the wrought-iron balconies, with their stylized flowers, arrows, scrolls, esses and fretwork, have lost many of the wine-coloured cut-glass pine-cones which topped the support brackets and put a delicate finishing touch to the balconies.

Now then, look closely at the old manor, but with your memory, your heart – your mind's eye, not your eyes so much, they're only the access, it's the way you look that counts. Look into the distance, look at the manor house as if you were looking in a mirror and try to see through to the other side, to the bottom of the lake, beyond the beyond, to the end of time. Go back in time, turn the clock back, come with me in your imagination; back to the time of Colonel Honório[1] – João Capistrano Honório Cota, to give him his full name, known to us all, a man of honour, the man you want to know all about, the man you've heard of already and know by reputation – we'll talk about him later, about his properties, or rather his father's – Lucas Procópio Honório Cota, a man known to us by hearsay, with a dark hidden past, tales told late at night, a shadowy figure, half legend half real, memories of him fading, the southerner come back from the backlands of Minas Gerais when the gold dried up, disastrously, and the mines fell silent; and they had to return and forget the stones and the gold, the impossible wealth they'd dreamt of, these cattle breeders, men of wealth, spendthrifts or skinflints, according to their nature or experience, now all landowners, lecherous, incestuous, nigger owners, land snatchers, paving this empty land with their children and slaves, riding hills and mountains, politicians and tax-evaders, they went planting farms, fencing corrals, setting up shelters and stores, scattering towns throughout the state of Minas, seeking the good growing lands, the red soil and other soils coloured by blood and tears – on his land, Lucas Procópio's, donated by him all legal and above board, they built Carmo Church and the town square.

Go back in time, try to anyway. See the house as it used to be, not as it is or was just now. Pay attention to the structure, keep in mind the baroque and its transformations, note the form of the manor, see it as a whole, by itself, suspended (no, time! halt your wheels and your sands, leave the house as it is, was just now, or used to be, just for us to see it, we want to see it; not possible with your destructive intervention, which merges and so distorts), for the moment, forget the signs, the silent messages of ruins, of disasters, of fate.

The house is in Carmo Square, where the church was sited. Carmo Church was the town's first stone and brick building. Afterwards Lucas Procópio had his house built (at the time only the lower part), and tried to parallel the style of the church, whose design and façade were meant to reproduce the experience the men had gained from the churches in Ouro Preto and São João del-Rei. But poorer, without the richly carved stone pediments which the baroque embellishes with its idle scrolls; and yet impressive, all white, with its stone door frames and corner stones, its panelled door, the two oriel windows, one either side, above the doorway, the cornices wrought in gentle curves and its single tower rising from the ridge of the gable roof. From the tower you have a bird's eye view of the rows of houses that sprang up at the back of the church, against the wishes of the founders, who wanted to see Carmo Church rise supreme, towering over the town in front of it. From the tower you can see the square, a smooth empty stretch of flattened earth occasionally disturbed by sparkling dust devils, the cross in the centre of the square, the streets running down from it, the white walls of the cemetery, the gaping red-jawed craters at the side of the road leading out of the town.

(Rosalina knew every inch of Carmo Square, for ever behind the curtains watching the church, the houses opposite, the teacher training college, the road. Her vacant listless eyes would scan the heavy silence of the square, the solitude of a stretch of open ground at three in the afternoon, the cloudless summer sky, the sun baking the earth, blazing back from the white walls, the donkeys standing hobbled by the cross, their panniers empty, waiting for their owners – slow and tired, grazing with hard muzzles, bickering over the odd tuft of grass which forced its way through the hard earth – someone coming slowly into the square, trying to avoid the sun, and her eyes would follow with the indifference of someone killing time, until the person turned the corner or disappeared out of sight at the far end of the street.)

If you wish, you can see Rosalina, follow her every move, just as she used to watch the passers-by, though not with her

15

glazed eyes, her listless indifference. But first, look at the house, leave Rosalina till later, there's plenty of time.

In Lucas Procópio's time the house had just the one storey, just like himself: thick-set, planted firmly on the ground, with its four windows and the door in the centre heavy, high, rough-hewn. His son, Colonel Honório Cota, increased his father's fortune and added to his estate, changing its name to Little Stone Ranch. A man without his father's roughness, more civilized you might say, paid a lot of attention to his appearance, prided himself on his bearing, a gentleman he was. Same with the house: he added a second storey to it and did it with taste. The ground floor lintels were heavy and straight, you might say they displayed the harsh, uncouth, morose character of old Lucas Procópio, while the lintels of the upstairs windows, set directly above the lower frames, were softened by a slight curve, embellished by the addition, above, of delicate cornices which continued the twist of the lintels.

When the mason Colonel Honório had sent for from so far away, just to refashion the house, said perhaps the best thing to do is put new lintels on the lower windows, with the same curve you want on the upper ones, I've seen plenty like that in Ouro Preto and São João, he pulled a face. The very idea, change things, he thought. I don't want it all changed, he said. I'm not knocking down what my father put up. What I want is to add what I've got to what he had. I am him, now, inside, in the blood. The house must be the same, that's how I want it. Him and myself. The man looked rather bewildered, couldn't properly make out that peculiar bond of people and house, he being from other parts, so the colonel cleared his throat and said don't you know your trade? Do what I'm telling you, then, think about it, put your brain to work and come up with a design. If it's good, I'll give my approval. The man was about to say something, talk about building practice, but the colonel cut him short. And see here, young man, he said, I don't want it to look like two

16

houses, one on top of the other. I want one single, whole house, him and me together for always. The mason saw the far-away glint in his eye and realized that the colonel wasn't talking to him any more, but to someone far off or to no one at all. He spurred his mule and went about his business.

The mason chatted to the townsfolk, asking questions, trying to find out what old Lucas Procópio Honório Cota had really been like. It's because of the house front, he explained carefully, in his reedy voice, afraid that someone might go and tell Colonel Honório that he was going about snooping into the life of the colonel's late father, the illustrious Lucas Procópio Honório Cota.

Precious little he found out, except the murky stories of an old-timer dispensing his own form of justice, taking off with his slaves into those forests, invading, bargaining, swindling, hoodwinking, settling, enlarging his domains, a cacique, an absolute monarch. That harshness of his didn't help with the design. Better after all to leave the lintels as they were. Perhaps he might agree to a cornice over the door, to add a touch of distinction. Yes he'll like that. As for the door, I'll make it double-leaved, nicely decorated, with good big panels, he won't want to keep that crumbling old thing, more like a barn door, begging his pardon, though he's not listening. What he won't knock out are the lintels.

Me and him together for always, the mason hummed over and over while he worked on the design.

Contrary to what Colonel Honório suspected, the mason knew his trade. He made that squat house rise up from the ground like a tree, he gave it life and lightness. The mason weighed things up, attempting to fuse in a single whole (he balanced cubic masses, he aimed for a clear-cut symmetry in the apertures of the house front, making it soar upwards, light and airy) those two – the misty figure of Lucas Procópio and this other one, Colonel João Capistrano Honório Cota.

The manor was finished. At first sight no one would say – you've only just noticed yourself, after I spoke about it – that the house you see here began as another house. But if you look carefully you can see in the one house, in the one person, the features of two different people : Lucas Procópio and João Capistrano Honório Cota. Me and him together for always, the mason hummed over to himself, as he rode back home.

You see how he made the door, with two leaves and decorated panels. He was right about it being better, wasn't he? Look how it blends with the upper windows, yet it still manages to fit in with the heavier ground floor windows. The mason pieced it all into the design, there's no single dominant line, yet just look how the door is the point of perspective. There's skill for you, the mason with his thin reedy voice, who'd have thought it, he was really good at his job.

I can tell you're not very interested in the manor, in the house I mean. You don't need to pretend, I can see it in your manner, in your eyes. Every time I mention a person you open them so wide I'm surprised they don't start watering. I know, I know, you want to know it all, everything all at once. You want to know the stories, the history, one can see that straight away. You want to know about Lucas Procópio, about João Capistrano Honório Cota, about Rosalina. Everything that took place. You'll perhaps be wanting to get out and about, leaving yours truly, your guide, behind and snoop around like the mason did to make his design for the manor house, so that you can write your story. You've heard about Quiquina already and you're probably wanting to go looking for her to find out what she'll say. That's mean, she never would say anything, she doesn't say a word. Even if she did, in her own particular way, you wouldn't understand, it's very hard to understand Quiquina, it was the same before, after what happened.

You say you do like old things. Maybe. People say one

thing and mean another. Perhaps you're only saying it out of politeness, maybe not. Maybe you're not even listening. You do really? truly? Well then, follow me, it's worth your trouble, the manor is very old. Look at the upper storey, Chinese-like, shaped like a pyramid and spacious to hold in place the rows of curved roof tiles. Just look how the coping reduces the bulk of the roof, looks quite oriental, you might say. Look how it – the roof – curves upwards at the bridge and the corners of the eaves, soaring on up. And see, it doesn't weigh the house down, it's like it was set lightly on top. Look at it all from different angles and get the feel of it, don't let your eyes stop in one place, be like the river which is for ever moving, changing even when it's still. See the effect, it's only an impression, but imagine it; note the illusion of the baroque, even in motion it's like a still stretch of river; note the play of light and shade, of volume and space, of straight lines and curves, of straight lines broken off but taken up again further on, of whorls and scrolls, you keep being surprised. Each time you look, each side, different times of day, you get a different picture, a different sight. The choice is yours, look : the house or its story.

That's enough, isn't it? I can see it's people you want. Bear with me just a bit longer, just to please me. Go back to where we started, the coloured windows. The panes of the upstairs transoms, bluebottle blue and purple, in the shape of a marguerite. The purple is the same as in the glass pine-cones. What perfection! They don't make things like that any more these days. How extravagant they were in those days!

But do as you please, go back to your naturalistic way of seeing things, seeing only the here and now : the eye doesn't move, the baroque does. You're right, the house is certainly in need of repair, painting, renovation as they say. There's even grass growing up on the roof and on rainy days there's an endless spattering through leaks in the tiles.

(But hush, now. Rosalina is coming to the window.)

2

The Honório Cota Family

When Colonel João Capistrano Honório Cota had the upper storey added to the house, he was little more than thirty years old, but he was already as serious as an old man, reserved, conscientious. He paid a great deal of attention to his dress, to his sober appearance. He wore a double-breasted worsted jacket and a linen waistcoat with a heavy gold watch chain across it; only his trousers were like those of everyone else in the town, being of duck, except the ones he wore for special occasions (baptisms, funerals, weddings – then he wore a suit, all the same), but always extremely well pressed, with a beautiful crease. It was a pleasure to behold:

With his leisurely, unhurried gait – the world could wait for him – throwing out his narrow chest, his careful gestures, his deep voice and slow speech, he would walk down Church Street, uttering greetings in a polite, gentlemanly manner to the people he met coming in the opposite direction and to those who appeared at their windows often with the sole intention of watching him go past. You could recognize him from way off: tall, thin, gaunt, like a large stork. Being so tall he might have been clumsy, but he wasn't, he always gave you the impression of a man of upright, dignified stature. He neither threw his legs to the side nor did he walk with them apart, but stuck them out straight, as if he were measuring his steps, knees stiffened into a straight line. When he was on horseback, on his way to Little Stone Ranch, on his white horse with the patterned leather and silver trappings, then he really did look the part, a fine imposing figure of a man. He looked like one of those knights of old, straight out of the pages of *Amadis de Gaula* or *Palmeirim de Inglaterra*,² on their way to war after being admitted to the knighthood.

No one would guess, said the older folk, that that one there's a child of Lucas Procópio. He was in league with the devil, old Lucas, who'd think this is his son, with the solemn, courteous manner of an honourable man? Lucas Procópio should be here to see him. You don't have to be a bully and run riot to prove you're a man. Oh, we respected him all right. After a time his word became law. Old Lucas Procópio, that is. We certainly had respect for him, plenty, but it was more out of fear, on account of the demands he imposed on us. It was a respect we didn't make much show of though, it wasn't given freely, like the respect we feel for Colonel Honório Cota, a feeling that comes from inside yourself, sort of quiet like. You take pleasure in going to the window and greeting him in the proper manner. Good afternoon to you, Colonel, how d'you do, sir.

The colonel went trotting by on his white horse, sitting bolt upright, as stiff as if he had a corset on, and raised his hand to his head in a wide sweep as if he was going to take off his hat, but merely touched the brim with his fingertips in answer to the greeting. Sometimes you would hear his deep voice speak a word of greeting. No one could remember ever having seen him stop by a window for a leisurely talk. Conversation is reserved for house visits, there's a proper time and a proper place for it – the colonel didn't excuse himself, he just told you, as if he'd been asked for a piece of advice. He didn't speak down his nose at you, he didn't need to raise his voice for everyone to hear him. We bowed our heads in silence, we listened, we respected him. Who would think of contradicting such a circumspect and dignified person?

So there he went trotting by on his horse, on his way to Little Stone Ranch. He would stop off, first, at the warehouse to talk over the orders with Quincas Ciríaco. Quincas was the son of one of his father's old overseers. Now he was his partner in the coffee warehouse and the de-husking machine. Quincas was the only person with whom he spoke more freely, talked at length (they'd been kids together), indulged in idle chat. Quincas Ciríaco did more listening than talking though, he liked listening when João Capistrano held forth. When he was standing, Colonel Honório Cota didn't lean against the piled-up sacks of coffee, nor, when he sat down, did he let his body slump in the chair, rarely even leaned against the back of the chair. He sat as if he had a heavy sword stuck firmly in the ground between his open legs and was resting his right hand on it. He never relaxed his old-fashioned self.

And Quincas, he just listened, hardly speaking at all, just punctuating the other man's words with a comment or a nod of agreement. Although he was now a man of substance, of independent means, Quincas still had, deep down, like a past you can't forget, that tongue-tied respect we all had out of fear of Lucas Procópio Honório Cota. Of his arrogant, bullying manner: shouting, cracking his stockwhip in the air. No, João Capistrano wasn't of the same stuff as his father. He remembered João as a boy, the two of them galloping in the fields, into the forests before they were cleared ready for the coffee to be planted. That whiff of good-smelling air that came from the coffee plantation. Come on João, your father's calling, he could hear the voice over in the slave quarters. João would quiz the air, straining to catch the sound of the voice.

Since boyhood João Capistrano had been a serious man, he never joined in, always kept a respectful distance. That sad look in his eyes was already there when he was a boy. Quincas Ciríaco seldom heard him laugh and he couldn't

22

remember ever seeing him split his face. Never more than a slight curling of the lips, showing the tips of his teeth, his eyes asparkle : Quincas knew he was laughing. He was just laughing inwardly. Where had João Capistrano got this way of his, he sometimes wondered. It was very difficult to see his father in him. Except for his face which had Lucas Procópio's features (his fleshy lips, his thick bushy eyebrows). João Capistrano must have buried his father deep down inside himself.

At times Quincas would fall pensive seeing João Capistrano hold forth in his leisurely fashion. Occasionally, when Capistrano got to talking about the great plans he had for his life, for his ranch, for the business, and got excited in his own way, his eyes all aglow, a slight quiver in his bony hands, Quincas Ciríaco would imagine he glimpsed his father's shadow in him. But it was a different Lucas Procópio, composed, balanced, thoughtful, not that whirlwind of a man. Quincas tried to change the subject, trim the sails of João Capistrano's more extravagant ideas. He didn't like seeing Lucas Procópio standing there in front of him. He didn't want Lucas Procópio for his partner. He was afraid the old boy would come back to life and come claiming possession, giving orders, lording it. Like before.

When he was a boy he'd often sworn to himself that he would rid the world of that scourge. He would imagine himself lying in wait, with his father's double-barrelled shotgun, the cartridges packed with buckshot : Lucas Procópio keeling over with two bullets in his chest (one wouldn't do, he always imagined two, one mightn't finish the old devil off), his clothes soaked in blood, foaming at his filthy mouth. Good riddance, you old thug, you fiend.

All right, João, let's be less ambitious, think ahead a bit he'd say, to rid himself of the unnerving shadow of Lucas Procópio's presence. In reality, he knew it was just fancy, João Capistrano was nothing like his father, he would tell himself afterwards. Yet there were those bushy eyebrows, those thick lips. . . .

So where did he get his personal manner from? From Dona Isaltina, naturally. It was she who saw to his upbringing when Lucas Procópio died, when the boy was just ten years old. But even when Lucas Procópio was still alive, Dona Isaltina competed with him in bringing up the child, trying to curb in the boy the father's brutish nature, teach him manners. Make him a decent person (she didn't have to try that hard, João Capistrano was always rather aloof, he really didn't enjoy going with his father and only went along when Lucas bawled come here, my lad, I don't want a pansy in my house), make him a man like her own father and brothers, who lived in the capital, her father a serious, refined man who had been a member of parliament in the Emperor's day, and who at his death she reckoned was virtually worshipped in Diamantina, where Lucas Procópio went to fetch her away to get married. She taught him his letters, passed onto him everything she knew, then wanted to get him a tutor from São Paulo, but Lucas said that was going too far, he didn't want his son getting to be a college man, one member of parliament in the family was quite enough! He said this knowing how much it upset his wife. The main thing for her was that he shouldn't be anything like his father, spawning illegitimate children all over the place, without a thought for his position, bragging about it, even being called father in her presence by his godchildren, that rabble of half-breeds who came for his blessing.

Yes, he had certainly inherited his manners from Dona Isaltina, his courteousness, though he wasn't effeminate, but what about the heart that yearned for wide open spaces? No, not his heart, Dona Isaltina was lively and cheerful, excessively so, even, when her husband was not around. João Capistrano's eyes had in them the tormented sadness of a man locked in a struggle with his ghosts. João tried to paint for himself and for the locals (in vain, because the older ones had been familiar with Lucas Procópio and they knew that the picture he was trying to push was like a counterfeit coin which you take just for fun, when it's only a trifle and seeing who it's from), as patiently as if he were building a wall a few bricks at a time, a different picture of his father. When João Capistrano talked of his father with the same respect and reverence that are reserved for the virtuous, Quincas Ciríaco lowered his eyes, allowed him to go on for a while, then changed the subject as soon as possible.

No, Lucas Procópio was not the man Capistrano made him out to be. Really, he knew it himself, he was just playing a sort of game. Wasn't he doing his best, without letting us see that he meant to change them, to efface the most obvious signs of his father? Isn't that what happened with the name of the ranch? And with the manor house? He said one thing and did another. It was the mason who told Quincas Ciríaco that story about the manor house : me and him together for always. It's only when you know that you can see the manor is really two houses. He is his father after all, Quincas said to himself, falling silent. João Capistrano went on his way.

Quincas Ciríaco tried to forget the shotgun, the target seen a thousand times in his dreams, the grim figure who even now appeared to him in his sleep. No, he couldn't be my father, never, thought Quincas. How could he even have thought such a thing? You start thinking, the thought takes hold of the reins, next thing you know you're at the brink. Why should he imagine that what was said about others was meant for him as well? Every child that's born on Lucas Procópio's lands is like him. Not necessarily in features, but in temperament, in speech. This fancy took hold of Quincas Ciríaco, plunging him into anguish as he lay awake at night. He tried comparing himself to his father, the overseer who lived with his mother. That started him feeling different from his father. How was it possible, how? There was his mother stuck in the house, pretty, very pretty she was, so obviously virtuous and pure. His father on horseback, off on business, riding all over the properties, passing on orders. Quincas kept watch to see if Lucas Procópio ever came to the house when his father was away. Never. Not even at night, when it was dark and his father was away from home. But you can't get rid of these feelings, you keep gnawing away, like a dog growling over its bone in a dark corner. He looked for the likeness, trying to find his own features in his father, the overseer, striving after a peace of mind denied him by the oppressive presence of Lucas Procópio. With hate inside him, gritting his teeth like someone – not a watchmaker – trying to put a watch together, he would try to emphasize his father's features in himself : he took to imitating his father so that there would be absolutely nothing in him of Lucas Procópio, the swine. Only later, much later, did he see, looking with care at the two portraits, his own and the other's (that was how he thought of his father), how much he looked like his father, he was his spitting image, as they say. But the evil was done by then, bitterness in his heart, remorse for having had the thought, all churned up inside by those sleepless nights.

Let's talk about something else, he'd say to João Capistrano. What about the accounts? Or, perhaps, let's get the spike and broach one of the sacks to see what grade of coffee's in it. We should be getting a big load today, must be ready to get it away immediately. Pass those bills of lading over to me, laddie. Then I'll be off to the Mogiana office to see if that shipment has been despatched yet. Things like that, to drive away the ghost of Lucas Procópio, a right bastard he'd say now that he was sure he was not his father. And he would put the shotgun down, he didn't have to shoot Lucas Procópio now. The warehouse, with its narrow corridors running between the solid square piles of sacks, seemed to become brighter and he could smell the warm, rich, stuffy aroma of the coffee beans, the sharp stench of the hessian sacks, instead of the smell of wet

26

grass on Little Stone Ranch, formerly known – for him always would be – as Haunted Ranch.

When João Capistrano Honório Cota decided to move into town and live in his father's old house, he was harbouring certain plans, at that stage still very vague and hazy, which had come to him during his solitary expeditions about the Little Stone properties, wafted on the scented breeze from the coffee plantation. He was borne along by fragrant dreams of high honours that he did not dare tell anyone, not even Dona Genu or Quincas Ciríaco : for years those plans were to stay in embryonic form. When he sent for the mason to add on the second storey, Dona Genu – who was a sensible woman, with both feet on the ground – said João, what do you need such a big house for? The ground floor is quite enough for us. No, said he, I'm going to be needing lots of rooms, lots of bedrooms and lots of drawing rooms. And with a sort of shyly affectionate gesture, pointing at his wife's belly, so that she blushed, I'm expecting plenty of guests out of there.

But he wasn't really thinking about those guests, although he wanted them badly enough. He imagined the house full of people, day and night, the noise of people talking, vast quantities of coffee being served, the port glinting in jovial hands. Their children, the townsfolk, relatives from far away come to witness and take pleasure in his fame. What this fame was exactly, he wasn't sure. The stuff of dreams. Only later was he to experience the definite, conscious longing for power and glory.

So he sent for the mason. And the mason came, and with him carpenters skilled in carving and other specialized craftsmen, the locals alone being inadequate to undertake the building of Colonel João Capistrano Honório Cota's splendid manor house.

And everyone came to watch the second storey growing brick by brick, stage by stage. Every day there was something new and everyone enjoyed watching Colonel Honório Cota's great undertaking. And when they saw how it

27

pleased him, they laid on the praise, redoubled their flattery and kowtowing. The more inquisitive of them wanted to know what the façade would be like when finished, if the balconies would have wrought iron railings, if the buttresses under the eaves would be visible, if there would be cornices, how the ornamental work would look, and they all received explanations, since he was now well-informed, after so many close conversations with the mason and the craftsmen. He knew all about the materials they were using, everything of the very best. Good for Colonel Honório Cota, giving the town a boost, we said, openmouthed with amazement and pride. We need a man like that as head of the town council, in charge of the county council, the State government. And we started talking about getting the streets paved, about running water and all manner of improvements for us all, about progress, justice and freedom, and other preposterous and exaggerated ideas. The colonel listened in silence. He didn't encourage us, he didn't influence us, but you could see that these grand ideas delighted him deep down inside. When they got to talking too much, in the chemist's shop, at the meeting place or in the church square, blowing their ideas up out of proportion, the colonel soon put a stop to their chatter : the time's not ripe, he may have muttered in the innermost recesses of his soul. Anyway, this show of nonchalance, this example of lofty good sense, merely added all the more, in our estimation, to the superiority of this good, upstanding man, who had come among us to sweep from the sky, once and for all, the heavy black cloud, the living presence of Lucas Procópio Honório Cota.

When the house was ready, the brickwork rendered and painted white, with blue window frames, the ornaments were added, those coloured cut-glass pine-cones, for instance. Next came the furniture, the wicker chairs, the china-cabinets, the marble console-tables which banished to remote corners of the house the old rosewood and maplewood furniture of the late Lucas Procópio. Then there were the cut-glass chandeliers with their thousand glistening facets, the heavy ceiling lights, the spittoons of English porcelain with painted flowers, there were even milk-glass pitchers, music boxes and silver caskets with no specific use. Also, to our great delight, there appeared a black grand piano, which was absolutely enormous, we'd never seen anything like it, and a gramophone. Then there was the grandfather clock of unbelievable size and beauty, all in red lacquer, with raised arabesques traced in gold – where on earth did he find that, and when, we wondered, as we listened to its dainty chimes, the silvery notes striking the hour. Even Nitti, the watchmaker, who was called in to see if the clock had suffered any damage in transit, to balance it correctly and synchronize the movement, was open-mouthed, said he'd never seen one like it in all his life, it must be terribly old. Because the clocks he was used to, with their chased jacaranda cabinets, were made by local joiners, only the movement came from abroad. People came from far away to listen to the clock, feast their eyes on it (the more daring would even timidly touch with their fingertips, as if deciphering an inscription on stone, the arabesques with their oriental patterns), charm their ears with the silvery tone of its dainty chimes, that same music which later, when the clock had stopped, was to strike the hours of our remorse. Then there was the pendulum clock for the pantry, but we'd seen plenty of those, though none as fine as that one. He did everything to perfection and the children added a noisy accompaniment to all this to-ing and fro-ing, keeping it up even when Colonel Honório was around, just as if the circus had come to town.

And so the colonel began to lord it in the manor. You could see him and greet him with all the courtesy that was his due, when he deigned to emerge on the balcony. Some of us even went out of our way just to enjoy the pleasure of walking past the manor and doffing our hat to that grand personage. Everything there was going just great, words couldn't describe it, just silent admiration. Quincas

Ciríaco was the only one who had a thought for a possible calamity, for what fate might bring, for what was to happen.

Despite all this, the colonel was not a happy man, you could see that. When he emerged from his wild dreams, which Dona Genu was far from even imagining (a load of nonsense, she thought, where does he get his brooding from? Old Lucas Procópio, he was all wild talk), she could see a film of sadness veiling his big dark eyes. She knew the cause of his sadness, or so she thought. He doesn't say because he doesn't want to upset me. But I know, don't I, she said to herself, gently stroking her belly, which was starting to grow again. Another one, another one, yet he hasn't a single one. Dona Genu became more unhappy at the sight of the dejected look João Capistrano had in his eyes when he was silent.

The children didn't come or they didn't survive. They were premature and stillborn, or they didn't live beyond the first six months. João Capistrano thought back on his own life, his father lording it when he was a youngster on Haunted Ranch, or Little Stone Ranch as he called it now, he remembered the curses, the moans, the thick blood of the Negroes. Occasionally, he would confide his sorrows to Quincas Ciríaco, who listened in silence, his only words of comfort being : that's how things are, João, God's will has many paths. Quincas was given to reading prayer-books and lives of saints handed out by the missionary friars, in secret he even read the ones from the Protestants, who were disapproved of when they came through the town.

And off would go the Negro Damião, followed by young Quiquina, but with no one else in attendance, carrying another wasted mite to the cemetery, the blighted fruit of Dona Genu's womb. What on earth did Quiquina see in the funerals of those scarce-born babes? So Colonel Honório and Dona Genu went on filling the red earth of the grave-yard. The rooms in the manor house seemed to get emptier and emptier.

And yet, João, God's will has many paths. One day Rosalina appeared, born in January, under the sign of Capricorn, as Quincas Ciríaco found from his almanac, and by Christmas she was still flourishing and beautiful. The colonel was delighted, wanted to show how pleased he was, have everybody share in the miracle. He gave more money to Carmo Church, paid for the church-front to be painted and for some of the repairs Father Gonçalo was in need of. He even commissioned a new crib, such as ne'er was seen, with life-size figures of the saints and the Three Wise Kings, and all manner of animals : the bits and pieces were all made on the spot, large and carefully fashioned, from the water-wheel, with running water, to the ox-cart, and everything else within the bounds of imagination. The comet hung glittering above the words : peace on earth to men of good will.

Dona Genu and Colonel Honório didn't for one moment dare to hope that it might be a male child, a boy to continue the family name, which was what he wanted most of all. If God's will has many paths, it was better to go along that one thankfully and with a pure heart.

At the baptism – which they delayed a while, in order to see just how God's will was faring (she wouldn't die a heathen, at the last moment she would be baptized anyhow, with water from a cup or anything wet) – Quincas Ciríaco brought her a gold medal which he made a special point of having blessed at the shrine in Aparecida do Norte, to be on the safe side, to be more reliable, you might say. He hoped that when she grew up to be a young woman, her grace and beauty would soften the wild brutish destiny of Lucas Procópio Honório Cota. None of those features, the bushy eyebrows which lingered on the face of João Capistrano and made him return, like a sleepwalker, to the territory of Haunted Ranch.

Now the manor began to swarm with guests. Night after night there was jollity, like a perpetual party. Dona Olympia, who gave piano lessons to Dona Genu (poor thing, she was no good at it, her fingers were too stiff, an old monkey can't learn new tricks, she'd say, wanting to give it up, but Dona Olympia insisted, her husband wanted her to go on, so she carried on suffering) – Dona Olympia was invited to come and play those local waltz-tunes that everybody could sing, and they served coffee, madeira, port, or cane-brandy for those who didn't want to try something new, as the case might be.

Colonel Honório Cota was happy with his position of importance. Even relatives from far off, on his mother's side, from Diamantina, or on his father's side, from Ouro Preto and São Paulo, people of some status, travelled the backlands all that distance to come and visit their cousin. Other visitors included the priest, the local mayor and councillors and the other colonels and ranchers from the area. Even Senator Dagoberto, when he was in town electioneering, was a guest at the manor, and the bishop plus all his apparel and his secretaries would be an honoured visitor. The only one who viewed it all with a degree of scepticism was Quincas Ciríaco, who brooded – he wasn't very sociable and only came with Dona Castorina to see his god-daughter of a morning, when there weren't so many people about. What's all this about, Quincas old friend, having doubts on my score? Don't you approve of my way of life? João Capistrano asked him one day. No, it's not that, João, it's just the way I am, you know me, I don't feel at home with a lot of people. He didn't take offence, he never got annoyed at the things Quincas said. In any case, he was surrounded by people, he wasn't going to attach that much importance to his taciturn friend.

This was the atmosphere in which Rosalina grew up and was educated, she had the best education available in those days. She grew into a pretty, well-built girl, with the lads all running after her, with one eye on her inheritance. She was sixteen now. As time passed and Rosalina grew up, so the dream of power and wealth began to grow and take shape in the colonel's mind. To start with they were hazy, meandering dreams, but they gradually took shape and colour and the dream turned into decision. The colonel's determination was iron hard. Colonel Honório was not a politician, which was unusual for a man of means at that time. Unlike his father, who laid down the law, appointed and dismissed the council, João Capistrano didn't get involved in political infighting, he only cast his vote according to tradition, which would mean following the example of Lucas Procópio, voting the way he would if he were still alive. With his usual prudence and circumspection, avoiding making remarks or stating opinions, he supported the government party. There were two parties, the PP, known as the Frogs, and the old MRP, also called the Parakeets.[3] The Parakeets had been in control of the town for more than twenty years. To be precise, the parties were the same as in the days of the Emperor, liberals and conservatives, having changed their names along with the change of circumstances.

So it was a surprise to us, though to him a logical, inevitable outcome of his visions, of those long thoughtful silences, when one day Colonel Honório began to comment on the running of the town, on the behaviour of some of the councillors, even of the mayor. They shouldn't do this or that, that wasn't the way to go about it, it was all wrong. How could they let the place stagnate, do nothing for the town, no worthwhile piece of public works? What they did do, they made a mess of, made you feel ashamed. We agreed with what he said, because of the manor house. In no time he was being ironical, making remarks with tongue in cheek. And ironical comments from a man as retiring and circumspect as the colonel were effective, they hit the target. Not even Senator Dagoberto was spared this time.

All this quickly reached the ears of the mayor, who was the leader of the Parakeets. The Frogs were croaking with delight. That was just what the frog was needing, they said, in fun, behind Colonel Honório's back. Dona Genu,

33

who was beginning to realize what her husband was aiming at, thought it a load of nonsense, he'd taken leave of his senses. Quincas Ciríaco said nothing. He kept to the warehouse or went off to his little ranch; he didn't come to the manor house any more, but no one noticed because they were so taken up with the wheeling and dealing. One day the mayor came round to ask for an explanation and Colonel Honório gave him a piece of his mind. Who do you think you are? I expect more respect from you, you peasant. Do you think I'm a parakeet, think I'm going to muck in with you? The colonel had made his choice, we were no longer in doubt, he had joined on the side of the Frogs. Thereafter the fight was on, the insults, the mudslinging, even obscenities, the closing of the ranks. Colonel Honório grew in stature, he was becoming a colossus.

In the manor house, at night, when the town lay sleeping, Colonel Honório Cota was like a house with its windows ablaze with light. He would be reading, looking for old papers in the chest where they kept Dona Isaltina's belongings, the things she had brought from Diamantina. He visualized himself as mayor, member of the lower house, perhaps even senator; these dreams of his were boundless. He was high-minded, had great plans for Brazil. He embodied his grandfather, imagined himself making long speeches in the Constituent Assembly under the Empire. Dom Pedro[4] was in a terrible mood, you could see he would end up doing something silly. João Capistrano Honório Cota was now Deputy Cristino Sales, his grandfather. He sat next to Bernardo Pereira de Vasconcelos,[5] one day he even interrupted José Bonifácio,[6] he could actually see his face, because of the Independence watch with his portrait inside. When Your Excellency is at the rostrum, you dignify not only this House, and your own Province, but this Nation, etc. He read his mother's books and when, in a basket of stuff, he came across the *Letter to the Electorate of Minas Gerais*, by Bernardo de Vascon-

34

celos, he really grew in stature. In his deep, powerful voice he read aloud Vasconcelos's letter as if he had written it himself. Dona Genu, who was in the bedroom, shuddered with fear that he would be heard in the street, and what would people think? Madness, a screw loose, loony.

People didn't just think, they were talking. The Parakeets' broadsheet, printed by the notary, called Colonel Honório Cota an addle-brained Don Quixote. But he was too proud to take any notice, he knew his history, he wasn't a turncoat, Bernardo de Vasconcelos had been called worse by the Marquis of Baependi. Sticks and stones, he said. I know my Brazilian history, I'm no ignoramus, not like that stamp-licking scoundrel of a notary. He'd better watch out for himself in that office of his, thundered the colonel. Let him start sneering at me or making snide remarks and I'll take my horsewhip to him. As a matter of fact, it didn't upset him. He remembered an old picture with a tall, thin horseman just like himself, bony and thin-faced, lance at the ready. He looked for the book and the picture among his mother's belongings, but didn't find them, and not finding them he put memory to help imagination and created a new likeness for himself. If we'd looked closely (you never notice these things at the time, only later), he did have something of the Knight of the Faith, and of the Sad Countenance, too.

Not that we laughed at him, who'd think of laughing? Nothing had any effect on Colonel Honório Cota, who moved forward fearlessly, righting wrongs, tilting at windmills. We continued to regard him with respect, even with a touch of fear, now. We got such a kick out of being in the presence of the great man. He was a bit of a nuisance to his colleagues in the party, though, because of his crazy ideas and the difficult words they'd never heard, which he had come across in his old books and papers, those mummified expressions he picked up in the letter of Bernardo Pereira de Vasconcelos. It all had a meaning for him, it was all part of a glorious struggle. Right from the start, an action which only he understood and few noticed was to stop using his silver Independence watch, which had been a present from Senator Dagoberto and had the picture painted by Pedro Américo[7] embossed on the outside and the portrait of José Bonifácio on the inside. He didn't throw the watch out, he wasn't given to pettiness, he just hung it from a nail on the drawing-room wall, never wound it up and there it stayed for ever after. The colonel went back to using his old gold hunter.

The rise and fall of Colonel João Capistrano Honório Cota was soon over. Apart from one or two deaths, small fry, everything went fine. The elections came, the colonel won by a handsome majority, there it was for all to see. The odd thing is, that wasn't what we did see, afterwards. Afterwards, what they did was something like this : they took the records to the notary's office, for him to register the result and draw up an affidavit which would be sent by post to Belo Horizonte, ahead of the records. But they made a slight alteration : the votes that had been cast in favour of João Capistrano Honório Cota and his party were credited to the Parakeets and vice versa. The affidavit was sent off to the capital all right, but the records went somewhere else, to the back of beyond, we never knew where, to which town. Did anyone know? No one ever found out. It all happened so quickly, the Frogs didn't even have time to celebrate with fireworks, shooting off guns and shouting their heads off, because the ones who celebrated victory were the Parakeets. The manor house was soon full of people waiting to hear what João Capistrano would say, to see what he would do. Amid the angry shouts and general indignation, Colonel Honório Cota's deep voice could be heard. We are going to the courts, I won't be robbed of my victory, he said, with a fine, booming voice, full of self-assurance. You could see how pale he was, his eyes were sunken, his hands trembled more than usual.

The lawyer, Dr Plácido do Amaral, was entrusted with

the case and set off for Belo Horizonte loaded with law books, statute books and old texts. In his wisdom he assured them of victory, it had been a bad business, very dirty, planned by that dago upstart, the notary. When the records were compared with the affidavit they would see it was a gross, a flagrant error, or so he said. The Parakeets sent their own envoys to Rio de Janeiro and Belo Horizonte to discuss the matter with Senator Dagoberto and their other friends in high places. When Dr Plácido do Amaral returned he was not as hopeful as when he had set out. We'll get an annulment, new elections, at least, I'm sure of that, that's what the law says. He approached the Parakeets, conferred with the senator, who came specially to the threatened stronghold, and as discussion followed discussion, the situation began to change. All at once the visitors started to disappear from Colonel Honório Cota's house. He found that he was the only one who was still indignantly saying we shall go to the courts. His companions would merely nod in agreement, then say they had an important engagement and escape from the embarrassment of his company.

João Capistrano sought out Quincas Ciríaco to ask his advice. He had forgotten his old friend, now he came back to him. Quincas Ciríaco listened to it all in his usual brooding silence. Quincas knew the whole story, but he listened to his friend's version. Then, João, he said, don't you see, can't you see, are you quite daft, can't you see that you've been betrayed, double-crossed in the most contemptible fashion? What! exclaimed João, going white as chalk. Quincas Ciríaco thought he was going to have an attack and die on the spot. But he had to go on, he couldn't hide the truth from Capistrano. Politics is like that, João – muck-raking. You don't know it, you're a good man, first time out of port. He paused a moment, choosing his words with care so as not to hurt his old friend more than was necessary. You've been discarded, João. But João looked at him vacantly, not taking it in. He explained: the

Parakeets and your Frog friends have come to an agreement, they've divided the spoils, half of the posts for each side. The mayor is still a Parakeet. João Capistrano closed his eyes, he felt for a pile of sacks to lean against, so as not to fall. Quincas Ciríaco expected something terrible to happen. What is it João? What's happening? Say something João. João Capistrano said nothing, gave no sign of life. The doctor, the chemist, thought Quincas quickly. But there was no one around and he couldn't go out, leaving João Capistrano alone in that state.

You mean to say, said João Capistrano after a while, struggling to reassemble his remaining scraps of consciousness. Quincas Ciríaco gave a sigh of relief and waited for João Capistrano to come to completely. Accept the inevitable, João. See the way it is. If you want to go on with it, just realize that politics is like that, you can't change it – muck-raking. At this, João Capistrano suddenly grew in stature, from being a prostrate, dejected, vanquished creature, a nobody. I shall go alone, quite alone, against everything and everybody, I shall go alone and knock at the door of the courts. Quincas Ciríaco was about to say the game's not worth the candle, when the government wants its own way you can put the law in your pipe and smoke it. He thought it, but didn't say it. I have means, I can sell my share of the warehouse, I'll take what I can get for Little Stone. Who do they think they're dealing with? I am the son of Lucas Procópio Honório Cota! And he went on, not addressing Quincas: he knew – I was against, I thought he was in the wrong, I wanted to be different – but he knew the proper way to deal with this riffraff. The only language they understand is a good whipping, the bastards!

It was Lucas Procópio's voice again, Quincas Ciríaco saw that. And I thought that voice had gone for good! Now it's here again drumming in my ears. Be off with you, you devil, out of my sight or I'll kill you, you swine. He patted his shotgun, aimed straight at Lucas Procópio's chest. One shot and he'd be down. No, not one, two, the man has nine lives. Isn't that him come back to threaten me? João Capistrano's glazed eyes were certainly not fixed on anybody, they had an otherworldly look in them, they were clouded with dark shadows. Quincas Ciríaco closed his eyes so as not to see that mouth, those bushy eyebrows. A bearded man, with a whip in his hand, was bawling at him.

But silence flooded back into the warehouse and Quincas opened his eyes to see who was there : Lucas Procópio or João Capistrano. Slumped on a stool, his long arms hanging down limply, his head sunk on his chest, it was João Capistrano, and he was staring at the stone floor as if he was looking for something among the coffee beans scattered about, only he knew what, something that was lost for ever.

Quincas Ciríaco took him by the arm to take him home.

We saw them go by. They walked slowly, in silence, eyes downcast. The people in the street walked on more quickly; those who were at their windows stepped back to watch from a discreet distance.

And people no longer had the courage to greet Colonel Honório Cota the way they used to : they knew that he wouldn't return their greeting, wouldn't raise his hand in that wide sweep, touching the brim of his hat ceremoniously with his fingertips. Colonel Honório Cota returned to his former abode to put away his sword, his helmet and his armour, he stood his lance in the corner. He went back to being what he was before, or rather he became gloomier and more withdrawn than before. Only Dona Genu shut herself away to weep over this terrible misfortune, why had he got mixed up in that business? Rosalina, who was by now a young woman, tried to give him support, but her way of doing this was to copy her father's silence, and with it his morose, sombre air of injured dignity, his quiet, undying, unforgiving hatred. Occasionally she would venture a tentative endearment, taking his long, thin hands

39

in hers and stroking them. He would look across at her and his dark eyes would glisten with a pinpoint of light like the beginning of a tear. He would withdraw his hands, he daren't indulge his emotions in that way.

And so Colonel Honório Cota ceased to return the greetings, the courteous salutes still addressed to him by those with less on their conscience. He only left the house to meet Quincas Ciríaco or to go to Little Stone Ranch, where he now spent days on end, alone. If you addressed him, he was never impolite, but his reply would be monosyllabic, quietly strong, abrupt. If it's a business matter, step into the warehouse, that's where I can be found, was the most you would get out of him. And in business matters he became a different person : hard, inconsiderate, merciless.

When Dona Genu died, a year later, the whole town thought the time had come to repair the damage, set matters right again. He would be amenable to friendship once more, the manor house would again be full of people. He would see that we were with him in his grief and misfortune. That we had forgotten, we were good at heart. The coffin, the bier and the wreaths were set up in the drawing room and the manor house was packed with locals, their faces solemn in mourning for the loss of such a good person as was Dona Genu : we were showing that we suffered too.

Colonel Honório, locked himself in his room. He only emerged when it was time for the coffin to be closed. In the drawing room, he looked down on everybody, without speaking a word. He made straight for the huge grandfather clock, the one I told you about, and stopped the pendulum. It was three o'clock. We waited in agony, expecting him to do something else, say something, some were already sorry they had come. None of the things we expected happened. He didn't refuse our greetings, he accepted our condolences with lowered eyes, answering that we shouldn't have gone to the trouble. People said that at one point he wept, but no one actually saw him – cry? that man? On such occasions people invent a lot. In the funeral procession Colonel Honório walked just behind the coffin, he didn't help carry it, leaving that to us, he had Rosalina on his arm. Like him, she did not weep or sob, her eyes were red and moist, glistening with tears which we saw because we wanted them to be there.

Dona Genu's death did not bring about the hoped for change in his relations with the townsfolk. He became more withdrawn, he would pass us by with unseeing eyes, staring into empty space, somewhere far off. The only change we noticed was that he began to go for long walks with Rosalina in the evenings. After supper, off the two of them would go, walking at a slow pace in the direction of the charity hospital, up above the town, from where they could make out the hills receding into the distance : green at first, turning blue, then grey, in the direction of the border with São Paulo. There the two of them indulged their sorrow and loneliness. Until night began to fall and they returned home.

With a pang in our hearts, we did our best to forget, tried not to imagine the colonel's hollow cheeks and sunken eyes. We discussed pleasant topics. But it was impossible not to see. God would not let us forget the grief that cast its shadows over the town's streets.

And so time passed, because it had to pass. Time had to pass for another death to occur, so that we could again visit the old manor house and see its furniture, its grand piano, the treasures which fascinated us; the milk-glass pitchers, the cut-glass ornaments, the music-box on the marble console-table, the speaker of the gramophone, untouched for years, the grandfather clock still standing at three o'clock.

That was when Colonel João Capistrano Honório Cota died. Everything happened the same, just like a repeater clock. The house filled with people, we were going to pay our respects, convey our condolences, offer our compassion to Rosalina to see if she would accept us.

The scene was repeated, we witnessed it with our minds back in the past. There we were again, like one of those film serials in which the hero has been left in a dangerous situation and you don't know how he's going to get out of it and continue his feats of derring-do. We hoped that the scene would be repeated, so that there could be a more suitable outcome, not the way it stopped before, only hinted at.

The scene was repeated, everything as before. Rosalina was locked in her room and we waited for it to be time for the coffin to be closed, to see if she would appear. People talked about trivial matters, to take their minds off what was bothering them, but nobody ventured to mention what they were all thinking about. Had it been prearranged? Would she be coming? She wouldn't? She would?

There was only one difference. Rosalina, or so it was rumoured, no one knew where the rumour started, Rosalina wouldn't come, nothing was going to make her. We looked at Quincas Ciríaco, waiting for some word of command from him. Quincas Ciríaco had taken over from Colonel Honório Cota, he was the one who should give orders in that house. Even the priest went over to have a word with him. I'll go and fetch her, she'll come, Quincas told the priest. All of a sudden, this is what we saw:

Rosalina coming down the stairs, looking more than life-size, head held erect, majestic, condescending, just like a queen – her eyes fixed on a point way beyond the wall, with stately steps, not a moment's hesitation; she was carrying a shiny object in her hand. Rosalina was every bit a figure cut out of a history book, like those lords and ladies in stories, not quite real, ethereal, moonshine. Anything could happen, we might be waiting for the bride to descend the palace staircase, with her gown trailing over the velvet carpet, followed by pages, nobles, the retinue:

we could be awaiting the arrival of the queen. There was nothing we didn't see, even things that were not there to see. You could hear people breathing, the slightest sounds, there was something ghostly about it.

We made way for Rosalina. Just when we thought she would go over to her father, she turned towards the wall and the shiny object she had in her hand was the gold watch belonging to the late João Capistrano Honório Cota, the one we loved to see him take out of the pocket of his white waistcoat, a beautiful, unusual timepiece, a genuine gold hunter. She hung it on a nail, next to the Independence watch. All the clocks in the room had been stopped, we just heard the silence ticking away. Only those who were in the pantry could hear the pendulum clock spinning its web.

Telling it now, it's difficult to believe. You arrange, balance, put together, weigh things up, work things out according to a design, try for harmony, symmetry, rhythm. That's just how Rosalina did it, choosing every movement : she looked at her father in his coffin, covered in flowers, and entwined her fingers as if about to pray, but she didn't. She turned suddenly in the direction she had come from. We watched in deathly silence : Rosalina walked back up the stairs, exactly as she had come down.

The one who cleared the atmosphere and brought the house back to normal, breaking the spell and restoring the peaceful silence of things at rest, the one who really showed what he was worth was Quincas Ciríaco. I was very fond of him, he was like a brother, Quincas said.

3

Silken Flower

Rosalina pulled back the curtain and appeared at the window. Carmo Square was empty, parched and glaring. Two in the afternoon. Only. Just now she heard the pendulum clock striking in the pantry. The donkey by the cross, the red earth. Quiquina had gone to deliver the crêpe-paper roses. The procession, the litter bearing Our Lady of Carmo all decked out for the festival. Tomorrow, from her bedroom, hiding behind the curtain, she would watch the procession set out. She wanted to see the paper and fabric flowers, those flowers which she alone was able to fashion so skilfully. Dona Genu had insisted on her learning. It was a Japanese called Tamura – she'd never seen a Japanese in her life – who taught her. He didn't stay long in the town, only a month. But it was enough for her to learn, she had to learn quickly. Mummy got these ideas into her head. Wanted her to be accomplished, thinking that she would get married. The piano – she'd never played it again since her mother's death, since things started to happen – the piano lessons with Dona Olympia, the fabric flowers.

Why was Quiquina taking so long? Funny, me get married. What's funny about it? I could easily have got married. Emanuel was keen enough. Not now, before, before things happened. Daddy was making plans for me, then he forgot me, got himself involved in that madness.

What was the need, he had everything. No, they couldn't treat him like that. Nor her. He didn't deserve that. So good, so silent, sorrowful. She must bear hatred for ever. I shan't forget, one shouldn't forget. Now it's just the two of us, alone in the world, her father said. When Mummy's funeral procession set out. We wept afterwards, we couldn't hold back the pent-up tears any longer. So that no one should see we'd been crying. In front of them. No one is to know, this death belongs just to us, what they say is all pretence. Didn't you see? With that riffraff that's the way it has to be. Or the way Lucas Procópio dealt with them. The only language they understand is a good whipping, that's what Father said. Grandpa Lucas Procópio. All those stories, contradicting one another. Daddy didn't get it straight, probably he didn't know it properly, when Grandpa died he was still a boy. He probably didn't remember him properly, everybody wanted to forget Grandpa. Why? The portrait in the drawing room offered no explanation. Make a flower to put on it. Nothing to be seen except that face, those big eyes, those bushy eyebrows, those fleshy lips half hidden by his beard. The stories they told. When he was alive, Damião loved to tell stories about Lucas Procópio. But when we children approached he would change the subject. Quiquina didn't know Lucas Procópio. She sometimes stands for ages looking at the portrait, then crosses herself secretively and runs back to the kitchen. Why does she do that? Lucas Procópio scared people, even though he was dead he still scared people. Colonel Honório isn't like him, they used to say in the days when she was still on speaking terms with them, before it all happened. Then the manor was engulfed in silence : emptiness, the hours dragging by, sluggishly, cats lying in the hearthplace of melancholy. The clocks stopped. Except for the pendulum clock in the pantry. Two o'clock.

How long was it since Quiquina went out? Over an hour, at the very least. Can anything have happened to her? No, nothing. She must have stopped on the way, standing there open-mouthed, overhearing people's conversations. Just as well she didn't come telling tales afterwards. Quiquina's expressions when she was upset, her eyes bulging, her grunts. You go and deliver the flowers. Come straight back, we've still got dozens to do, she said slowly, speaking clearly, explaining things properly. There are times when you can't get through to Quiquina.

The church door was closed, she couldn't be there. In the priest's house, she sometimes went to ask him for a saint card. The little pictures of saints pinned on her bedroom walls, in the kitchen, in Quiquina's quarters. What did she see in them now? When she was a child, she too used to run after the priest asking for pictures of saints. Quiquina wasn't a child any more : she was old, much older than herself, old enough to be her mother. She used to lose her picture cards, Rosalina did. Quiquina always kept hers. When the missionary friars came, they brought coloured cards, much prettier, with perforated edges etched in gilt. She always mislaid them. Then she would search the whole house, like a mad thing. Has anybody seen my saint cards the priest gave me? Inside her school books in the drawers. She would search high and low. Quiquina, have you seen my saint cards? Like Mistress Beetle in the story she would say won't you, won't you marry me, I've got money, you can see. Quiquina would deny it, stamp her feet, about to cry. It was her, she suspected; Quiquina was pinching her saint cards, she could see it now. What did Quiquina want all those saint cards for? To go to heaven. When she was a girl, all right, but what did she see in them now?

Quiquina saw to the sale of the flowers. She clinched the deals, worked out the prices. She was good at setting prices. A bit cheaper for the church, though nobody gets them for nothing. And who could refuse to pay poor Quiquina? Quiquina planting herself in the doorway, motionless, wordless, waiting for her coppers. How much for a dozen carnations, Quiquina? Cloth ones. She worked

46

it out on her fingers, then held up her hands to show the price. Cloth ones were dearer, it was harder work and everything was so expensive. She didn't get involved, leaving it all for Quiquina to sort out. Where did Quiquina get so many customers? Because it didn't occur to anyone to approach her direct, they were afraid to speak to her. They would clap their hands at the garden gate and call for Quiquina. Flowers for Dona Rosalina to make. It was better for her, kept her hands busy and her mind off things, helped her to pass the time. Even travelling salesmen, who came to town to sell to the haberdashery stores, knocked at her door to order flowers. They bought dozens and dozens, for resale in bigger towns, cities. That was better business, flowers for the salesmen. Flowers for city dos, for women's hats (it must be nice to wear a. hat, what would she look like in a hat : in the dressing-table mirror, in her bedroom, she imagined herself wearing a hat), for brides' bouquets, the filmy organdy roses, fashioned so lovingly, were the ones she liked best. Those delicate, graceful roses, the ones they bought most of. Here in the town they had scant success. In the town all they wanted were orange blossom, she was sick of them. Quiquina, don't bring any more orders for orange blossom, if you can help it, she would beg, I'm so fed up with them. Quiquina would nod agreement, but whenever there was a wedding, along she would come with an order, laughing quietly to herself. Why did she laugh, what was so funny? It was just Quiquina's little joke, Rosalina didn't get angry. Or lilies for first communion, she was fond of those. She took special care with the starch, stretching the cloth tautly on the marble top of the console-table, they had to be stiff and smooth. The special shaping iron for lilies, the whitest velveteen that Quiquina could find. The iron well heated and clean, so as not to soil the material. When she was a child, before there was a Mr Tamura, they used real lilies. The priest had to bend over, she was very small. Dona Genu made a point of it : one's first communion ought to be made early. The priest placed the wafer on the tip of her tongue, she couldn't keep her eyes off his thick fingers, the yellow tobacco stains, it ought not to be allowed. Back from the communion table, head down, contrite, part genuine, part pretend, she listened to the remarks. A little bride, she looks just like a little bride. Emanuel wanted to marry her, she was no reject. The real lilies a bit faded, their white flesh bruised, from clutching them so tightly to her. The cloth lilies didn't come apart ever, always stiff and beautiful. They were the most successful, after the paper roses. When the missionary friars rounded up the kids, the church full of people. Then the sermons about hell, eternal damnation, souls in purgatory, they were supposed to pray for them, and about heaven too. The harmonium playing. The girls singing, herself all in white, a little bride singing. Eagerly waiting her turn.

Why didn't Quiquina come? Why was she so nervous? Nothing could have happened, nothing happened to her, Rosalina. She sought within herself the reason for her nervousness. Nothing special, a day like any other. Those long, empty days which she filled with her flowers. The slow, still hours. The grandfather clock stopped at three o'clock. Her father, moving more slowly and deliberately than ever, stopped the pendulum with trembling fingers, with the hands standing exactly at twelve minutes past three. Immediately afterwards the funeral procession began, Mummy going away for ever. Later on she was to repeat the procedure, just like performing mass. The gold watch on the nail on the wall, next to the silver one which was there first. She meant to do something obvious, decisive, for them all to see. She was trembling, her hands trembled, her whole body trembled with a faint hum, she thought she was going to faint. She had to be hard and cold, without emotion, just like her father stopping the grandfather clock, three o'clock. That's our stamp, the stamp of the Honório Cotas, she said proudly.

48

Better put Quiquina out of her mind, stop thinking about her. She tried to fix her eyes on the square. The white church, whiter still now because of the sun's dazzle. The sun flooded the square, glinting on the stones, shimmering in the air in waves like you see through distorted window glass. The training college which she had attended. Not a single memory of that time. She didn't want to remember, just look. Look at the little donkey which had eventually managed to shake off its halter. The first time she had noticed the little black donkey, it was still haltered. Those donkeys were a bit like her life, stuck in that window. It had struggled like mad to get free. Now it was hopping about, braying, like a circus pony : the man in the red tailcoat cracked his long whip in the air, the ponies pranced about the ring. When its owner comes back, the donkey will be well away. Has anyone seen a donkey that looks like this, he'd go asking around the whole town. No one would be able to give information. No more dirty little black donkey, left alone waiting in the church square. A hard-working donkey, with its bamboo panniers. The donkey, the man in the red tailcoat, the whip. Contrary to her expectation, after all those manoeuvres, the donkey stayed just where it was. Silly thing, it could have run away, far away, to Little Stone Ranch, for instance.

At Little Stone she had a beautifully caparisoned pedigree pony. Where was he now, that pony, Firefly he was called? His coat was so beautiful and smooth, not a hint of tick on it. He's gone, Firefly ran away, she cried at the thought that Firefly wouldn't ever come back. Firefly dead from a snake bite. Firefly did come back, he was found in a pasture, way off, his coat plastered in mud, covered in burs and ticks. What a job they had cleaning him up ! The donkey scoured the hard earth with its muzzle until it found a tuft of grass. Silly thing, if it moved closer to the shadow of the church it would find a juicy patch of tasty grass, surely it would like that. The donkey didn't see it, what it really liked were those scraps of grass that forced their way through the dry ground. In the patch by the church there were even some of those little yellow flowers, the sort you see everywhere. The donkey could eat the flowers as well as the grass, gorge itself on yellow flowers. Donkeys don't care for flowers, what they like is fresh, green grass, when they happen to eat flowers is it just because they don't notice?

She left the window and went back to the table, to her flowers. No, today she wouldn't carry on with the paper flowers. She wanted to make a huge rose, nicely shaped, an organdy rose, all filmy, in case a salesman came wanting one. Or – if it turned out particularly pretty – she'd keep it in the dressing-table drawer and try it in her hair. She would perform in front of the mirror, pretending to be a beautiful, elegant woman in Rio de Janeiro, going off to a party on her husband's arm. Quiquina wasn't to see her. She would lock the door, open the dressing-table drawer and fetch out the prettiest roses she had made and had kept because she couldn't bring herself to sell them. A bit self-conscious, as if she were committing some secret sin, coquettish. She was too old for such things. A pretty, extremely elegant woman : white dress trimmed with lace, her arms loaded with gypsy bracelets, diamond ear-rings sparkling in her ears. How pretty you are, he would say, stroking her hair and arms. On Emanuel's arm, and he all earnest, unsmiling. And she was pretty, all she needed to do was take more care of her appearance, change out of those dowdy dresses; she always looked the same, always those black dresses, perpetual mourning softened only by a white lace collar. But then she didn't need to change, she never left the house now, always at the window, always seeing to her flowers. It was hardly worth taking the trouble to doll herself up for Quiquina, she would think there was something wrong. Only when Emanuel came. Quiquina astonished, open-mouthed, seeing Rosalina dolled up as if she was still thinking of marriage.

The clay pipe, its embers glowing in the dark, she liked to stay puffing away in the dark. Quiquina laughing with her mouth wide open, dropping her pipe, she was laughing at Rosalina wanting to get married. No, of course she wasn't thinking of marriage. Emanuel was keen enough. Her father. You're not to look at boys, you mustn't encourage this rabble. After what has happened. These folk are just no good. One has to have some pride. If you lower yourself too much, you'll drag your arse on the ground. He even used coarse expressions now, didn't mince his words. Nobody's going to tread on our pride. They'll see.

Eyes closed, she strained after the dainty chimes of the pantry clock in the silent well of the house. She cast a stone into the still, smooth waters of the weir and the ripples spread outwards from the centre where the stone fell, as if you could see the petals of a rose opening out, opening until the yellow pistils appeared. She came down the staircase slowly, very very slowly. All those faces turned towards her, waiting to see what she would do. The tremor coursing through her body like waves of electricity. Her father stretched out in the centre of the drawing room, the four lighted candles. The smell of candles and flowers lingered in the house, clung to her clothes, stuck in her nose. Quiquina cleaned everywhere, but the smell was still there, coming from inside her. Then it disappeared, but came back again when she thought about it. Just like now, she remembered and back came the smell. At least the paper and cloth flowers didn't leave any smell, always clean, always pure, everlasting. An everlasting in the weir, the flower kept on floating on and on. The chimes of the pendulum clock spread out inside her like the stone in the weir. The flower.

It can't have been long since the pendulum clock struck two. The anxiety of waiting for Quiquina made her think more time had passed. She hadn't heard the clock strike again. It was only because Quiquina was late that she noticed the time, normally she didn't bother much, the hours were all the same to her. If it weren't for Quiquina she would even stop the pendulum clock, so that there would be nothing in the house to tell the time. Time would just be night and day, the two halves one can't stop. She opened her eyes, felt the delicate smoothness of the satin with her fingertips. A pleasant feeling, peacefulness, almost happy. Her eyes wandered slowly over the drawing-room furniture, the silent piano, which she'd never touched again, the vases, the house full of flowers, the flowers she made to keep her hands busy and her mind off things, then Quiquina collected them, made an armful of them and went off to sell them, just like now, she went out carrying the roses and didn't come back, like now, why hadn't she come back yet, can anything have happened to her? I couldn't live without Quiquina. She's getting old, is Quiquina, very old. When a Negro has white hair it shows they're very old. No, Quiquina would still live for a long time. What would it be like afterwards, when she was alone, all alone in the manor house with all the locked rooms. Even though Quiquina couldn't speak, she missed her. Quiquina bustling about the house, busy in the kitchen, in the garden, helping her with the flowers, her presence was a sign of life, of time. Quiquina meant that life was going on, that she wasn't dead, that her life was not just one long nightmare from which she would never wake up. Quiquina growing old. Quiquina bringing people into the world, delivering babies. When she was needed they came and called her even late at night. Not very old, not all that old. Daddy said she was about ten years younger than him. Yes, she is old, she must be pushing seventy. My God, if she dies what will become of me, alone in this huge house? I'll go mad, I'll die, and that'll be that. Nobody comes here, I'm not interested in anybody. Our pride, we're not to run after folks. Only Quincas Ciríaco, my godfather. His son Emanuel still comes : his manner, with his hat on.

'My godfather', Quincas Ciríaco, had died, leaving Emanuel to look after things, the warehouse, Little Stone Ranch, when she needed money Quiquina went to get it from him, he never came, except at the end of the year, to show her the accounts, the two of them so ceremonious and polite. He was keen enough once. Now he was married, he couldn't even think of it. A glass of port or madeira perhaps? He never accepted, always in a hurry, had some matter to attend to. She would dress with more care, she waited anxiously for the end-of-year visit. Nobody else. We quarrelled with town, we quarrelled with life.

Why was it her eyes didn't seem to see properly today, just glimpsed things, and from there she was taken off on her travels, into her memories and fantasies? She made an effort not to think, just let things exist quietly, on their own, without her, cold. But things in that house weren't cold or silent, a pulse was beating in her body, reproducing strange noises, like a door for ever banging if she lay awake at night. Now he's coming downstairs, the studs of his boots echoed in the corridor. Her father, or grandpa Lucas Procópio? Did Quiquina hear it too? But she wasn't at all afraid of her family ghosts, she wanted them to come and make her life less empty. The house was alive at night, or in the daytime when that silent emptiness cast shadows as if it were night, as if she could hear a heart throbbing in the pendulum clock. Whose heart? Her mother's, her father's, Lucas Procópio's? You couldn't tell. Perhaps the house had a heart. Nonsense, houses are made of stone, bricks, mortar.

There she was again, being borne off into the shadows. Like someone trying to stave off sleep (sleep weighing down her eyelids) and struggling back to waking time with a jolt, to the cold existence of things, so she now attempted to handle objects and feel their hardness. She ran her fingers over the table's surface, feeling its veins, sensing its filaments, sliding over its stains, pausing at the

53

scissors, the pliers, the wires, the steel shaping-iron, the pot of starch, then nervously creasing the silk, the velveteen, the organdy, all that paraphernalia she used for making her flowers. To overcome the anguish that now came from deep down inside, tearing her flesh, she began to say the names of things, out loud, ritually. As if she were repeating a lesson, as if she were listening to Mr Tamura giving her a lesson about those innocent, delightful flowers. For roses, organdy, satin or silk. Camelias, of velveteen or linen. For carnations and for the tiny violets one uses cambric, it is best. The shaping-iron must be hot. First you dye, then you starch. Mr Tamura's slit eyes – how did he still manage to see when he laughed? – blinked, his speech was distorted by wrongly pronounced consonants. After it is well starched and ironed, you stretch the fabric over glass, a marble surface is better, so that it will stay quite smooth, without any wrinkles, when it is dry. And she, or he, went on, violet, carnation, camelia, rose, apple blossom, marguerite, lily. When she got to poppy, her eyes felt heavy with sleep. Was it Mr Tamura who said from the poppy we get opium, the opium poppy? At night, before she went to bed, orange wine, when the madeira was finished. Sweet, she had to drink a lot of it. Quiquina was not supposed to see, she only saw afterwards when the decanter was empty. Rather tipsy, a pleasant sleep starting to numb her limbs, that itchy sensation in the fingertips, nice, pleasurable, her vice. Sometimes she had to get up at night and take bicarbonate for her stomach.

Now it was her eyes which scoured the walls, saw the stains, the cracks which she kept forgetting to have repaired (she didn't want people in the house, she could do with a hired man, to clean up the garden – a jungle, Quiquina has to do the weeding – to scare off the kids who jump over the wall and throw stones, jobs like that, but it couldn't be anyone from the town, only a man from another town), her eyes skimmed over Lucas Procópio's portrait and came to rest on the grandfather clock, covered in dust, it even had spider webs, she had pledged herself never to touch the clock again, although everything in the house was spotlessly clean, an obsessive cleanliness, she was a meticulous person, well brought-up, accomplished, Dona Genu's work. Her eyes came to rest on the two fob watches hanging above the console-table. The watches belonging to João Capistrano Honório Cota, she said with mock seriousness. Her father used to bring the watch close to her face, as close as the chain allowed, to show her the time. She asked him to teach her how to tell the time. He settled her on his knee, explaining the way the hands worked. The second hand ticked away hurriedly. Inside the Independence watch there was an engraving of a man without a neck – unless it was because of his shirt collar and his coat collar – he had a long nose, long hair like a woman, slit eyes like Mr Tamura's or like a circus elephant's, a lipless gash of a mouth, a man called José Bonifácio, the patriarch, her father said or was it her teacher at the training college? A vague desire to pick up the watch, open the case and have another look, after so long, at the face of José Bonifácio, the patriarch. But she couldn't handle the watches, she must never handle those watches. The watches worked a spell, though stopped they carried on ticking just like that lost soul in the house at night, with the windows open, the silent starry night outside, the wind whistling in the corners of the square, stirring the curtains, the doors banging, there was always a door banging in the depths of the night, when she was sleeping, immersed in sleep.

But now she was not asleep, she was keeping an eye on things. Things had no life, so they said, no mystery about them, exposed. But she saturated things with noise, she gave things a sap of life. She could see how everything was cold, contained, clean, as clear as a spring the very moment it spurts from a rock. Then it collected into a pool, lower down, near the bamboo hedge. The gilt-framed mirror on the wall (a lake) would reflect her body, but from where she was she couldn't see : the mirror was empty, mirror-glass. No wish to see herself in that mirror – in the other, all right, in her room, when she put the rose in her hair and she was a lady out for a walk; Emanuel offered her his arm – that mirror held in the depths of its waters images from the past, the candles sputtering, the bodies laid out, the dead hands crossed over their stomachs, the rosaries draped over them. When she stopped before her father's coffin, she began to shake, she wanted to feel those cold, white, yellowing hands, so that she would know the texture of dead hands, she had never felt a dead person's hand. But no, she didn't want anyone to see into her secret heart, no one was to see any action she had not prepared beforehand.

A door banged in the kitchen. Is that you Quiquina? she shouted. No reply. She got up and went to see if Quiquina had arrived. Quiquina was standing stock still in the middle of the kitchen, near the table, a look of surprise on her face. Now she was laughing, she pointed to the wad of notes on the table. Quiquina settled accounts when she pleased, Rosalina didn't bother. Quiquina probably kept more of it for herself; she didn't need it, when she needed money she sent to Emanuel for it; silly Quiquina, she could keep it all. Quiquina pinched the saint cards the friars distributed, pretended they had got lost, she didn't see them; later they would turn up pinned on the wall in Quiquina's room.

You took a long time, Quiquina. The Negress gestured vaguely. There's no more starch, I shall need more, to make some roses, said Rosalina. But Quiquina stared uncomprehendingly, so she said I don't want to make any more paper ones today, I'm fed up. What I want to make is a huge rose, for myself. Quiquina laughed approvingly, with an affectionate sparkle in her eyes. What on earth would she do if Quiquina were to die suddenly?

She went back to the drawing room. The rose, the

organdy delicate and filmy, for a ball. She had never danced, she imagined what a waltz must be like : light and airy. Emanuel. She would go over to the window, to wait for the starch. Quiquina had brought her tranquillity, she wasn't nervous any more.

The square again. The donkey hadn't made off, it wasn't like Firefly, it was cropping a non-existent patch of grass. It could surely go over by the church and browse in the shade, so much better, feed on the yellow flowers. Why did the donkey persist in getting burnt by the sun instead of being comfortable in the shade? It stopped grazing and pricked up its ears. A drone in the distance, far far away. The droning grew louder as it came nearer, approaching. The first strains of a whining singsong. She looked up the street to where it became a road and swung past the cemetery. A cloud of dust, the whining sound quite audible. The nasal singsong coming from the distance. An ox-cart was on its way to the town.

4

A Hunter without Ammunition

Must be around two o'clock, said the man, looking at the sky. He was on foot, walking along the road by himself. Aye, wouldn't be more, judging from the sun. He shielded his right eye with his hand – his left was sightless – (the sun beat down, the air was a dazzling glare flashing with myriads of almost audible streaks) and took a long look. There's a mountain of a sky for you, what a mass of blue, he said. The sky was vaulted, dazzling, vast because there were no clouds – except for a tiny cottonwool scrap of white cloud floating on the skyline, where the road disappeared from view on a bend, in the direction he had come from.

It wasn't like the sun in the outback, which never let up, scorching everything (a few small, resigned trees, all knotted and twisted, stunted, with dry leaves, not a hint of fresh, moist, shiny green, like they were always covered in dust on account of the dry, itchy feeling you got in your nose just from looking at them, back there, where he'd come from a long time back, he recalled, comparing), but still the sun was strong. He knew that under the first shady tree, like that one just ahead, which overhung the road, bushy, casting a good shadow, he could stop walking and rest, while he waited for the first buggy, truck or ox-cart, he would ask for a lift on the back, as far as the town, which must be close, judging from the signs of life he'd begun to notice.

He certainly couldn't go on any further, he had come from far away, he was tired and hungry. The last town, where he'd stayed a couple of days, was many miles behind him. He'd left at daybreak, the sky barely beginning to brighten, still grey. He had come at an easy pace, no hurry. But the best thing now would really be to wait for the first lift. He was getting tired too, by now, of travelling alone, with no one to chat to, left to his own thoughts, rambling.

He'd rest in the shade of that tree. Then he would sniff the nice keen air, that felt refreshing, a little chilly even, because of the breeze from the coffee plantations. They covered the hills and mountains he had travelled through like the cells of a honeycomb. There was a scented breeze, a constant current of air wafting down the corridors, those lanes between the rows of coffee bushes on the hillsides.

He went on a bit further. In a moment he reached the shade of the tree. He slipped his gun off his shoulder and with an affection tinged with sorrow patted the knife-scored butt, his initials scratched on it the day Major Lindolfo made him a present of that there fowling piece, when he was still a kid, so that he could go hunting with him, back in Paracatu, his birthplace.

A good man, the major, my godfather, I never seed a hunter like him. If the major hadn't died, he wouldn't have quit, left Paracatu, gone roaming all over, without a roof over his head or a steady job, from town to town, ranch to ranch, like a Judas, a wandering Jew. Could've stayed on in one of them towns he'd come through in his own part of the outback: Vazante, Patos, São Gotardo, one of them places where the surroundings, the life and the customs were those he knew from childhood. Could've stayed in Vazante, for instance, that was a nice place, nice people, hospitable people who didn't poke their noses into your business. One of the ranchers, Clarimundo, who had stacks of cattle and an enormous great ranch, had

59

even made a point of his staying, liked the look of him and the way he kept the chat flowing. I like somebody like you, to natter to in the evenings, was what he said. Wanted him to stay and join the workforce, work with the oxen. Or any other job you like. Choose, you've a right to choose, with the problem of your eyesight. As long as it's a decent job of work, nattering is for your spare time.

He wasn't a hard worker, but didn't want to let on to Clarimundo while he was on the ranch, finding the odd job to do so as not to seem idle. What he did like was a good long natter, he'd take off across the fields into the woods, rifle slung across his back, and find a good place to lie in wait, ready to pot at birds. Work without stopping, from dawn till dusk, was not for him, a free man; I wasn't born to be a slave, was what he'd say.

Forgive me, Mister Clarimundo, I have to be on my way, he said. And where will you be going, Clarimundo asked. Around, I'll keep going until I find somewhere peaceful like, a place that suits me. So you mean you don't like it here, you don't care for us, said Clarimundo. It's not that, mister, of course I like it, I like it a lot. It's just my fate to keep moving on. A promise, he lied. Clarimundo had looked at him, laughing. What fate's this you're talking about? You'll be turning into a pilgrim or a preacher, you'll probably end up at one of those far-off places I've heard about, Congonhas or Matozinhos, where they do miracles. No, mister, I ain't no preacher. Not that I'm an unbeliever, I believe in God and all the saints, my mother brought me up to respect religion. I'm just not fond of such things. I'm more given to travelling, I'm a rover. A hobo, you mean, said Clarimundo with a guffaw, catching on in a trice. No, mister, I've always been a good worker, you can ask (there was nobody around to contradict). It's just that since my godfather Major Lindolfo, you must at least have heard his name, since he died, I've changed course and I made up my mind to roam the outback, not go against my destiny and see where I end up, let God take charge and see where He wants me to get to. That's my promise. Don't laugh, Mister Clarimundo, God'll punish you.

Clarimundo looked thoughtful. Wonder if he believed me? He liked to peddle tall stories, cock-and-bull stories, idle tales. This story of his destiny pleased him, he repeated it more than once. Every time he met someone who wanted to engage him on a more permanent basis, upwards of a year, out would come the story of his destiny, of the promise he made after Major Lindolfo died. There was a good side to it, too, because that way he could paint Major Lindolfo's exploits in strong colours, those impossible hunting expeditions in which truth just bobbed about in a stream of fictions.

What he was looking for was a man the likes of Major Lindolfo, a wealthy man who wasn't over bothered about work, who'd leave him to his own devices and, whenever it crossed his mind, which was always happening, would fetch out his fine double-barrelled shotgun, with its leather case, fill his haversack, whistle for the dogs, and he didn't even need to say come on Joey, bring your popgun and let's go to the woods, because he was already ready, he'd been watching for some time for the major to start getting the itch. Them was the good times. He wouldn't find another man like his godfather, there ain't no more like him. It was great, the two of them camping in the forest, by the riverside, day after day, eating cavy they'd caught themselves.

His gun on the ground – the ramrod was a bit rusty, it needed polishing – the pouch with the powderhorn and the pocket for buckshot next to him, the little bundle with his clothes and few belongings beneath his head for a pillow, there he lay, enjoying the fresh air. It'd be nice to have just a wee bit of powder, but it was all gone, the powderhorn was empty. A little way back he'd come by a thicket that was chock-full of birds. There wasn't that much to hunt around here, he could see that. Only the occasional clump of trees put in an appearance here and there, and he would gloomily imagine having a shot. They had a mania round here for tearing down forest land and burning it clear to plant coffee, that put an end to the bird life. It was a shame to see the poor creatures scorched to death, their perfect little eggs dried up and burnt, you could tell they were partridge eggs because you knew what they looked like. It was wicked, such a waste too.

Better not to think about it, too sad. He looked at the blue blue sky, the unchanging green of the coffee bushes, beginning just over the fence and spreading over the entire valley, in their tedious symmetrical lay-out. He was already fed up with this landscape, so different from the woodland, from the part of the world he'd come from, the backlands of Paracatu. At times he felt homesick, he wanted to go back. Heavens, what a distance! One day perhaps, again. How different it all was from Paracatu, Vazante, São Gotardo, Dores, all those places he'd left behind him on his way.

It happened in Divinópolis, after he'd been travelling for a year, his journey broken by brief sojourns at ranches where he did a few odd jobs to earn his keep and then went on his way. It was in Divinópolis that he first got the idea of staying on a bit longer and saving enough to buy a second-class ticket on the East Minas Railway, to the end of the line, a place they said was called Tuiuti, where another branch began, another region, the Mogiana, or Southern Minas Railway.

He'd never travelled on a train, it was a good idea. He spent hours on end in the station square, watching the trains shunting, the engines belching smoke, the whistles. The uniformed railway officials with their peaked caps, the linesman with his coloured lantern. That was a job, yes sir, a government job. If he had a political patron, he'd land one of those jobs, and then he'd put down roots, never leave the place, he could even get married, he was no child, and have a family, dreams like that. But it was too much to hope for, too much of a dream; he imagined himself travelling in those trains, leaning back in his seat, eyes alert, glued to the window, watching the landscape fly by; chatting to the man next to him, one of those travellers he saw when the express went through. Must be nice, made you feel important. As soon as he had enough money he'd be a traveller as well, he'd make for that place called Tuiuti. He checked with the ticket clerk how much a second-class ticket cost, worked it out, he still didn't have enough, he'd need to work some more, that was a disappointment. He chatted to the engine drivers, wanting to know if the train went through many big towns. The railway workers laughed at his curiosity. To him those names, Formiga, Campo Belo, Três Corações (you have to change there, if you're going to Tuiuti, he was going to Tuiuti, he'd made up his mind) were mysterious names, like names out of a story book, heard in a dream.

He wiped the sweat from his face, stretched his arms. If he wasn't so hungry, his belly turned over every so often with a rumble, he'd sure like to have a nap. He needed food, there was nothing left in his knapsack. He looked about him, close by, to see if he could find any fruit. Nothing, unless he looked further afield. Tired out, he wasn't going to get up. Better sleep. But sleep, how, hungry as he was?

Hell, this is no way to live. Maybe it'd be better to stay longer in the town he was making for, get himself some sort of work to keep body and soul together and sort things out? Workhand, handyman in a house would be fine, not a ranch hand, he was fed up with bush, the bush is for snakes The last time he took on heavier work was in Muzambinho. He did a hoeing job with a mobile gang, on the Hide-and-Seek Ranch. The manager wanted him to stay on as a tenant farmer, against the harvest

63

coming when he'd need more hands. No, he'd not stay for anything, the work was too heavy for him. Some days he got blisters on his hands and the sun burnt down on his topknot so's he thought it'd burst. The manager wasn't bad at all, he'd liked him, but the foreman never gave you a let-up, wanted to have the hide off you. Slave I am not and that's a fact, am I a nigger? he would say.

Feeling the pangs of hunger, he began to think seriously about what he was going to do. He needed to think of something, whatever it was. Next to handyman in some old lady's house, another good job would be in politics. No, he wouldn't do for that, he talked too much, he knew, and they don't care for that. And then there were always disturbances, fights and shooting. He didn't like the idea of shooting people, he imagined his own body riddled with bullets, stretched out on the ground, the warm blood spurting from his mouth. His pleasure was potting at birds, his fowling piece was very old, but still good, it never failed him. You just rammed home the powder, put the lead shot in and bang! the wee thing fell in mid flight.

He got very excited on big game hunts. When Major Lindolfo went hunting puma, deer, even coyote – it was the devil hunting coyote, unless you were a really good hunter like the major, coyote hides in any bit of undergrowth, he camouflages himself, when you think he's in one place, the cunning devil's off away, so nobody would believe us when we told them Major Lindolfo shot a coyote today, a huge one, so big. But what he really liked was the little stuff, he was a birdman. Small slugs, birdshot. The major really overdid it, he didn't bother about using the animal skins, so he fired buckshot. The row it made, crikey!

With an empty powderhorn and no shot, what was the good of being a hunter? If only he had a bit of powder to take a few pot shots, something to do. . . . A dog was a good thing, didn't need to be like Major Lindolfo's, sharp-nosed pointers, good tracker dogs, great deer hounds like Tornado, snarling game dogs like Burrower, a great all-rounder. A short-legged dog with a sharp muzzle. Crosspatch was a hell of a brave dog, he went into the burrows after the cavies. If Crosspatch was there he could play with him. He'd pretend to throw a stone into the undergrowth over yonder, the dog would start up, ears pricked, one leap and he'd be there.

He picked up his gun, aimed at a small bird that flew past, it was a grassquit. Not having powder he made the noise of the gun with his mouth. It was just play, if the gun was loaded he wouldn't be wasting shot on a grassquit, that'd be sheer wickedness, grassquit wasn't game, it had no use except to chirp the way it did. Worse still is killing the songthrush, that's real cruelty, only heartless people do that. The nice thing about the strongthrush is to listen to his singing, the trills he makes. Lindolfo had one that sang like nobody's business. He was the one who looked after it, cleaning its cage day in day out, he even made a little perch for it. There was a goldfinch too that he caught in the woods and gave as a present to the major's son, Valdemar. The boy played with the bird all day long. He would rub a cork in a bottle, imitating another bird, and the goldfinch would sing fit to burst, you'd think it was going to die singing. Birds are silly creatures, boys are silly creatures.

That there Valdemar, always catching colds, he was for ever after the goldfinch. He taught the boy how to set a birdtrap in the barnyard, there were lots of pigeons there in the afternoon. Some days Valdemar would make a scoop. He wanted to make him a walking-stick rifle, but Major Lindolfo wouldn't let him, too dangerous. Not now, Joey, when he's bigger I'll give him a shotgun for a present and he can go hunting with the two of us in the woods. Valdemar grinned with pleasure, looking forward to the day when he would go hunting with his father, but inside what he really wanted was the walking-stick rifle, or so he said afterwards. Valdemar was something of a fibber, poor laddie, and played up to his father.

Good memories them, as good as a nice dream, just like a dream really. He closed his eyes and tried to recall the glorious days when Major Lindolfo was alive, when the two of them used to go hunting in the forest. They would leave in the dark, when the dawn gave little signs of its coming, with a supply of meat-cakes for the trip. Oh his empty stomach! like a bottomless pit! The boy would come out onto the verandah to see them off. Go inside, child, be careful with your cold, your mother will be angry, it's very chilly.

The boy Valdemar was a sickly child, always catching things. One day he fell ill, the fever was so high you could feel the heat of it from some way off, he was delirious, he begged his mother to stay right by him, he wanted her close to him. The days went by and the child didn't get any better, not like the other times. The major went about grim faced, not saying much, despatching people to the town, he sent for the doctor. He was far from thinking about hunting, Joey was afraid he might even make some silly promise about never going hunting again. The child talked of nothing but the walking-stick rifle. The major looked questioningly at his wife, all right Lindolfo, she said, let the child have his wish, it may be his last, and she burst into tears. It was heartbreaking. He went off and made a fine little rifle for the boy, with a piece of melted down lead at the base of the barrel, the butt made of smooth wood, it was a beauty, took him days to finish it. When the fever abated a little, the child found the rifle by his side. You should have seen how happy he was. He stroked the gun, pointed it at the window : the blue sky swarmed with birds that only the boy could see. He said thank you with his eyes, his sunken eyes glowing like a cavy's in the dark when you turned the light on it. Then he became delirious again, pointed over to the dressing-table where there was a print of Our Lady of the Concep-

66

tion, saying that she was releasing lots of pigeons just for him to shoot, and twisted and turned in his bed trying to find his rifle. His mother called Major Lindolfo to help with the child. It was awful, gave you the creeps, you had to come away so's not to cry.

So one day he died, it was the saddest thing he ever saw, because it was a child, children should never die. Dona Vivinha, we thought she'd die of grief. She went about the house in a daze, couldn't settle in any room, carrying the rifle around with her. She was like a demented creature, of course you should be sad and cry, but not so much that God might think you're doubting His will. God's will is just, we said, but Dona Vivinha even blasphemed, she couldn't be consoled. Joey, take that damned rifle and throw it out into the fields, the major said. Or Vivinha will go mad.

That was a long time ago, he had quite forgotten the story, hadn't thought about it for a long time. Not since he left Paracatu. Whenever the story of the child threatened to come into his mind, he would switch his thoughts away to lighter matters, some form of amusement. This time there was no way out, he started remembering the major at dawn, the two of them leaving for the hunt, Valdemar on the verandah waving goodbye, and suddenly he was overcome by the depressing memory of the child dying. He opened his eyes, the air swam before him. His eyes were wet and he felt the tears start welling up. He was alone there, he could cry, there was nobody watching. But he didn't cry, what he did want was to forget the boy Valdemar hunting pigeons with the angels. He tried to take his mind off things by staring at the cloud of mosquitoes that hovered around a bush, he thought he could even hear their droning noise. When you want to forget, every little thing reminds you, it's difficult. It was almost certainly a mosquito that bit the boy and gave him the fever.

He closed his good eye, leaving his wall-eye open. He

couldn't see a thing, just a milky glare. Thank goodness the other was good, God's will is just. His right eye saw everything, even at a distance, clear as anything, missed nothing. Except he had to turn his head sideways to see better. Didn't matter much when he was shooting. God's will is just, maybe he'd be worse off without his wall-eye, might not see good with two eyes. God's will is just, but that child. Enough of that, it's not right to keep questioning God's actions. If God took the child to Him when he was little, it was because He needed him. If he was alive maybe he'd be a bad lot, perhaps a criminal even. That's it, God's will is just, he felt better about it. The child vanished into thin air, now he could smell that good smell brought from the woods by the breeze that rustled in the broom thicket where a yellow butterfly was fluttering. He twisted his head in the direction of the road to see if a cart was coming, or somebody at least. Not a thing, nobody, just the empty red dust road. What a deserted, forgotten place! There he was alone, adrift in that big wide world.

His head on the bundle, he found a more comfortable position. Now he was drifting far away. The major came in sight on the road, on his palomino. A cloud of dust behind him. Come on Joey, quick, the child is very sick. He climbed up behind the major and held onto him. Sereno, the horse, galloped on. It was dark already and still they weren't there. Then Dona Vivinha appeared on the verandah crying and saying it's no good, you've come too late, you and your crazy hunting, he's died just this minute. It'd been him had made his godfather late, the major barely gave him a glance, his eyes blazing like coals. Down to the river, he heard the major say, but where did his voice come from when he didn't open his mouth? He was beginning to suspect what was going to happen. Down to the river, quick! On the river bank, waiting. He heard a noise in the water, a cavy showed its head. Crosspatch pricked up his ears, one foreleg raised. The major shone the lantern straight in the cavy's eyes. Not me, godfather! For the love of God! He couldn't speak, the major wasn't listening. A stream of light from the lantern blinded his good eye. The major was aiming at him. An explosion. Buckshot, the devil! He woke in a fright. He was afraid of dreams, he was having a bad day. He wiped the cold sweat from his face. His hand over the place where he was shot. There was a buzzing in his ears, was he still dreaming? The buzzing began to get louder, it was clearer now. A distant singsong droning in the air. He looked up the road and saw a cloud of dust. The interminable whining of an ox-cart. He saw it quite clearly, he wasn't dreaming : the carter's lad, the lead oxen, the carter at the side. When the boy came into the shade of the tree José Feliciano was already on his feet in the road, his gun on his back, his bundle hooked over the gunbarrel, waiting.

Hey, you boy, he said to the carter's lad. The boy looked at him, said what might have been a good afternoon and slackened his pace. Because he didn't see the man, he said where's the carter I saw just now, when you came in sight back there along the road, don't tell me he's vanished – trying to be funny and win the boy's sympathy. Dad's back there, on the other side, at the back end of the cart, the boy said, pointing with his goad.

José Feliciano waited for the cart to pass and fell in step with the carter. Afternoon, friend, he said. Sun's damned hot, enough to scorch the hide off you. Aye, said the man, and carried on walking. Think I could get a lift on the back of your cart? I can't keep going, I've come a fair way, had some dizzy spells, cramps in me legs, I get it from time to time. I'm feeling a bit weak, think I must've picked up some bug at the last ranch I stayed at, back in Guaxupé. The man gave him a close look, José Feliciano tried to look poorly. You can get on, said the carter. The cart wasn't full, the sacks of coffee were only piled halfway up the canvas fixed to the supports.

He threw his bundle onto the cart, jumped up after it and sat there with his legs dangling outside. Well, it wasn't quite what he'd hoped for. A buggy would be better, an ox-cart's very slow. But when you're on shanks' pony, anything with a wheel is a lift. The cart moved off again. The man went up front and prodded the lead oxen, shouting their names. Then he came back to the cart and had a good look at his passenger.

Where did you actually say you're from, young fellow, he asked, to get the conversation going. I've come from Guaxupé, said José Feliciano. Is that where you're from? asked the carter. No I'm not, said José Feliciano, who was working on the story he was going to tell. No, that's not where I'm from, I just worked there for a time. I'm journeying, come from way off, a place you've likely never heard of, Paracatu. (Right, I haven't. Which way's that?) In the outback, in the north of Minas, a long way from here. You can travel for days on end and you'll still take a long time to get there. I've been travelling these roads, getting the odd job here and there, the sort of thing my illness allows. From Divinópolis to Tuiuti I came by train, on the Western. Then I ran out of money and I've been putting up at ranches I come across. (Are you ill, young fellow?) I've never been really ill, but for some time now I've been off-colour, dizzy spells, cramps in me legs, a heaviness I can't explain. I'm thinking of looking up a doctor in town, get a prescription. Is there a good doctor there, d'ye know, seeing as you're from these parts? Dr Viriato's a good man, said the carter, a friend to the poor. He fixed me all right. Not me exactly, my boy Manny there, he got some sores nobody could deal with. I even made a vow to take him to the shrine at Aparecida, if he got well. He did, and I've got Dr Viriato and God to thank for it. You know, young fellow, I haven't settled that vow to this day. Do you think it matters if a fellow puts it off a bit?

José Feliciano saw that he was on firm ground, the

man was religious; if he thought up a good story, he could count on him. No, he said, as long as you do it, God don't mind waiting, you just choose your time. That's how it was with me. Sure as I'm standing here, I'm settling a promise. My godfather, Major Lindolfo, from Paracatu, had a son, a fine strong boy called Valdemar. Just imagine, one day the child fell ill, a raging fever nobody could cure : medicine man, faith-healer, doctor, not one of them. So I made a promise I'd go wandering these backlands for three years or so. Every place I stop that's got a church, I light a candle to the Virgin there. José Feliciano stopped short, afraid to get onto the subject of the Virgin, not a good idea, might get punished. Perhaps he should try to retrieve matters? But the man didn't give him time : and did the boy get well, get cured? Never had another thing, said José Feliciano, saddened by the thought of the boy dead and buried back in Paracatu. He's at school in Belo Horizonte now.

I don't know your handle yet, and I haven't told you mine, said José Feliciano, the subject was bothering him. Mine's Silvino, Silvino Assunção, at your service, said the other. Look here, young fellow, I'm getting to like you. You're good for a chat, that's what I like.

Mine's José Feliciano, or Joey Bird, they call me Major's Jack too, you can take your pick, I answer to all three.

Silvino Assunção laughed at the way he said Joey Bird and pointed to the fowling piece lying on the bottom of the cart. A good type this Joey Bird, good for a natter when you were travelling. Pity the journey was nearly over, they'd soon be there, less than an hour.

Aye, said Silvino, a nickname's always a good thing, it picks you out. I don't have one now, when I was younger I was nicknamed Silvino Smoke, goodness knows why. Then they forgot, now they call me by my proper name, all of it, Silvino Assunção.

It was my godfather gave me this nickname Joey Bird, Major Lindolfo, the best hunter I ever saw. Later, if there's time, I'll tell you some stories about him. What were you saying when I put my oar in . . .? Nicknames, said Silvino. You know, you should stick to that one of yours, Joey Bird. In the town, if you don't have a nickname, they'll slap one on you straight away. And some of them vex people. When a fellow gets annoyed he don't want to hear nicknames and that's just when a nasty one sticks. Well then, I heard one that was funny, I'll tell you if you like. There was a man in these parts who couldn't stand nicknames, said he'd kill somebody if they gave him one. What do you think, the man was always whistling and when he whistled he made a mouth like so, like a fowl's arsehole. We started calling him Arsehole. Only behind his back, say it to his face and he'd go mad with rage, start saying he'd shoot somebody.

José Feliciano had a good laugh, that there Silvino was really quite a lark. When he went back home one day, he'd tell that story for his own, they'd all split their sides.

I see you like a good story, said José Feliciano, getting ready. I'm not averse, friend, said Silvino. If there's time I'll tell you one, said José Feliciano. And, feeling his stomach rumble, you haven't by any chance got a bite of something to shut my belly up, have you Silvino? Forgot my grub, haven't had a thing to eat since dawn. There's a bit of tack still in that saucepan, said Silvino. And there's some sugar candy as well, in that bag. Silvino went up front to have a word with the boy. He shouted the names of the oxen once more and came back to José Feliciano. Friend Joey, are you out of a job? Right now I am, said José Feliciano. If you like, I'll have a word with my boss, he's needing people for ploughing. I don't care much for ploughing, said José Feliciano quickly. What I want right now is a spell in town to get myself well again. What about a coffee warehouse, mused Silvino. No go, it'd be too heavy for you, lugging sacks of coffee about. Before Silvino got to fixing him one of those jobs, José Feliciano interrupted : what I'd like, really, is a job as a handyman, or something, in a town house, gardening, odd jobs, you don't happen to know of anything? Not right now, said Silvino. If I hear of anything, I'll let you know.

José Feliciano ate all the tack. Now he was sucking a piece of the candy. The cart plodded on, jerking up and down over the ruts in the road. A good bloke, right friendly, José Feliciano was thinking. It's not every day you meet the likes of him. He saw that Silvino wanted to chat some more. But first he aimed to finish his chunk of sugar candy.

By the looks of it you're a hunter, said Silvino. I was, said José Feliciano modestly. And a good one, back in Paracatu, when my godfather, the major, was alive. Nowadays I keep this here gun just for fun, to take a few pot shots at birds. Once a hunter always a hunter. Just a while back I was thinking about it, when you turned up. (Should he tell one of those stories about himself and Major Lindolfo? The one about the coyote, perhaps, just to leave Silvino open-mouthed with disbelief? He felt too lazy, that was a very long story and the journey would be short, to tell it properly, with all the trimmings, required time.) I'm a good shot, though, he said. A bird in the air don't fool about with me. I can't show you, Silvino, because I've got no more powder, if I had I'd show you.

A hunter without ammunition is a sad creature, alone, without a friend in the world : not a soul. He's like a man in the dark, turned in on himself, on his own nature. A prey to all sorts of temptation. That's when the devil turns up, evil thoughts come to the surface. A pot shot takes your mind off things, helps pass the time. It keeps a man's spirit looking outwards, in the daylight.

Silvino Assunção looked Joey Bird straight in the face, had a close look at him, to see what he was like. He saw that he had a wall-eye, his left. You don't mean to say, friend Joey, that this here cloud in your eye is from powder or from shooting. . . . He laughed. Though he was a peaceful fellow, José Feliciano didn't like people to poke fun at his blind eye, God's mark as he called it. But this fellow had been so kind, he decided not to take offence, carry on talking. No, it's not. It's a mark from God, so's to see the wickedness of the world all the better with the other eye. Without meaning to, he'd had a dig at Silvino. I'm sorry, friend Silvino, I didn't mean to give offence. Not at all, friend Joey Bird, we say things without realizing. I don't hold myself offended, said Joey Bird, you've been so kind to me that I'm the one to apologize.

The town was close, he could see the church tower already.

Are you from here, from the town, friend Silvino, he asked. Not from the town exactly, no, said Silvino. I'm from a little place near here, I was born on a small farm. I'm always backwards and forwards carrying coffee. I've not got much on today, usually the sacks of coffee are piled up as high as the props. The cart trundles along singing on the bearing. A fair treat.

A good singer this cart of yours, it whines good, said José Feliciano, to clear the air after his sharp reply. You should see it all loaded up, said Silvino. I give the singer wedge a good greasing with ox fat and coal dust, and it sings a treat. They know it's me coming from way off.

José Feliciano decided to change the subject. Is there much game hereabouts, friend Silvino? I'm not a hunting man, but I know there's some, said Silvino. There's wild pig, cavy, capybara's getting scarce, the usual things you find everywhere. I meant small stuff, said José Feliciano. For me to have a bit of sport. There's not much, used to be more, friend Joey. With the clearing and the firing, the game dies or moves away. But you'll always find the odd thicket, if you want, and being a good shot like you say, you can bag a brace of guan, heron, quail or partridge. There are some hunters who like that, say there's good hunting. Well, that's fine for me, said José Feliciano.

74

Later, when I squat somewhere and find myself a little job, first break I get I'll be off shooting in these woods you've been talking about. If we – God grant, I'd like to – meet up, I promise you a brace of guan at least, for some broth for your lad, does he like it? Silvino thanked him, God willing they'd meet up quite often, he was in and out of town all the time.

The cart whined its way up the hill. The white walls of the cemetery. A little further and they would be there.

Nice big cemetery, said José Feliciano. Aye, it's not bad, said Silvino. It's got a wrought iron gate with letters and words traced over the top, that's what I like best. In olden times folk took more care, seems they had more patience. I'm not fond of cemeteries, said José Feliciano, but if the gate's like you say, then I'll have a good look at it when we get there. You know they wanted to give me a job in a cemetery once, he began, inventing. I wouldn't have it, and it was a good job, mind you, a good wage and all the other conditions. I wouldn't do for that, burying people, having to deal with corpses from the poor-house, in open coffins, without lids. They drop the poor devil in the grave any old how, then they use the same coffin for another wretch. I couldn't bring myself to do it, I've got too much feeling in me. Aye, said Silvino, thoughtfully. That's right, it may be a good job for some, but for the likes of us, like you say, feeling people, it won't do. Must harden the heart. After a time I guess a grave-digger gets a heart like the soil, he don't take note even when it's a relative has died. It's all like soil, useless stone, dead men. José Feliciano said that's why I wouldn't do it, I'm no good for that sort of thing, death, any death, even someone I never saw in my life, the tears start coming, I have to try hard not to cry. You know, feelings. . . .

The two of them fell silent, thinking about death, sad events, how pointless life was. José Feliciano stared ahead, he was miles away in memoryland. The boy Valdemar, the little white coffin covered in flowers. Dona Vivinha weeping, couldn't seem to let go of the toy rifle, on the point of going out of her mind. The major silent, his face set, not a tear in his eyes. People like that suffer the more, a good cry relieves things. Don't make no difference though, what a bugger of a life! Shit, what's a bloke live for, just to see things like that?

At the cemetery gate Silvino brought the cart to a halt. That's a lovely gate, Silvino, said José Feliciano, laying it on. All the places I've been to I never saw a gate like this. And I've covered some ground, you know. That's a fine piece of tracery. Was it done hereabouts? Thought as much, the smith what did that knew his job. There's bits of it look like Dona Vivinha's lacework. What's that it's got written at the top, those words? Don't know, said Silvino, I can't read letters. They tell me it's in priest's tongue. I know a little bit of priest's lingo, said José Feliciano. I actually assisted the priest when I was a boy. I'll see if I can read it. He spelled it out slowly, pretending he was reading under his breath. He'd never assisted at mass at all, what he knew was barely enough to read the notices on the church door and a children's almanac. Aye, it's very difficult, I can't remember very well, he said. I know it's about death, the dead. That's nothing new, laughed Silvino. Even I know that, though I can't read. Let's get moving, he said, with a prod at the nearest ox.

The cemetery was left behind, now they could see the street which the road gave way to.

What's that, Silvino, José Feliciano almost shouted in astonishment, pointing at a huge crater, like the bed of a broad dried-up river, which stretched from the side of the road almost out of sight, where it fused with the valley, red and black. Ah, said Silvino, you've never seen a crater before? I've seen cave-ins from alluvion or erosion, said José Feliciano, but a thing this size, never in all my life! This time he wasn't lying and he wasn't overdoing his praise. He was actually afraid to look down into those jaws with the dark red gums, with a few small trees growing down inside and the beginning of a stream. How awful, friend Silvino. Seems like the earth is being eaten all away. Devil's work, that's what I think, this hunger for earth. Ain't the townsfolk afraid it'll reach there one of these days? It'll end up devouring the streets and the houses, swallowing up everything.

Accustomed to travelling that way almost every day, Silvino didn't bother much about the craters. The landscape like something in a nightmare. The boy Manny, he didn't like it, got the shivers, went numb. When he caught sight of the great hole he turned his face away so as not to see. Maybe the boy and Joey Bird were right? he wondered, as if he were seeing the crater for the first time, because of Joey Bird being scared. Devil's work, the jaws of the crater, like a punishment, eating away at the town like a raging sore. Don't be afeard, there ain't no danger, he said, they're moving that way, in a different direction, the movement has stopped on this side. I never think about these things, best not to. The lad there's got a thing about them, childish fear. You know, when he comes to town by himself, on the horse, when he gets here he breaks into an almighty gallop, so they tell me. But you're not a child, you shouldn't get scared like this.

He wasn't a child. But the craters had merged with the still fresh memory of his recent dream, Major Lindolfo shot him full in the chest, there was no point him shouting. If he went near the edge of the craters, to see the bottom of the hole, the earth would give way beneath his feet, he would be sucked down. A waking dream, just as terrifying as the other. The cart swayed and, as it rocked gently and he had his eyes closed, he seemed to be asleep again. With his eyes closed the picture of the craters grew to frightening proportions.

He opened his eyes and saw the first houses. No one at the windows, the town lay sleeping in the heat of the day. The white glare of the houses in the sun was painful to the eyes. The shadows of the craters faded away. The cart

77

came to a gradual halt in the square, until the last snatch of its whine died out. Silvino called his son. Manny, this young fellow, Joey Bird, was frightened of the big hole, like you. Manny, very thin, stood looking stupidly at the stranger, with his eyes wide open. We've got good reason to feel scary, ain't we Manny? said Joey Bird, to be nice. The lad grunted something, his face split by a grin, could be.

Friend Silvino, tell me something. I'm very inquisitive, you'll have to excuse me. Tell me, whose is that spendid house? Ah, said Silvino, that's the late Colonel Honório Cota's manor house. You can lavish your fine words on this one, the praise is in place. It's a bit dilapidated now, mind you, there's even grass sprouting on the roof, creepers. When Colonel Honório Cota was alive things were very different, the manor sparkled, it was a joy to see. Whenever I had to come by here, I'd slow down a bit, just for the pleasure of looking and to raise my hat to that fine figure of a man. After, he got a great sorrow in his heart, a dreadful sorrow. All because of politics, to do with government, you know, and he got all gloomy, grumpy, brooding. In the end we were even afraid to raise our hats to him. Seemed he didn't see you, had his eyes looking inwards. He let things slide and the house went to pot, no one to look after it, just God and the rain. A bit soft in the head, that's what happened to him.

José Feliciano was admiring the manor house. The building was big and heavy, it was wearing well, with just a bit of attention the manor would look like new again. He wouldn't mind working there, he might get a job as a handyman, you never know.

Friend Silvino, he said, who lives in the house now? His daughter, Dona Rosalina, Silvino told him. A spinster lady, since her father died she's locked herself in, never goes out any more. They say she's on her high horse, more like she's ill, I think, not in her right mind. All by herself in this big house. Well, there's a nigger woman,

Quiquina, but she don't really count. I don't know how a body can stay shut up like that, all on her own, with nary a one to have a talk to. If she were out in the wilds, perhaps, there are people who live out in the bush, but in the town . . .? I don't know, sometimes I think the townsfolk is right, she's too proud as well as a bit touched. Her folk were always a bit funny, not all there, you know.

José Feliciano didn't attach much importance, he was thinking of finding a job at the manor. That would be great. A spinster lady, a nigger woman, no man. Nobody to boss him about, to be pestering the life out of him all the time. Foremen were always making you do something or other, never gave you a minute's peace, worked you to the bone. He wasn't made of iron. A nice little job. And bound to be little, if any, heavy work, he'd have time off. He'd pal up with another hunter (one hunter always smells out another), get himself a dog, and away he'd go exploring the countryside around. Just like in Major Lindolfo's time.

Friend Silvino, you said not all there, a bit funny, and so on. You don't mean crazy, fits, rages. . . . Nothing like that, friend Joey. I didn't say it myself, it's what the townsfolk say, you know how folks talk. Aye, folks say too much, they overdo it, said Joey Bird, already championing the manor. It's more oddness, said Silvino, the blues, a bit of nervous trouble. Now I'm letting my tongue run away with me. I never heard a single story and I've never had a single word with her. I've never knocked on the door to ask for anything, not so much as a drink of water. She's probably quite civil and normal. If you think about it though, she's got her reasons. The late Colonel Honório Cota quarrelled with everybody, he fell out with the town. After what they did to him, some folk think he had all the reason on his side. . . . What did they do to him? asked Joey Bird. Ah, Joey, that's a long story, too long for now. My lad there can't wait any longer to get moving. You don't need me to tell you, in time you'll get to hearing.

José Feliciano had made up his mind : he was going to work at the manor house. Unless the lady didn't want him. Do you think I might get a nice little job there, he asked. Don't ask me, said Silvino. I've never known of anybody working at the manor since Colonel Honório Cota passed away. Why don't you try? You never know, it might work. . . .

You're right, friend Silvino, I'll be getting off here. I'll try, won't hurt me, and maybe God'll help me the way he did meeting us up. You've been very kind to me, real kind. Nowadays you don't find a man like yourself, with a good heart, every day of the week. On the way back, when you come past, if I'm at the manor, please stop so's we can have a chat. It passes the time and it'll be a pleasure for me. God bless you, friend Silvino. Bye for now.

The cart began to clatter on, the whining started again. Off went Silvino, a good man, a kindly soul, and his son Manny, that God gave him as driver's lad.

Left alone in the town square, José Feliciano eyed Carmo Church, the priest's house, the houses on the other side of the square, the teaching college. A nice square this. All it needs is a bit of garden, some greenery, some flowers to decorate it. Why don't they do something about it? I quite like it here. If the town is all like this, and if the lady there wanted him, he'd never leave the place. A heavy gust of wind whipped up a dust devil that raced from the centre of the square towards the church. That's not a good thing, a dust devil's never a good sign. First the dream, then the craters, and now the dust devil. Could it be an omen for him? Wouldn't it perhaps be better to rest a while, then try a different track? That's silly, such things don't exist, imaginings. Silvino was right, he wasn't like Manny who looked the other way every time he passed the giant hole. If you've got a clean conscience, everything's all right. No point in running away. God is strong. What will be, will be. Try and miss the trap and you fall right into it. Wasn't that like the story Dona Vivinha used to tell? She didn't accept the will of God, when the child died she dragged herself around blaspheming, close to going mad. Go on Joey, take this damned rifle and throw it out into the field. Dona Vivinha, God preserve her. Dona Vivinha told that once upon a time there was a man who had a bad dream, the sort that makes you wake up and think about saving your soul. Your little daughter will grow up, said the voice in the dream, she will grow into a young woman, and when she can bear a child something will happen inside you, an idea you can't carry out and yet the only way you can get rid of it is to let it have its way. She will turn into a pretty young woman, nicely dressed, alluring, a beauty. Though you don't want to, you will end up sleeping with her and taking her maidenhead. The man didn't say a word to a soul, he mulled over the dream for days on end. Till one day, without a goodbye, he took his belongings and vanished, alone, for ever. He hid away far into the outback, not a word was heard from him, by word of mouth or by letter. Time passed, the man began to age, the daughter who was a girl became a woman. The mother died, the daughter was left alone in the world and decided to make her own way. And off she went, following a path which she didn't see was being mapped out for her by an unknown hand. Finally she reached that place, far away in the outback. There she met a man of mature age and kindly disposition, a sensible man, just the sort she was looking for to look after her, for she was tired of suffering and of being an orphan. She bewitched the man, he courted her, the way things happen. You shack up with me, said the man, in God's eyes we're married, when a priest comes by he'll give his blessing. The young woman agreed, but she didn't tell him anything about her past. She said she had come from a different place, not the one she'd really come from, invented a story for herself, even changed her name. She knew that when your father leaves home without a word something is wrong, somebody's cracked or got a disease that's catching, or a crime, something that will bring dishonour on the family. Dona Vivinha spoke carefully, pausing a moment just to see our distress. And so time passed. One day, when they were so happily married the folk there said there had never been a love like theirs, so peaceful and deep, a mirror for all husbands, the bad husbands the world is full of – one day she had to speak out, her heart begged for rest, still waters, that man who was her husband was the listener she prayed for, the peace we all need when we have a full heart, one day she went and said this isn't my name, it's not like this, it's quite different, she went on for a long time and the man pieced together the stories she said were of her real life and realized, with a terrible anguish, that his wife was his daughter, that the story she was telling was not just hers, but his as well. While running away to avoid it, he had done exactly what the dream told him, to the letter. The ugliest sin of all, one without remission and without God's forgiveness. After that the expected happened, curses, bloodletting, the man took his axe and cut this vein here, the one they call the carotid artery.

Plain silly, Dona Vivinha liked to tell stories, the sort that stopped you sleeping, had you eating your heart out with suffering. Children and soft-hearted people shouldn't listen. He wasn't a child, Silvino was right. Foolishness was for scary folk with nought to do, stories to pass away empty evenings. There was no such thing, no gaping hell, no ghosts. Dona Vivinha wasn't too good in the head, hadn't he seen how she behaved when the child died? And then, if it was like she said in the story about the man, what was the point him running away, if some day he'd bump into that house anyway? With life, it's a case of forwards nobody knows, behind you've already seen. Better stick with God and stop fussing. God is great, as big as the whole world, as endless as the darkness. He was a tiny wee bird, alone in God's heaven.

He tried to dismiss those gloomy thoughts. Life goes on, no point in griping. The ox goes the right way about it, shuts up and chews its cud.

He looked at the manor house, and everything was bright and clean : the sky was cloudless and shimmered with light. The house stood so firm it seemed to rise out of the ground, with its thick walls, its panelled door, its many windows and the curtains swaying gently in the wind. The general effect was a pleasant feeling of shade, of a cool interior, of welcome and of peace. He took hold of the door-knocker and knocked. No one answered. He thought he saw a curtain move, someone behind the curtain. Anybody at home, he shouted at the window. No one came, better go away, what made him get hung up on that house? There wasn't any shortage of handyman jobs in the world. He was preparing to go away when the door opened. A short fat old nigger woman, with a few white whiskers on her chin, was stood there, staring him straight in the eyes.

Good afternoon, auntie, he said. I've come a long way, I'm from other parts, not here. I've been on the road since early morning. You always meet a kindly soul, you hope to. Just a bit back on the road I was given a lift in an ox-cart, that made things a bit better. (He needed to talk, keep talking, it was his way of making contact with people). It's as I say, there's always a kind soul to give you a hand. I never lose faith in Our Lord. He always gives a hand, He shows His kindness through others. You believe, I can see it in your eyes, women is always closer to God. Being a man I don't go in for praying much, but I always turn to God in times of distress. (The woman was silent, not a word of agreement, she just nodded vaguely. Maybe she didn't understand, perhaps she was a bit daft? Better go away, this is one hell of a start.) As you see, auntie, I'm thirsty, do you think you could let me have a drink of water? Then I'll say what I came for. (Maybe she didn't like being called auntie, perhaps she wasn't one for familiarity, these old nigger women like being called auntie, surely can't be one that don't. Perhaps she simply didn't understand. He went through the motion of raising a glass to his lips, so that she would see he was asking for water.) A drink of water, missus, nobody refuses that, it's simple charity. If you don't want to, I'll be going, sorry I troubled you. . . .

The black woman turned away and went inside. As she did he looked through the half open door to the interior of the house. Then he looked at the window where he thought he saw a movement. Just an impression, there was nobody, the lady of the house must be somewhere inside.

The black woman came back with a mug of water. He drank it, wiped his mouth on his shirt sleeve and thanked her. He stood waiting for her to say something, just a word, so that he could carry on. She said nothing, so he went on do you think, missus, I'm sorry I talk so much, but I'm a bit of a cadger at times. If you're in need, you can't wait to be asked, you have to swallow your pride. Swallow your pride or you don't get nothing else to swallow, do you? Me, I always ask, I'm not shy, that's what I'm like, if you understand me, begging your pardon. I'm asking, I'd like to ask, do you think you could ask the madam if there's an odd job for me to do? I work good, jack-of-all-trades, that's me. I do weeding, look after the garden, I can chop wood, do a bit of bricklaying, even a bit of carpentering. Do you need somebody? I can help in the kitchen, the cleaning I mean, when I scour the pots and pans you can see your face in them. I'm used to doing jobs for Dona Vivinha, back in Paracatu, where I come from. Anything will do me, I don't turn no job down. . . .

There was no point going on, it was useless, like talking to a stone. The black woman gestured him to go away. Not one word. I'm going, he said. If I'm not wanted, I'll not stay, sorry I spoke. Aye, he thought, she must be a bit touched. Could it be a warning for me to get away?

He was about to leave when a voice called hey, young man, come over here. A light pleasant voice, couldn't be the nigger woman, old women don't talk like that.

It was Rosalina, from the window. Concealed by the curtain, she had listened with interest to everything the man had said. At least this one's not from here, she thought. That's what he said. From Paracatu, I heard quite clearly. She liked the look of the man, his straightforward manner, his ready tongue. She hadn't heard human speech for a long time, with Quiquina walled in her silence. Emanuel's visits were rare and even then hurried. She would dress up ready, remembering earlier times, let him go on talking, just for the pleasure of listening to a human voice. Afterwards she would go on, for days on end, repeating what Emanuel had said over to herself, hearing his words in the air. Until they faded deep in her heart. She liked the man, she was particularly impressed by the rifle he had slung across his back.

Good afternoon, ma'am, he said. I was speaking to this here . . . Yes, I heard what you said, Rosalina interrupted. It's not what you think, said Rosalina, she's dumb. You mean to say she didn't hear what I said, I said my piece for nothing? he said. No, she can hear all right, said Rosalina. She's dumb, but she's not deaf. You want a job, if I heard right. That's right, ma'am, anything will do. Just for a day, or do you want to stay and work at the house? she asked. If I can and you wish, I'd like to stay and work here for good, if I suit. Tell me something, she said, you're not from these parts. . . . No, ma'am, I'm not from here, I'm from up country, a place called Paracatu, you've probably never heard of it, m'am. I don't know anything about it, she said, but I know where it is.

Another thing: can you use salt in this gun of yours? Yes, of course, he said. What for? Oh, there are some lads, she said, who keep annoying me, they throw stones at the windows, climb over the wall, they won't leave Quiquina alone. I don't want to do them any harm, just frighten the little imps.

José Feliciano had a good laugh, laid it on a bit, he saw that Dona Rosalina liked it. You can leave that to me, Dona Rosalina. It won't even need salt, a few shots in the air are enough to frighten any lad, they won't come back. Anyhow, me being here, you know, ma'am, they have more respect for a man. How come you know my name, she inquired, ready to retreat. Seeing Dona Rosalina hesitate, he said, it was the carter. He only said that your name was Dona Rosalina. Nothing else. He's a decent man, like me, I don't care to poke my nose into other people's business. It doesn't matter, she said, I'm not interested in what they say about me, my father or my grandfather. If you want to stay here, don't come to me with street gossip, from meddlers, dishonourable people who don't keep their word. I don't want to know what goes on in this town!

Seeing how excited Rosalina was getting, he tried a different tack: don't get me wrong, Dona Rosalina, I didn't mean anything, I had no intention to offend. Anyhow, I'm a reliable person, if my godfather was alive, Major Lindolfo de Sousa Veras, back in Paracatu, who brought me up, you could easily write and ask about me, he would only say nice things about yours truly.

That's enough, she said, recovering her composure. You needn't explain, it's over and done with, I understand. By the way, what is your name? My name's José Feliciano. But I'm also called Joey Bird or Major's Jack, the choice is yours, as you wish. I shall always call you José Feliciano, she said, that's your real name. Keep this Joey Bird business and Major's Jack for outside, for the riff-raff. All right, he said, that's the way I like it myself.

Well then, the job . . . Come inside, she said, and we'll talk about it.

José Feliciano was making for the door which Quiquina had left ajar, but Rosalina stopped him. Not that way. Through the garden gate, in the wall over there.

5

Wheels within Wheels

So José Feliciano, or Joey Bird, or Major's Jack – as you wish – started work at the manor. Rosalina called him José Feliciano and always addressed him formally when she gave him instructions : not the way she addressed Quiquina, he saw that immediately. José Feliciano, you can weed the garden, it's an absolute jungle. Now you can help Quiquina with the cleaning. Next you can take these flowers and go with Quiquina to deliver them. I don't know, you can ask Quiquina, she will show you, you will learn bit by bit. You can go to the warehouse and tell Mr Emanuel that I sent for money, he knows how much.

She meant to keep him at a distance, to avoid familiarity. She saw at once that José Feliciano was not what he claimed to be, that he was really very nosy and inquisitive. In the first few days she was close to sending him away, because he asked so many questions, wanted to know so much. He didn't stop at the usual questions, she wouldn't have minded those; every so often he came with a leading question, trying to bridge the gap – he wanted to know about her life, about her parents and relatives. She had to clip his wings, he needed to know his place : she was the mistress, he was just a servant.

Rosalina certainly knew how to command respect, she was a lofty personage, like Colonel Honório Cota. In her presence (when Colonel Honório Cota was alive and mixed with the townsfolk : she wasn't a child any more, nor was she yet a woman, but you could see in her bearing, her movements, even in her expression, the great lady she was to be, the sort that just to look at you lower your eyes respectfully) we behaved considerately, there were things we didn't say, we watched our language, we admired in silence.

Sometimes we wondered what she would have become, in her passage through life, if it weren't for the election and the family deaths which hindered her ascent. She was not supercilious, you couldn't say that of her : there was a power within her, a haughtiness, her way of taking her place in society, her station in life. Ah, Rosalina was not like the rest of us creatures, ordinary mortals. Those who merely suspected, when she was a girl, what was going to grow out of that lanky body, subsequently understood what it meant when they saw the mysterious light which her presence cast over the town. She was a true daughter of that Colonel João Capistrano Honório Cota, of late and dear memory, to whom we doffed our hats respectfully. It was all so long ago, one forgets. . . .

Just a servant. He realized immediately that he would never be like Quiquina, whom Rosalina treated with a mixture of friendship, respect and affection. She called Quiquina just by her first name, using the familiar form of address. Yet even Quiquina, who had been her nanny, knew that authority, the reins were firmly in Rosalina's delicate hands.

If Rosalina didn't send him away immediately, there were certain reasons. One day she came close to dismissing him. That was when, after looking at the two portraits in the drawing room, he said Dona Rosalina, who is the man in that picture there? My father, she said unthinkingly. Suddenly her face set into a frown, a sign that he shouldn't go on, but he didn't notice, and the other, he said, that's your grandfather, isn't it? What was he like,

Dona Rosalina? I've been told . . . If you want to know these things, she said, raising her voice, almost shouting, if you want to gossip, go and talk to the townies you've been hobnobbing with, do you think I don't know? Me, he started. I have no say in your life outside this house, nor the company you keep, but within these walls, no! What do you mean, Dona Rosalina? Don't be angry, he said. I didn't mean any harm, I don't take no notice of what they say, I'm just like that. I spoke more for the sake of talking. You know, ma'am, it gets lonely here . . . I get to feel like talking, ma'am, Quiquina's dumb, me doing all the talking gets wearisome, I need to hear somebody's voice occasionally, to chase the ghosts away. All right, I'm sorry I spoke, he said, noticing the hard expression in Rosalina's eyes.

One of the reasons why Rosalina didn't send him away was precisely what José Feliciano said : people need to hear a human voice, to get away from their ghosts. A man is not a solitary being, a lake of silence, he needs to hear the music of human speech. If you don't take note of what words mean, if you don't sniff their essence, but just hear them, human speech is rough and brutish, full of strange sounds, of highs and lows. Now listen, not just with wide open ears, listen with your body, if possible with your belly, with your heart, and see now, just hear the sweet melodious song. Just the song, the music.

Rosalina listened to José Feliciano. His voice gave new life to the manor house, its music filled the hollow shell of the big house, chased away the heavy shadows among which she had been living, almost unawares. Now she wondered : how could she possibly have lived so long without hearing a human voice, only Quiquina's grunts and the desperate signs she sometimes made when she couldn't make herself understood? Listening to her own voice. But you never hear your own voice properly, with your ears. It echoes inside your body, in the depths of your soul, like a sound coming out of the earth. If you think of a record, when your voice is recorded, people don't recognize themselves. Suddenly, awoken by the song, she saw what a desert her life was. How could she have lived like this for so long? How, my God? She was turning into a thing, burying herself in a dark hole, she and her world were the same thing. While inside her the life-blood clamoured, that force which through the green fuse drives flower and beast, and makes the world this closed-in place which spirit alone cannot penetrate.

And the voice, which to start with was too loud and made her ears ache, awoke her to the brightness, the light of things, to life. She was not really aware of the moment when her slow awakening began. Suddenly, one night, she found herself in front of the mirror going through the ritual she always performed in her room before going to bed. With the silk rose in her hair, she observed herself in the mirror. Yes, I'm still young and pretty. She let her eyes droop voluptuously, filling them with an expression of love. A passion, a blossom, but no one to pluck it. Her fingers adjusted the rose in her hair. Suddenly she checked her gesture and remained quite motionless, like stone. She stayed like that for a time, quite still. Who was that figure in the glass that she didn't recognize? A slight tremor began to make her eyelids and her face muscles twitch. She took the rose from her hair and kept looking at it in the palm of her hand, as if she had not seen it before, as if she herself had not made it. Rose, she said. A cloth rose, a silken flower. A white, baroque rose. And her eyes began to acquire a new brilliance, her reflection in the mirror blurred, she thought at first it was something to do with the glass. But her eyes slowly filled with tears, tears, she saw with amazement, because she hadn't cried for so long, she could not even remember the last time. And she wept silently, without sobbing, the tears running down her cheeks and dripping onto the white silk rose.

The second good reason why she didn't send José Feliciano away was because his presence gave her a sense of security. From time to time she was startled by a bang in the garden : it was José Feliciano with his fowling piece. She would smile, almost a happy smile. The children now left the manor house in peace, they didn't climb over the wall any more to steal fruit (why did they do it? If they asked, she would give them the fruit, she was not hard hearted, what was she to do with all those oranges and jaboticabas? So she was thinking), to annoy Quiquina, they didn't throw stones at the windows any more. Just as he said, he didn't need to use salt : at the first bangs the lads realized there'd been a change and scattered, with shouts of it's buckshot or it's salt. José Feliciano smiled with satisfaction, flattered and pleased with himself, because he was showing his usefulness.

Another reason why José Feliciano was kept on at the manor was because he was practical. Doing different sorts of odd jobs on his long journey south from Paracatu, he'd learned to do a bit of everything, unusual, as the master craftsmen would say when he was boasting about his own work. So it came about that he knew a bit about most things : carpenter, bricklayer, electrician, painter, he could unblock drains and repair taps. He only disliked permanent jobs, such as he'd often been forced to take on during his journey – hoeing and harvesting in the coffee plantations. Hoeing was no job for him, I'm no slave, he would say with the flyest face you can imagine, sometimes playing on his supposed illness, other times on his useless eye, or yet again on his promise to wander like a nomad, a promise which he had really never made nor even intended to make. He had learned these minor skills on Major Lindolfo's farm, from the tradesmen his godfather had come from the town, or from the farmhands themselves – he had nothing else to do, he was observant and he was a member of the household. He performed these services with growing skill, until the major could do without the tradesmen from the town and would call on him when necessary.

That was how he came to ask Dona Rosalina if he could buy some tools to do the jobs he kept inventing to while away the time. Even he was sometimes amazed to discover in himself such willingness to invent work. Rosalina only told him to weed the garden, plant a few beds of tomatoes and vegetables, help in the kitchen and with the cleaning, accompany Quiquina to deliver the flowers and stop by the stores and drapers' shops in the town, go and fetch money from Mr Emanuel. He told himself that it was the silence, the loneliness, that weighed so heavily in that house : Quiquina dumb, Dona Rosalina shut inside herself, she was a woman of few words. Only very occasionally did she lift a corner of the veil and start talking, and even then she seemed to regret it afterwards, cutting him short just when he was thinking that the ground was favourable, his for the taking. Try as he might, he could find no way of knowing how to predict Dona Rosalina's sudden changes of mood. Like a dog which fails to sense its owner's mood and is chased away when it comes with its usual games. He spoke differently to her : Dona Rosalina, to be straight with you, I was never one to keep doing the same job, I don't stick to things. But with you it's different, ma'am, it's a pleasure to work for a grand person like yourself. It's the heart that counts, Dona Rosalina. People who are big hearted, try as they will, can never be petty. That's the way I see it, Dona Rosalina. Rosalina would look askance when he pitched his praise too high. But she enjoyed listening to him, he was so straightforward, had such a lively tongue. If he weren't so nosy it would be really nice to have a long chat with him, talk about her life, about her past, about the things she was tired of thinking over by herself. Even after what happened, after her mother died and her father shut himself away with her, cutting himself off from the world, she still used to go to mass on Sundays and went to con-

93

fession occasionally. When her father died, she even stopped going to church : the manor was her territory, its boundary was the garden wall.

So José Feliciano began to put the house in order. He felt like his own master doing these extra jobs. He repaired the rickety chairs, the damaged tables, replacing the tops that had woodworm, he soldered leaking pipes, turfing out the bits of cloth which Quiquina stuffed in to try and stop the water spurting out. He got rid of the roof leaks, replaced tiles, touched up the crumbly plaster in the drawing room, he even thought up a plan for painting the whole house. I shall need more men for that, Dona Rosalina, he said, when he put the plan to her. She listened in silence, alarmed by his over-ambitious ideas. No, it would be too much of an upheaval in her life, too many people in the house, particularly people from the town. It would be like suddenly finding herself naked, as if she had opened the doors of the manor to the town. She couldn't possibly consent. No José Feliciano, I don't want to, she said. Thank you for your trouble. Your intention was good, very praiseworthy, I'm quite touched. But I don't want to. The house shall stay as it is until I die. Just as it is, as Daddy left it. He wouldn't like it. But Dona Rosalina, what does your late father, God rest his soul, have to do with it? José Feliciano ventured. Nothing, José Feliciano, she said. Or rather, he does. But that's my business, no one else's concern. In any case, I thank you for your interest, it shows you are keen and that is good, I'm pleased and praise you for it, as I said. If you like, you can carry on doing the things that need doing, but don't invent anything major. Thank you, José Feliciano, you've no idea how grateful I am.

Even though his project was turned down, he was pleased. For the first time, Dona Rosalina had behaved like any normal human being, she wasn't up on high, shut away in her fortress of silence, the haughtiness that became a daughter of Colonel Honório Cota. You get wrong ideas, he thought. You judge a person by what you see, and you don't see what can't be seen, what's hidden in the cellar, the lumber of suffering, that people aim to keep locked away, because if other people see that they realize that a grand person is really quite tiny. . . .

But when he thought he had Rosalina in his grasp, she would change. She would change so abruptly that she didn't seem to be the same person as a few moments earlier.

Time moved on, more quickly now, since Joey Bird had arrived. We noticed the changes. How could we fail to notice, when so much was changed in the house? We didn't see changes in Rosalina, she was still a closed book, whenever she saw someone approach and start making the first gesture as part of a new try at greeting her, she would quickly turn away. Rosalina aloof as always, retaining as always that undying hatred, the same silent unrelenting hatred of our Colonel Capistrano Honório Cota, of lasting memory. What we noticed mainly was the manor house, curious as to what was happening inside, merely imagining the possible changes in the great little lady, Rosalina, who was after all an Honório Cota. Some recalled wistfully the good days when Colonel Honório Cota was on good terms with us, when he rode past, cutting a figure on his horse, and returned our humble greetings with the sweeping gesture of a person of quality. And they wondered if by wishing very hard it would not be possible, with God's help, that she would one day come among us again and forget the past. We kept the manor under surveillance. We saw Joey Bird's work and were thankful for his presence in the town. We watched the house front, with its many windows whose broken panes he replaced one by one; the blackened roof revealed the marks of time, but no longer that state of abandonment with tufts of grass sprouting through chinks in the walls, threatening to make cracks; the repairs to the plastering under the eaves were a sign that the manor was convalescing, was no longer a ruin. We felt our hearts swell with hope. If only it were given a coat of paint, we thought. But Rosalina wouldn't allow that. . . .

But José Feliciano's labours were not limited to household jobs, to repairs to the house. Being a hunting man, he wasn't satisfied with letting off his gun to scare off the kids and with the sport of potting at pigeons in the garden of an evening. No, on Saturdays he made arrangements with a friend he'd found, Etelvino, who was very fond of hunting and even had a good little dog with the funny name of So-and-so, and off the two of them would go on Sundays to the surrounding countryside.

It was no lie, he was a good shot, he always came back with a brace of partridge. He would perform a courtly gesture, offering the fruits of his expedition to Dona Rosalina. She would accept, but with no more than a thank you, give them to Quiquina, she didn't want any familiarity, he was very impertinent, give him an inch and he'd take a foot. However, she was always waiting at the window when he came back from hunting. She kept hidden so that he wouldn't notice. José Feliciano was very sharp, he could see from way off that Dona Rosalina was at the window, waiting. She was pleased, she's pleased he thought. And he overdid the bowing and scraping when making his presentation, so she said, not to him, to Quiquina, but so that he would hear, Quiquina, I'm rather fed up with all this partridge, make me a steak.

That hurt him, so haughty, he thought. The townsfolk were right.

When she saw that he was sulking, that she had hurt him more than she intended, she merely wanted him to know his place, she tried to make up. The next day she offered to make him a loan, he could repay it later, when he was able, to buy a new rifle, the one he had was so old. . . . José Feliciano had his pride, he refused. He would think about it later, was what he said, already imagining

96

a brand new shotgun, with a leather case like Etelvino's and like one the major, his godfather, had. A hunter with a new gun, then he'd show Etelvino. If Dona Rosalina agreed, he might even get a dog like So-and-so, or like that Crosspatch of fond memory, and walk through the streets whistling on his way to the woods, so that his acquaintances would be well aware of his importance.

When he was absorbed in some job or other, Rosalina would watch him from a distance. She could see his left eye, white, the leucoma that veiled his sight. What was it, I wonder if he was born with it? She hadn't the courage to ask, for fear of offending him. He never mentioned his defect, though he was so fond of talking about himself and other people. The first time, when he first arrived here, I wonder if he spoke to me or to Quiquina about that cloud in his eye? She couldn't remember, she tried hard to recall the details of José Feliciano's arrival. It was a long time ago, she was so far away from those silent days when she lived alone in the big house with Quiquina. . . .

He roamed about a lot, he was always wandering about the town. When she sent him out to do something, she could expect a delay. He always came with a shabby excuse. Something happened over at the meeting place, Dona Rosalina, I'll tell you how it was. He would invent a long story, with all manner of incidents, in which he always had the hero's part. She listened without paying much attention, although she experienced a certain pleasure in the flow of speech and in the twists and turns of the narrative. That was his business, she had nothing to do with the town, with those people. His life outside the house was of no interest to her.

Of no interest? Then why were there nights when she tossed in her bed, unable to sleep, her mind swarming with depressing thoughts, when he was a long time coming back to the house? Whereabouts could he be so late at night? Before she realized she would be imagining him out in the street. He can't be a good man, she said, angry at José Feliciano and angry with herself for thinking about such an unimportant person. But it was difficult to stop thinking. Bound to be consorting with a prostitute, she said with hate in her voice. Pig, filthy beast. Tumbling with a whore, a pig like himself. At the Mares-Paddock, she heard him from her window, arranging with someone outside on the footpath. And at night, when he was late, the words echoed horribly in her ears. Mares-Paddock, that's where he must be. Mares-Paddock, it's a good name for it. That's what they are, mares. Filthy, beasts of the field, filthy like him. It's nothing to do with me, him coming home drunk, whistling. He's not a thing of mine. He's just a nobody who knocked on my door asking for work. Nothing more, just that. Drunk, he comes back drunk from the whores. I'm feeling like this because the house is so empty at night, it's dangerous.

Why was it that before the arrival of José Feliciano she didn't think about the loneliness, the danger of two women being alone in the manor? Rosalina was unable to find an explanation.

While Rosalina called him José Feliciano, when Quiquina referred to him she did as follows: she put her wrists together and waved her outspread hands like wings, then she stretched her left arm out straight, with her right arm across her body, her finger pressing an imaginary trigger, and sometimes completed the performance by making a sharp report with her mouth. So for Quiquina he was made up of two images: the wings of a bird and a shotgun – Joey Bird. She didn't always need to go beyond the first gesture, we knew that she meant Joey Bird. When people asked Quiquina what she thought of Joey Bird, she would grin broadly and blink her eyes, which sparkled more than usual, then she would twirl her thumbs at her temples and make funny faces, so we knew what she thought of Joey Bird – a mischievous imp. Sometimes they would pretend not to understand, for sport, so that she would repeat her pantomime. Quiquina, is he mad? She shook her head, not at all. She would repeat the scene, he was just mischievous. They laughed at her sly humour. Quiquina was really very funny.

Buying flowers from Quiquina was a great sport, which some people took so far that it bordered on the perverse. But Quiquina always found someone to defend her. Don't treat her like that. Don't you see it's uncharitable to mock those who bear God's mark? She didn't like being helped, she could easily look after herself. She got her own back in the price, she imitated the person behind his back, stuck her tongue out and made the funniest faces you've ever seen. And those who started by laughing with the idler ended up laughing at him instead. Quiquina had a very warm spot in the town's heart.

If a new salesman, one of those travellers looking for a bit of fun on those lazy afternoons in the drapers' shops and the chemist's, decided to take advantage of Quiquina's innocence (they didn't know Quiquina, she was very quick in business matters, she knew the value of Dona Rosalina's flowers), there was always someone who would intervene. Young fellow, don't start that or you'll come off worst. We like a joke but there's a proper time for games. Truth to say, we are very very fond of Quiquina. Then another, a more reputable person, would say if that's all you mean to offer for the flowers, keep your money, I'll take them and I'll pay more. The salesman would realize straight away that he was on dangerous ground, he might even lose a very profitable market for orders. I was just joking with her, can't you see that? What did you say her name was? Quiquina, I'll give you twice what I said, I'll take the flowers. She grinned with satisfaction and behind the salesman's back stuck her tongue right out, poking fun at him. We had to explain everything to these new salesmen, who were not strong on tact or intelligence. That she was dumb but not deaf, they didn't need to shout; she was dumb but not daft, in fact she was very sensible; she was not one of those local idiots often found in small towns, but she had a place in all our hearts. The town defended its child keenly and with dignity. We had our pride.

You see the town did like Quiquina. We enjoyed her quiet comfortable presence, her tranquillity. Quiquina was tranquil, she was big-hearted, you could see that. Because of our longstanding remorse, we needed to love someone from the manor, since Rosalina rejected our love, our friendship, our outstretched hand, even our eyes. Oh, that old warring hatred, nurtured by the pride of the Honório Cota clan. We would have preferred her to be like old Lucas Procópio, a lawless, unforgiving man, given to fits of anger, more extrovert, who spat it all out when he was hopping mad. We formed an opinion, imagined the story of his life, pieced together a picture of him with the scraps of secondhand reports of what he had been like, a picture of an outsize Lucas Procópio. The only person who could have corrected the portrait of Lucas Procópio sketched by the town's imagination was old Maldonado. But he, poor thing, was no good to anyone, far advanced in age, sunning himself on his doorstep, decrepit, lost in the clouds and in his meaningless mumbling, soft in the head. No use going to him. So we had to rely on our imagination, on the myth we created. We wanted Rosalina to be like Lucas Procópio, insult us to our faces, so long as she spoke to us. But no, Rosalina had taken after that Colonel João Capistrano Honório Cota, whose nobility, pride and silence were an added mortification to our grievous remorse.

Quiquina was the bridge, the boat which carried us to that island. The bridge, however, which we could not cross, the masterless boat drifting in the silent sea of our dreams of a crossing which was impossible. People did question Quiquina about life at the manor. But if they asked for news of Rosalina she would become dumber than she really was, not a sign, her speech mechanism would fall silent. She would lower her eyes and very soon withdraw. We knew it was useless and they gave up asking. We were afraid that our questioning might lead to our losing the company of Quiquina as well, that bridge which, though not used, did exist. That boat which, though empty, did carry a little of our aroma, of the salt of our tears.

In the beginning the most distressed among us turned to Emanuel, maybe he could explain, they thought. Emanuel, though, was just as discreet and taciturn as his father, the late Quincas Ciríaco. What do you want to know for? Haven't you done enough already? he said. Come on, Emanuel, we meant no harm, we just wanted to know. If you want to know about her health, he replied sharply, she is well, thank God, and she doesn't need a thing. I take care of everything in accordance with the wishes of her late father, God rest his soul.

And the manor became gradually more lofty and inaccessible on its rock.

The town was very fond of Quiquina, she was a useful person. She not only brought Rosalina's flowers to our market; when she was needed to deliver a baby, she would be there, always ready to help. If Dona Aristina for some reason couldn't be in attendance, people turned to Quiquina for help. She wasn't a professional, but she had acquired a good deal of practice from helping Dona Aristina with her midwife duties. Many of the youngsters who climbed over the manor house walls in those forays of theirs and pestered Quiquina, had come into the world with the help of her deft, affectionate hands. When their parents got to know of the mischief they got up to, they would tell their children off, was that a nice way of behaving towards Quiquina? But boys will be boys, she would acknowledge, forgiving them. It's hard work getting a boy to be respectful. They only understand by being frightened. This was why Quiquina kicked up such a fuss and hurled the stones back at them as hard as they came. In the street they were better behaved, they went past with their tails between their legs.

The arrival of Joey Bird was in one way a relief to her. She no longer needed to bother herself with the boys up on the wall, to keep an eye on the garden, to watch out for the stones. That was what Joey Bird was there for. He would load his gun, aim into the air and the explosion would scare the kids, the pigeons would fly away in alarm. The fowling piece was the first virtue Quiquina found in Joey Bird. At first she didn't like the look of the man, she had her likes and dislikes. On the whole she didn't like strangers, the Italians least of all, because they did such a lot of shouting. He'd come from far away, nobody quite knew where the place was. She looked on him as an outsider. Nothing good would come of it. That man is no good, you can see at once that he's no good. He's not one to get too close to. A lot of gab, full of wiles. He tells lots of stories, he's always telling stories. You never know when he's telling the truth and when he's lying. He's not serious either, always got his mouth wide open laughing. Laugh like a drain, you can't have much brain. When laughter arrives, sense flaps its wings, the bird is flown. She certainly hadn't wanted Joey Bird to come into the manor house, she motioned him to be on his way. It was Rosalina who got it into her head, and when Rosalina gets an idea that's the end of it. She's been like that since she was a child. She was really keen to have him go on his way, hunt for a job somewhere else. On top of everything else, a hunter, a loafer obviously. But Rosalina called him, hey young man, come over here. God could easily have stopped him hearing. The two of them led a peaceful life, the two women by themselves, very close to one another, since Colonel Honório Cota died. She could be Rosalina's mother, she was there when Rosalina was born.

What a happy day it was when she was born. The

colonel and Dona Genu gave thanks to God, Our Lady, all the saints, they didn't know how to show their gratitude for such a fine present from heaven. They wanted everyone to share their happiness. That one she was sure would survive, she prayed hard to God for her to survive. She looked questioningly at Damião in her distress. Damião replied, no. That Rosalina, God wouldn't be calling her to Him so soon. You could see in her eyes, everything about her, that she would survive. She wasn't going to be yet another little angel. Oh, Our Lady of the Rosary, mother of black people, please let God not take her to Him. The little corpses that Damião took to the cemetery every year, every time Dona Genu's belly grew big again. Some of them weren't even whole, just bits of creatures, abortions. Even so she would go with Damião on those sad journeys to the cemetery. It was fate, a curse. You shouldn't believe such things. But there are some things that keep happening and you can't stop thinking things. Dona Genu had those little angels just for the red earth of the cemetery. The mouths of the craters were there to devour everything, ground and people. One day they would end up devouring the cemetery, out of sheer greed, the fleshless bones of the old corpses, from the earliest times. Even old Lucas Procópio. Probably sick him up again. Didn't everybody who knew Lucas Procópio say that he was a real blackguard, one day he'd end up shot through the heart, in an ambush.

He wasn't killed though, he died a natural death. Her mother used to tell her about the things Lucas Procópio got up to, she'd cross herself. Devil take thee! That's one the craters should have swallowed alive. Her mother never had a good word for him. For him a slave was really a slave, no friendliness, no forgiveness. When Colonel Honório Cota talked about him, he spoke respectfully. You'd think he was talking about someone else. It had all come from Lucas Procópio. Everything bad. The spirit of Lucas Procópio grew bigger. The tormented soul of Lucas Procópio was restless, couldn't find peace. Weren't they his, those steps she heard coming downstairs at night? Nonsense, there's no such thing, God is supreme, God is merciful. It was God's will that Rosalina should survive, to prove that fate doesn't exist, that man makes his own way. Within lines traced by God.

While in one sense the presence of Joey Bird was a relief to her, in another way it brought her a lot of bother. She had to keep hunting after him. Where did he get to? He would be nearby, talking to her, telling her his long stories, those interminable tales about Major Lindolfo, Dona Vivinha, the boy Valdemar, people she'd never heard of before but who were now part of her life. Suddenly he would vanish, sniffing all over the house just like that there Crosspatch on a shoot. When he could see that Rosalina was busy in her room or with her flowers, he would be off prowling about the house, even fiddling in the drawers. He was always wanting to know about Rosalina, about Colonel Honório Cota, about Lucas Procópio. There are some people who like to know things just for the sake of it. But he wasn't like that, he must have some other reason. What did he want to know so many things for? Must be to tell the others, gossipmonger. Why didn't he do what she did? She was without speech, that was God's will, but if she wanted she could tell by using her fingers, her hands, even her eyes. They would understand, they were dying to know. Could Joey Bird be telling them that Rosalina was drinking at night? Oh, if the town got to know about that. Better to send Joey Bird on his way. Wouldn't it be better to make Rosalina see that nothing good could come from that man? Rosalina knew what she was doing. But she didn't realize that he was telling the others what went on in the manor house. If she were sure, she would open Rosalina's eyes.

Joey Bird had one white eye, when he wanted to see something better he turned his head. That white eye disturbed her, she never knew whether he could actually see. Because with him it could all be pretence, the man was a bad lot, you could see that at once. Could it be that Rosalina didn't see that? Why didn't she send him away? He's a great help, I realize that we needed him, said Rosalina. Didn't need him at all, the two of them had always lived alone without needing any Joey Bird. It's true he did keep the garden tidy and he chopped wood for her. And she did need some help, she was old and tired. But why did it have to be that one-eyed man? Of course it had to be him, it couldn't be anyone else. Because he came from other parts. Not from the town. Nobody from the town was allowed into the manor. Not since Colonel Honório died. Only Mr Emanuel. Mr Emanuel came very rarely, only at the year's end. You might say nobody came into the manor house, Mr Emanuel was like a member of the family. Quincas Ciríaco's son, now there was a good man. If there were more like Quincas Ciríaco in the world, things wouldn't have happened the way they did, the manor would have carried on being full of people, happy parties, like when Rosalina was born. Quincas Ciríaco, such a sensible man, giving advice to Colonel Honório, when he took leave of his senses.

When Mr Emanuel came to see Colonel Honório, to ask his blessing, Rosalina would get herself up like for a party. If she didn't want him, refused him, why did she doll herself up like that? How are you supposed to understand a young woman, particularly one of those Honório Cotas? All funny people, didn't see things the same way as other people. Could he ever have said anything to her? No, Mr Emanuel was very reserved and timid. Wouldn't even look at her, except out of the corner of his eye. Mr Emanuel would stand there twisting his hat round, talking to Colonel Honório, but watching her out of the corner of his eye. When she noticed, he would change the direction of his gaze, as if he were looking at the clock that the colonel stopped when Dona Genu died.

Like he was trying to see the time. Surely he knew that nobody wound that clock up any more after Dona Genu died.

Then it was Rosalina's turn to repeat things the way her father had done it. She came downstairs like a bride, no – like a queen. Nobody noticed how beautiful she was, everybody was afraid of what might, was going to, happen. Jesus must have gone up to heaven the way Rosalina came down those stairs. Like she had a cloud around her. The little picture on the card, Jesus walking on a cloud. The saints terrified, no, it was the soldiers with lances who were covering their eyes, blinded by so bright a light. Rosalina came down the stairs as if she had thought it all out beforehand. Was she altogether in her right mind at that moment? Jesus was joyful, though, he'd overcome all the evil things they had done to Him. Rosalina was the saddest thing in the world. White, not a drop of blood in her face. At one stage she thought she would faint away.

Now Emanuel was looking at the clocks: the gold clock first, with all the patterns. He would look from the grandfather clock to the gold hunter, then to the silver watch. All stopped. He didn't want to know the time, it was mainly to avoid Rosalina's eyes. Very shy was Mr Emanuel. He would never be alone with her, that was when the colonel was alive. He always asked nervously where his godfather was. He would stand twisting his hat round, a nervous habit. Hidden in the pantry she used to keep a secret watch on that strange courtship. Emanuel didn't tell her, nor anyone else, about his love. A love like that is beautiful: respectful, preserved in silence, unspoken.

What lovely eyes and what a good-looking man Emanuel was. If she'd wanted, her life could be quite different now. Rosalina didn't want to get married, goodness knows why. Even to Mr Emanuel, who was like a relation. She would have to leave the house. Or even if she didn't have to leave the manor, her father would be alone. She would have to break the pledge the two of them must have made in secret, even without words. Open her heart to the others, the doors of the manor to visitors. Her father didn't ask that sacrifice of her, but she knew that by going against his hinted wish that she should marry Emanuel, she was obeying the desire that was deepest within his heart. By disobeying, she was pleasing, she was the best daughter in the world. Like him, she was just like Colonel Honório. You could see the one was a copy of the other. That quiet, careful, aching hatred. Rather she were like old Lucas Procópio, the way they said he was. God help me, devil take him, said her mother. We knew that Lucas Procópio didn't suffer, that evil creature never suffered, only other people suffered on his account. But you really suffer for people like Rosalina and Colonel Honório. You suffer more because you can see how they are suffering. Like an Indian child suffering but refusing to cry.

Perhaps she was sorry she had refused Emanuel. At times Quiquina thought so. When Mr Emanuel came to settle the accounts, those rapid visits, as if he were visiting someone he didn't like who was sick, she would get herself up, pick the best dress in her wardrobe. On one occasion she coquettishly put a white silk rose in her hair. Didn't want her to stay in the room. Go and make coffee, Quiquina. Emanuel is fond of coffee. She said Emanuel, not Mr Emanuel. She said Emanuel like when they were children and played together and she called him Emanuel. The two of them were always up to their games in the coffee warehouse. Afterwards they became formal and from then on he was Mr Emanuel, they were just acquaintances.

Mr Emanuel, you needn't explain the accounts, I know they are correct, I trust you. Will you take a liqueur? Perhaps a glass of port, I will join you. No? Quiquina, bring the coffee, no one refuses a cup of coffee, it's an obligation. He was in a hurry, he didn't stay half an hour even. He was still afraid of looking at her, when she looked at him he averted his eyes, he even seemed to blush, and he stammered, like the time when she put the white rose in her hair. He looked at the white rose in astonishment, unable to understand, or perhaps he did understand? He was no longer in a position to love her, he was a married man, he'd picked a really nice girl called Dona Marta. Why did Rosalina do that? Could she still be thinking of catching him, having some sort of affair with him? Mr Emanuel was bashful, reserved. He couldn't even stand Rosalina's eyes looking at him. Why did she do it? Girlishness, she's like a girl in some ways. Because she didn't come through her girlhood properly, when she became a teenager – adolescence is like a girl bursting into flower – she was hit in the air just like those birds that Joey shot down with his gun. That's all he was good for. To scare off those little imps in the garden. Weed the garden, chop wood, help with the cleaning, that was all right. For the rest he was a nuisance, a busybody, meddling in things that were nothing to do with him.

It was so good before, when the two of them were alone. When she went by herself to take the flowers. So good, Rosalina only talked to her, only she heard Rosalina's voice. Now he was there to drink in her words. In fact, Rosalina encouraged Joey Bird. When she wasn't busy you could see she liked chatting to him. As long as he didn't come with street talk, asking questions about Colonel Honório and Lucas Procópio. He was clever, canny, now he didn't ask about things that annoyed Rosalina. His conversation was pleasant, those stories about Paracatu, about Major Lindolfo, Dona Vivinha, the boy Valdemar, those strangers who came into Rosalina's conversations with Joey Bird. She couldn't imagine what Rosalina saw in those hunting stories. Rosalina even laughed. That laughter hurt Quiquina. Like a gesture of affection that had been taken away from her, a laugh that should have been just for her, for her alone.

He wouldn't leave the manor house, she was sure of that. It would be no use her telling what Joey Bird was up to, or invent lies about him. Rosalina needed a human voice, her grunts and signs were not enough. He could speak, he could find his way more easily into the closed heart of Rosalina. That key was one she didn't hold. When the conversation was getting lively and Rosalina was smiling, she always found a way of interrupting that intercourse which defrauded her. She would grunt like a dog whimpering to get the attention of its master. In her despair, she would get mixed up, be all fingers and thumbs. She would struggle to express herself somehow by means of her pathetic sign language. She would produce the strangest signs from her stock. She believed Rosalina understood her distress because she would always call her and ask her to do something. Quiquina, get the materials and the shaping irons ready. You shall choose the flowers we're going to make. She would smile contentedly, on that ground Jocy Bird couldn't compete with her. Rosalina was hers again, just hers, the flower of friendship opened like no other flower. Rosalina, she thought affectionately. Naughty girl, forgetting old Quiquina.

Because for Quiquina she would always be a girl.

From the very first days the town adopted Joey Bird, he was one of us. Here was another chance to build a bridge to the manor house, perhaps this would be the way to cross. It would be the broken connection which we tried to reconnect at the time of the two deaths : Dona Genu's and João Capistrano Honório Cota's.

João Capistrano Honório Cota at least received our heartfelt condolences, that day when we witnessed the first clock being stopped. For us the grandfather clock was the first, we only noticed later that there was another one hanging on the wall above the console-table. We thought then that he would be sociable with us again. But that's not how it was : he hadn't changed, he went on being the same João Capistrano Honório Cota, wounded and hurt; he accepted our condolences in the most formal manner possible, as good breeding directed, he couldn't throw us out of the house when we'd gone there to our beloved Dona Genu's funeral wake : he was the same unforgiving João Capistrano Honório Cota – in his silence he seemed to be throwing that death in our faces, debiting it to our already large account. With Rosalina it was worse, as was seen. We were unable even to tell her how deeply we felt the death of our great man, of João Capistrano Honório Cota.

Two vain attempts. The manor remained inaccessible. We would never succeed in reaching its nerve centre, never re-establish the lost connection. Because Quiquina, as we said before, was no use to us as a bridge, serving only to cross from the manor to the outside, we should never be able to cross it the other way. Quiquina's dumbness, and worse than this, the lack even of sign language when we asked for news of Rosalina, made her an impassable gateway. We said things to her, but our voice received no echo, no reply. We stopped thinking about Quiquina, because when we thought about her in relation to the manor house our sorrow became greater.

That was why the presence of Joey Bird was the cause of much cheerfulness and of all manner of speculation. Perhaps he would provide the tongue we lacked? Maybe those changes in the body of the manor house were taking place also in Rosalina's heart, the anxious ones wondered, those most given to dreaming and hoping. What Rosalina needed was a human voice, a single voice would be enough to open the way to the voices of the town, we thought. But our hopes were vain, as we saw. When they asked Joey Bird about life at the manor, he had plenty to say, too much almost. However, little of what he had to say was what we really wanted to know. Perhaps he doesn't want to say, said some; perhaps he doesn't know himself, said others. These things are hard to find out. After many roundabout questions, and after many thrusts and parries, one of us asked on behalf of all. Joey Bird, tell us straightforward, what about Rosalina? What does Rosalina think of us? A long silence, longer than Quiquina's silences, because Joey Bird *could* speak, fell over him and us. Go on, Joey, tell us, even if it's bad. We wanted to hear what we already knew. He looked at us very slowly, going round the circle one by one, as if he expected to find his reply written in our eyes. She doesn't think anything, she doesn't say anything. That wasn't much. We put the pressure on. Joey, who always had so much to say for himself, didn't want to speak now. Go on, man, tell us more, tell us the lot. You really want to know, do you? he asked, playing to his audience, savouring his reply. All right then, I didn't want to tell you, but you want to know. It's not much, very little really, hardly anything at all. Dona Rosalina simply doesn't want to hear anything about you. She doesn't want to clap eyes on you. As far as she's concerned the town has died and you've all gone to hell. Joey Bird's reply cut us to the quick.

If the town adopted Joey Bird, he was happy to be adopted. Everywhere you went you would find Joey. At the meeting place, in the circle round the South Minas Electric Company's lamppost, which the loafers were stripping in thin shavings and curls of wood. Joey Bird actually got himself a jolly good Cornet pocket knife and took part in the leisurely work of paring down the wood, bit by bit, to help along the conversation. The post was getting thinner in the middle, some day it would fall over. That's what the South Minas Electric Co. thought too and one day they had a steel belt fastened round the post, just at the height where the amusing sport was practised. Though the Company's iniquitous behaviour was initially accepted, it only needed Joey to raise his voice for everyone to start saying that behaviour like that was really a terrible insult. What a dirty trick! they yelled in unison. A slight, an insult to the dignity of a civilized town. That's what everybody thought and we cursed the Company. The Company, you see, was not local and not only did it charge an exorbitant price for its lousy services, but even had the nerve to threaten to cut off the electricity if we were behind with our accounts, or when some bright spark thought up a way of using a piece of wire to stop the disc in the meter, so that it only went round about ten days a month: that way the account was only a third – the right amount according to some – of what it should be.

An outrage, an insult, shouted Joey Bird, pointing at the steel belt. Oh, if this had happened in my home town, where Major Lindolfo, my godfather, could see it! That was the signal for the town's powder keg of hatred to explode. Colonel Sigismundo was passing when he heard the hubbub round the lamppost and wanted to know what it was about. When they told him (he too liked to strip off the odd shaving, it was a good sport), his just wrath knew no bounds. He called for a pick-axe, he'd knock the bugger down himself. If they wanted a fight, they could have one. When that shit of an inspector comes this way, let me know, he said, I mean to fill that louse full of lead. The inspector, who was in the vicinity, took to his heels and went to tell the manager of the Company. The manager didn't want to face Colonel Sigismundo, he knew what he was like. He decided the best plan was to write to company headquarters, telling them what had happened and requesting instructions. He got a letter back saying that a different procedure would be in place. Lamppost follows, the letter ended. And so it was that instead of the wooden post the meeting place got an iron one, the only one in the town. That was a novelty, a piece of progress. Joey Bird still tried to insist that the insult was just as big, in spite of progress and so on and so forth. But people felt he was overdoing it, the town's honour had been satisfied, imagine putting a steel belt just to insult people. See, clever dick! The Company realized who it was dealing with. At the same time we were peaceful, sensible, progress-loving folk.

Colonel Sigismundo, he liked the way Joey behaved, even wanted to have him in his pay, to do political work, but Joey said no, he couldn't possibly leave the manor house, Dona Rosalina needed him badly. Joey Bird's loyalty was praised a lot and he rose in our estimation.

As well as being a regular at the meeting place, Joey Bird used to drop in at the chemist's shop, the post office, where he would ask if there was a letter for him, he was expecting one (that was a lie) and the railway station in time to see the five o'clock express. On Sundays it would be the football pitch, he would act as linesman. Or he would go and play quoits in Carmo Square with a bunch of yokels. But what he liked best was going to watch the Italians play bowls in Italo Brentani's shed. The row the dagos made, the swearing, the obscenities yelled out with that musical lilt. They were great, the Italians! Joey Bird spent hours on end in Italo Brentani's shed. He could soon follow the game and he knew that the best bowler was Alfio Mosca, who had a sawmill in Uptown Street. The only one who could touch him was young Jacomino Guidorisi. But Joey Bird had a special liking for Alfio Mosca, he would bet money or a bottle of beer on him, he would give the odds and he always won.

When he was in the money, he would make for the Mares-Paddock to sow his wild oats and work off his desires on the mulatto girls. There was one he liked a lot, Marie, who was good in bed, full of tricks. Because he couldn't visit Bridge House, where the women were prettier and there was a better class of clientele, rich people, ranchers. He had big ideas, Joey Bird was a dreamer. But he consoled himself with the thought that, after all, all women are good, like a guitar it depends on the player.

When Joey Bird went by with Etelvino and the dog
So-and-so skipping along, on their way out into the
countryside (himself tall and thin, the other short and
fat, redfaced), they made a right pair, we died laughing.
At the faces he made behind Etelvino's back, poking fun
at him to show that in spite of all his special equipment
the fellow was a poor shot.

We knew that Joey Bird was a born liar, but we were
amused by his fibs, he was very funny. Joey Bird told
hunting yarns about the unforgettable shooting expeditions of Major Lindolfo in Paracatu. Only on special
occasions, when there were more people present, would
he tell the story of the coyote, the incredible hunt with
its mass of incidents which no one believed but pretended
to believe : first, because not everybody can catch a
coyote, a devil of a cunning, tricky critter, quick as a flash;
and then, the story was neatly put together – it grew a
bit with each telling, aided by our stupefaction, and he
invented a lot. But we still asked him to tell it, he was
very amusing, there was no one like him as a storyteller.
We even asked him to tell stories about ourselves. We
enjoyed ourselves chatting away, when there was nothing
else to do, to pass the time away : we became fond of
Joey Bird. Joey Bird had been one of us for quite a
time, very much one of us, looked on with affection and
warmth.

And so Joey Bird, or José Feliciano, or Major's Jack –
as you wish – was leading the sort of life he had dreamt
of. It was a bit like in Major Lindolfo's times, back in
Paracatu. If he hadn't yet found another hunter like his
godfather, if he didn't have the major's firm, strong hand
to protect him (he was always up to tricks, but he knew
that although Major Lindolfo lost his patience with him
occasionally and made all sorts of threats, it was only for
outside consumption : at home, when they were alone,

he always stroked his head, lovingly, like a mother with her young), if he had to make his own way now (there, he was always Major's Jack, he had a reference), on the other hand, in the town he was esteemed for what he was and he continued to add to his fame and glory through many exploits.

In the town itself he was completely happy. In the manor house, where the silence hung heavy and the hours crawled by slowly – the clocks still, even the pendulum clock in the pantry seemed to take no notice of time, so slow and lazy was the movement of its hands – those two figures that formed the constellation of his present life made him nervous, waiting for something to happen, because nothing ever did, something to account for the quickening of his heart-beat, his fancies, at times his fear. Nothing happened, the days and nights were always the same : the black woman in the kitchen sucking on her pipe, her sign language and her grunts, difficult to get through to; Dona Rosalina in her room or in the drawing room working at her flowers.

When he got tired of talking to Quiquina – he did all the talking, talking continuously, to overcome his nervousness at the goggling eyes and dumbness of the black woman (he was having a difficult time getting to understand Quiquina's sign language, her code of gestures and actions), when he got tired of Quiquina, he would go to the drawing room and stand watching Dona Rosalina at her patient, meticulous work.

Dona Rosalina, ma'am, he would say, do you mind if I stay and watch you work? She would shrug her shoulders just like Quiquina, as if to say it doesn't matter to me in the least. But he could see that Dona Rosalina liked him to be there and before long she would start talking. Her voice was so pretty, so musical, like somebody singing, that he would close his eyes and drink in her words. When he had his eyes closed, she was a different Rosalina. He pictured her person, her gestures, and he imagined the prettiest girl in the world. With the stuff of clouds, with tender thoughts and with his childhood memories of rivers, woods and birds, he put together a vision that was so endearing and gentle that he forgot the reserved, sometimes peevish creature he knew as Dona Rosalina.

Just what did she talk to him about? Of things past, of her childhood on little Stone Ranch, which for him was a dream place, which he had never seen. If only he could go to Little Stone Ranch one day. But no, when we visit a place it's always so different, so much less interesting than when we dream about it. She talked about things as if they were things seen in a dream. That pony Firefly which had once run away and couldn't be found. The pony now galloped in Joey Bird's dreams. That's the sort the boy Valdemar would like, the walking-stick rifle in his delirious fever, pointing it in the direction of Our Lady, saying she's setting loose pigeons for me to shoot at. Dona Rosalina talked not so much to him, but as if she were alone and he merely the spring that set in motion the machinery of her memory. She talked about her father with great affection, about her fussy mother, her years at the teaching college – never a fellow-student visiting, she was always alone. But it was all the stuff of dreams, her father was not real, her mother a pretend mother, invented on the spur of the moment, according to her changes of mood. They were not the same people he heard about in the town, the persons he would love to know about (more than once he braved Dona Rosalina's anger asking questions about them) but had now completely given up trying, for fear of losing her good will and the good position he'd found. She talked about those creatures bathed in a halo of light, floating on clouds, just like a child talking about his father, his mother and his horse. Because at times Dona Rosalina didn't seem like the grown woman of the present. She was a young girl telling stories about herself, making up a life for herself. Life and people seen through the bright eyes and open heart of a child. When he had his eyes closed, she was like a young girl playing with him in the far-off lands of Paracatu.

When he opened his eyes there was harsh, dull reality, without even a sprinkling of dream, untouched by the gold dust of memory. The staid, meticulous person he saw did not fit with the gentle, melodious voice speaking from way down inside, from another person. Only her eyes matched the voice and the subject of the stories. These never went as far in time as her womanhood, when the thread was suddenly broken and she changed, falling into her father's pattern. She herself suddenly appeared to become aware of the reality that still lived inside her. From time to time she seemed to be startled to find herself talking and would look at Joey with surprised eyes. She would come back to the ordinary world, to the harshness of things. What exactly was I talking about? she would ask, as if taking up the thread of an intricate story, fashioned in dreams, during hours of silence and solitude. You were talking, ma'am, he would say gently, afraid that the glass would be shattered, that she would come back to the everyday world – the delightful dream world was slipping from his grasp – you were talking about your pony, Firefly. Oh, my wee pony, she would laugh. Foolishness, José Feliciano, girl's talk. Anyway, I shouldn't be boring you with these stories. You don't bore me, ma'am. People should talk all they want, talk without fear, follow the dictates of the heart.

But she didn't go on. She talked of other things, her flowers – she explained how they were made – about Quiquina, about jobs that needed doing in the house. What if you were to teach me, Dona Rosalina, what do you say? What about teaching me how to make flowers? I might have a knack for it, you never know, he said one day. She thought that was funny, she had a good laugh about it. You, José Feliciano? You make flowers? Really!

that's no job for a man. Your hands are hard, used to working with a spade, an axe, your rifle, they wouldn't do to handle these silks and organdies. You'd end up ruining my materials. That would be very funny. . . . She realized she had been too forthcoming and tried to draw back. That fellow was very meddlesome, give him an inch and he'd take a mile, and so on, that's what she thought on other occasions, when he encroached. But the way he looked at her, his face was so frank, his good eye so clear, a good person, apparently, without ulterior motives – only his wall-eye bothered her, she didn't know if he could see with it and, if he could, what he did see through the cloud – stopped her going from one extreme to the other, changing back suddenly into the Rosalina he knew so well, the one whose guise she had grown used to since her mother died. No, José Feliciano, definitely not, was all she managed to say. What would people think of us, you turning into a florist? That's no job for a man! A man's place is out of doors, out in the country, dealing with the hard things in life.

José Feliciano let a few moments elapse, then said Dona Rosalina, I don't care a fig for what other people think or say. But I do, she retorted. He could see it was unwise to keep on, things might turn out like on other occasions. He didn't touch the subject again. Really, he wasn't all that keen on learning to make cloth flowers, it was more a way of filling time, of being near to Dona Rosalina and hearing a human voice, he was tired of Quiquina's dense silence.

Just as well it wasn't like the other times, those early days when he had to take care not to fall into a trap. Each of his questions could provoke such an unreasonable and violent reaction in Dona Rosalina, that he was afraid of asking anything. Later he realized that there were certain things he wasn't to know, a narrow strip of Dona Rosalina's life that he must not step onto. Particularly her folk, that eccentric old devil of a Lucas Procópio the town had so much to say about, the other, Colonel João Capistrano Honório Cota, gruff and moody, he'd heard many stories about. He noted that only she was allowed to talk about them, he must only listen. He was very smart and soon learned which was forbidden territory. The area of conversation was rather restricted, he had to be very alert not to overstep the mark. He knew, for example, that he must never talk about the town. But he enjoyed listening, it was nice to be near Dona Rosalina.

What an odd person she was, Dona Rosalina. He was disconcerted not only by her contradictory behaviour but by her mysterious nature. How could someone be like that? He could not understand, rack his brains as he would, he could not understand it. He got the idea that there were two of her in one : so when he thought he knew one, he found he was mistaken, it was the other one who was speaking. Sometimes more than one, she was so unpredictable in her behaviour, in her different manners. A confused agglomeration of Rosalinas in one Rosalina. He spent hours listening to Dona Rosalina, watching her least gesture, the slightest movement of her lips and eyes. He observed her from all angles, he followed her around and she never seemed to be one and the same person. Later, in his room, he tried to put his ideas in order, to put together the bits and pieces he picked up to form a composite picture of Dona Rosalina : a Dona Rosalina who couldn't really exist. Outside the house, he didn't think about her, completely forgot about her. He discovered that, no matter how much people questioned him, he could never talk about that lonely woman. His mouth must be sealed by his own will, just as Quiquina's was by divine intent. If ever the thought of Dona Rosalina came into his mind when he was in the street, he would expel it at once, because at a distance her person took on strange and lugubrious hues. While he needed the fresh outdoor air, the bright light of day, where time passed normally and life was ordinary, without any mystery or surprises other than the mystery of existence itself. The manor house was a grave, the craters, pathways shrouded in gloom.

No, she's not like other people, he'd say to himself. She wasn't like anyone he had known. Sometimes, at a distance, when he thought about Dona Rosalina, she put him in mind of Dona Vivinha, a little : Dona Vivinha after the child died and she wandered about the house like a soul in torment, the toy rifle in her hand, talking nonsense, not right in the head. She was like that for a few days. Joey, take this damned rifle and throw it into the bushes. Then it was all over and Dona Vivinha was herself again, except that she was sadder, permanently sad. Dona Rosalina wasn't actually like Dona Vivinha had been during those days, he just got that idea when he thought about her at a distance. Proud and a bit touched, that was what Silvino the carter had said. In the manor house, at close quarters, the shadows dispersed and she sometimes seemed a perfectly normal person, in her right mind, she didn't get those crazy spells like Dona Vivinha. When people live on their own they get out of their depth, lose touch with reality, he thought to himself. That's all, nothing else. That's not being touched, people talk too much, that's what. Silvino was right. When folk don't understand a body right, when someone's not just like everybody else, they say they're cracked, mainly to push aside a creature who needs an effort to understand, needs figuring out. Silvino was right about one thing – pride. Not that way, she'd said the first day. Through the garden gate, over there in the wall. This was her way of showing him that he was not her equal, that he must keep his distance and know his place. The distance she always put between them, if he came closer. It was silly, she didn't need to say that, he knew his place. Dona Rosalina was the madam and highly respected, he was just a servant, a skivvy. As if he would try to get through the barrier. If he sought Dona Rosalina's company it was more because of the silence in the manor house : it was so heavy, suffocating. He didn't have her strength of mind, she could stand years on end of that silence, time standing still, the loneliness. Not that way, through the garden gate. It stung him, even now when he remembered, it hurt. A dog chased away from the church door. Pride is not a good thing, some people get their deserts for it.

No, he was wrong, sometimes you're mistaken. In the first few days he thought things were going to be worse. Now he was accustomed, he had grown to like Dona Rosalina, he was sorry for her, thought of her with a certain fondness. Poor thing, so lonely, she had reason to be as she was. The clocks didn't go, so for her time didn't pass. My God, how awful ! It put you in mind of lying in wait for game.

Dona Rosalina was changeable, she never settled into any of the many Dona Rosalinas he kept discovering every day and adding together in the hope of one day perhaps being able to understand. He wanted to understand Dona Rosalina to make life at the manor easier, not to be always on tenterhooks, weighing his words, being cautious. Dona Rosalina slipped through his fingers as if by magic, like a will-o'-the-wisp. She was artful, with her gentle eyes, when you thought you had her caught, she would slip away. It was like hunting a coyote. Those coyotes in the out-back, wild, cunning, flashing amongst the undergrowth, mingling with the bushes, they seemed to be everywhere and nowhere. Major Lindolfo was always quick on the trigger. He would aim, press the trigger, the explosion would ring out, he would look : he'd missed, the coyote wasn't there, it was in another patch of undergrowth further along, like it was laughing at our confidence and our annoyance, having us on. Dona Rosalina was just like a coyote, he was trying to catch a coyote in that big house. She was always hidden in some part of the house, lost in time. Not Dona Rosalina's person, which was quite still and silent, working away slowly and peacefully at her flowers. He didn't know at this stage that what he was looking for in her was the other person: the spirit, the soul of Dona Rosalina.

And then she never looked her proper age, he could never tell how old Dona Rosalina was. Every time he looked at her, she seemed to be a different age. She went from the young girl who talked about Little Stone Ranch to a prudent, sensible, wise old woman. Dona Rosalina wasn't old, he could see that, despite the way she did her hair and those black clothes that no one wore any more. Dona Rosalina fashioned for herself a figure from older times, cut out of an old picture. She must be knocking thirty, was what people told him in the town, when he still bothered to question other people for information about Dona Rosalina and the manor house. Thirty was an age she never seemed to be, always either more or less. Sometimes he mentally let Dona Rosalina's hair down and he saw her as a very pretty young woman, with delicate, well drawn features; only her mouth was fleshy, red, seeming not to fit into the austere, stern face, with its clear, dark eyes, shining with a purity and a gentleness that soothed him, bathing him in waves of pleasurable warmth. If she wanted to, none of the town girls could compete with her in beauty. She was so pretty he started to see her in his dreams: all filmy, her hair flying loose, moving as if she were dancing on clouds and speaking words to him which he never managed to catch. When he had these dreams, he was always afraid to wake up, because the feeling of peace was so blissful, the feeling of a complete and happy life.

Time standing still, stifling. The clocks in the drawing room, their hands motionless. Time could not win in that house. Dona Rosalina outside time, a star over the sea, untouched by the roll of the waves.

At first, when he was still trying to find things out, when he first arrived, those clocks and watches puzzled Joey. The great, shiny grandfather clock, with the weights at the bottom, on the long chain. It must have a pretty chime, a ripple of bells filling the air with dainty, cheerful, rounded notes. Dona Rosalina, he said, why is this clock stopped? If you like, ma'am, I'll put it right, or I can take it over to Larisca, he's a good watchmaker, I've watched him at work. She didn't say a word, could she not have heard? Dona Rosalina, he said. I'm not deaf, she said crossly, her eyes turning dark and stony. There is nothing at all wrong with this clock. It didn't stop because it went wrong, Daddy wanted to stop it. Like the other two, those on the wall. I stopped one of them myself, when Daddy died. . . .

Although he didn't mean to ask, the desire was too strong and he said why, Dona Rosalina, why?

She shot him such a look that he was afraid. It's not your business, she said. You see to your work, do what you're told to do. You've no business wanting to know what only concerns me. Daddy and me. Ask the others, that rabble in the street. If you want to stay on here, don't ask me questions, do you hear? No questions!

6

The Breeze after the Calm

One by one she counted the chimes of the pendulum clock. After the tenth stroke she waited for one more. Nothing, just the silence of the house at that hour of the night. He hadn't come in yet, at the Mares-Paddock no doubt. Was that where he went nearly every night now? No, not every night, the money he earns isn't enough. They're only interested in men when they can get something out of them. Unless he's having an affair with one of them and she doesn't charge him anything. She just couldn't understand the life of women like that, she didn't know why she hated them. He might not be there, could be in some bar, drinking and listening to silly talk, she knew when he was coming, from his whistle, he always came back whistling, pleased with himself. Pig, why did she keep him on? Those filthy hands handling the things she touched afterwards. She had never thought of that before. Forget it, there was no reason for her to keep thinking about him, his life was nothing to do with her. As long as he works properly and doesn't bring that town gossip into the house.

The haziness from the wine, the warmth in her breast, in waves. She was not befuddled yet, still lucid. In a while, just a little while, the world would be floating, all soft and remote.

Quiquina doubtless still up. Not long before she had heard the muffled sounds of her cleaning the stove. Quiquina would not go to bed until she herself went up to her room. Quiquina on sentry duty, Quiquina her watchdog. During the day she would come in to her, stay near her, help her cut the cloth, prepare the irons. The daytime flowers, the scentless flowers of her life. After supper, when night fell, she would be alone in the drawing room, book in hand, passing time until she went to bed. This was when she was more alone than ever, the hours dragged so. During the day, the flowers kept her hands busy and took her mind off things. The hours dragging on, the unhurried silence. From time to time Quiquina's footsteps, her presence in the pantry and in the kitchen. At night she never came past the drawing-room door. Why? She couldn't make Quiquina out. Just her way, she's so good, never mind. If she needed her, all she had to do was call Quiquina and she would be at her side as if by magic. Quiquina mulling things over in the pantry; or in the kitchen snoring in front of the fire. Sometimes she would be in the dark and Rosalina imagined her eyes like two live coals, a cat's eyes in the dark, her pipe glowing. How could someone stay so long in the dark like that? Tonight the light is on, her eyes are not glowing. If she asked Quiquina to sit with her, she would come, stay a little while, then show she was sleepy, throwing her mouth open in an exaggerated yawn, and retire. Just a fib, Quiquina wasn't going to bed at all. A bit later she would hear (sharpening her ears, Quiquina made hardly any noise at night) Quiquina's soft footsteps in the pantry, the corridor, the kitchen. Why didn't she go to bed? She didn't know, Quiquina was watching over her.

There was the decanter open in front of her. She kept the bottle of madeira hidden under the table, she had to go steady with it. Quiquina wasn't to see. No doubt she thinks because I know she's still up I won't drink any more, won't get drunk. That's silly, I shan't get drunk, I'm used to it, only a drop more to make me feel drowsy and sleepy. Until he comes back. This sweet stuff certainly isn't going to bowl me over. Under the table, hidden. The madeira, she had to go steady with the madeira. The port wine, to offer him, he never accepted, when he came. Mr Emanuel, perhaps you'll take a glass of port? He never accepted, but she still offered. He didn't accept, he didn't want to be near her for long. Could he be afraid of having a drink with her? Did he realize, perhaps? She wondered if he remembered the days when he came to court her. He remembered, he couldn't have forgotten. When she kept her eyes on him, he would lower his, all red with embarrassment. Funny: Emanuel. When did she start calling him Mr Emanuel? Emanuel, Emanuel. It was nice when she just used his name. Then he got married. Now they were like strangers. A glass of port? He would take a coffee. His fingers would tremble, the cup clattering in the saucer. Is he afraid of me, I wonder? If it's all over, why should he be afraid of me? The dark corridor between the piled-up sacks of coffee. He stayed so little, he comes here so seldom. He could stay longer, it wouldn't hurt him. The two of them used to play in the warehouse, run between the sacks piled up to the ceiling, climb up to the top, right up to the top of the pile. The warm smell, the sacking had a shuddery smell, the good, warm resinous smell of the coffee beans. That's no way for a girl to behave, and grown up too, she's like a nigger child, said her mother. Let her, said her father, she's still a child, it doesn't matter. Her mother saw mischief in everything: can't you see that Emanuel is a grown boy? Can't you see that? You really are innocent, João Capistrano. She didn't know why her mother spoke like that, she couldn't see anything wrong in their games, their skylarking in the warehouse. But her mother kept on about it, it was time she became a young lady, gave up girlish habits, childish games. Come on, come on up, he said from the top of the pile. You can't do it, he taunted her, smugly proud of his prowess in getting to the top of the highest pile, touching the roof tiles with his head. Like a cat, with her dress hitched between her legs to make it easier and so that none of the workers down below could see her underpants. A cat, she was right next to him in a flash. See, stupid? She was panting heavily next to him. Up top under the tiles the sun was strong, it was hotter. Her face was red, flushed. There they would lie, she would do the talking, he would be silent just like his father. Since he was little he'd been silent, placid. Only once he was more daring. She wanted him to order her about, wanted very much to obey him. She told him he was daft, but that was in play, just words. To herself she played at calling him my lord and master. His face was funny, flushed like her own. Once, just once. Rosalina, Rosalina, her father called from down below. Emanuel! Her godfather, Quincas Ciríaco's deep voice. She was about to answer, but he stopped her. Shush, don't move, he covered her mouth. In order to cover her mouth he held her close to him. His body was hot and sweaty, his breath was hot, he was snuffling. Like Firefly once, sweating after a gallop, sniffing at her thighs, whinnying. Emanuel's hot breath on her neck tickled her, made her nervous. But she let him, she wanted him to, she let him. Now her breathing also became snuffly, through her nose, his hand was over her mouth. She could feel the moisture of his sweat-soaked shirt, his body on fire under his shirt. Her thighs were bare, she didn't bother to cover them, she let him see, blushing. She never thought he would do it, she wanted him to, never, that he would do that. She was showing her grubby underpants too. Nobody left in the warehouse, they'd gone away. But he carried on covering her mouth, their bodies locked together. Goodness knows how long they stayed like that, a long time, ages and ages. His breathing got faster, hotter. His excited eyes burned into her thighs. With his free hand he caressed her thigh, moving higher up all the time, his hand getting hotter, getting close to where she was burning hot. She didn't want him to, she let him, pretending to resist. Then he became bolder, more excited, panting heavily. His hand inside her underpants, just where she was hot and moist. She could have let him, she wanted to, just to see. But totally against her own wishes, she bit his hand, he cried out. A cat scratching. He looked at her in astonishment, not understanding, his face as red as a beetroot. She ran out of the warehouse. For a few days they were like strangers, didn't know one another. She didn't even look at him when her father was near. I wonder if he thought I had told on him? Stupid, as if she would. Then, suddenly, they started talking to one another again, they forgot the matter, as if nothing had happened. They forgot, friends again, children again. She wondered if he remembered when he looked at her. Not that old business, but later on, when he was a grown man, respectful, serious. Later, when he wanted to court her, he came to see her with the excuse of having business with her father. He remembered, he couldn't fail to remember. He was so withdrawn, so upright, like his father, her godfather Quincas Ciríaco, a true friend of the family. He never took the wine. Was he perhaps afraid of getting excited again? The wine.

She had to go steady with the madeira, the port wine was for him, even though he wouldn't take it, it was there, for him. The madeira was for her. It would be fine if she could just drink the madeira, the dry one, with the *R* on the label, was so good, so much stronger and more effective than those sweet drinks that Quiquina made. The bottle was half empty, in two or three days it would be finished, even going steady. Quiquina would have to fetch another. Go steady, she must be sparing. Be more sparing. But how could she, when the wine was so good? So that her account at the warehouse should not attract attention, so that they wouldn't start talking. She didn't care what the town thought of her, they could think what they wanted. But not the wine, the town must never know about her weakness. For the town she must be like her father, in her disdain, in her silent hatred, in her revenge.

Never, they would never know. She was as sparing as she could be with the madeira. She started with the madeira, then went on to the orange wine, or the jaboticaba liqueur, when the bottle of madeira began to get low. The orange wine and the jaboticaba liqueur were too sweet, they were sickly sweet, afterwards they gave her heartburn.

She poured another glass of madeira, thought she saw Quiquina in the corridor. Why did Quiquina never show her displeasure because she drank so much wine? Quiquina was always good, like a mother to her. Quiquina gave no sign, pretended not to be aware of what went on in the drawing room in the evenings. A silent agreement between them. Every time she left the decanter empty, the next day she would find it in the cupboard, full. Quiquina never let the madeira run out. She never once had to ask her, Quiquina would see to it. She just left the bottle on the table and Quiquina understood, she fetched more. She didn't hand the wine to her, but put it on the console-table, already uncorked. Maybe they thought at the warehouse that the madeira was for Quiquina. If she could be sure, she would drink more. No, they would be suspicious, they would know that if Quiquina were going to drink, she would drink hooch, that's what niggers like. Like that José Feliciano, he presumably drinks beer and hooch. Except that José Feliciano isn't black, in fact he looks a bit albino. But it's the same thing. What if she asked Quiquina to buy a bottle of brandy? She would say brandy, the other word was very vulgar. No, that would be going too far, taking advantage of Quiquina, she couldn't do it. If she did ask, Quiquina would buy it, she was so good to her. What if she said it was for a cough, I mean, something like that? No, definitely not. And what about sending José Feliciano. . . . No, not him. I wonder if he knows? He probably suspects, if he hasn't seen already, he's always inspecting the house, spying on me. Why did I go and let that man into the house? Quiquina didn't want me to, she didn't like the look of him. Nothing I can do about it now, I have to put up with him and make use of him. Anyhow I can't get rid of him, I need him too much. He wasn't likely to know, he was out every evening. At the Mares-Paddock, no doubt. She waited for him to go out, before she started. After he had turned the corner, that was when she opened the cupboard.

Brandy, if she asked, Quiquina would buy it. Why do they call it by so many names? Hooch, grog, all vulgar names. Whitecane was quite a good name, and that other one, cane-spirit, but she couldn't ask for whitecane, it would be ridiculous, her saying that. Firewater was a good name, it was so expressive. Burning-water, something burning inside her with a pleasant warmth. She tried it once. When Quiquina was not well and she had to make up a bottle of fever cure. There was a little over and she drank it. It was very strong, it burnt her throat and brought tears to her eyes. She coughed. But afterwards it was so good, that warmth in her chest, she felt her chest expand, a feeling of comfort, of confidence, almost of peace, happiness. Just for a moment a giddiness, everything shining. How things danced and shone, the impossible round-dance they danced in their brilliance. The Catherine wheel, the lights, the games. Herself as a child running, skipping in the square, singing; herself a child on her pony Firefly, at Little Stone.

No, that would be taking advantage of Quiquina. What if she invented an illness, she thought once again. Quiquina wouldn't believe her, she knew about her vice. But she would buy it. She couldn't, not humiliate Quiquina, poor Quiquina, so good, she loves me so much. Better carry on with this, a little madeira, then this sweet wine, this sugary liqueur. What if she asked Quiquina to make it stronger, not so sweet? She wouldn't do that, there was a wordless agreement between the two of them. When the bottle of madeira was empty, Quiquina bought another; when the decanter was finished, it turned up full again the next day. Quiquina should go to heaven.

And me to hell? She laughed awkwardly, twisting one side of her mouth. Mummy must be in heaven, I don't know about Daddy. Only Grandpa Lucas is in hell. They said so, she knew. Lucas Procópio knew how to live, Lucas Procópio was right. That was her father talking after it all happened and he shut himself away with her in the house. She wanted to be like Lucas Procópio herself. Lucas Procópio, though she didn't really know what he was, had been, like. He went to hell, the depths of hell, they said. Not to her, among themselves. She looked at his portrait on the wall, of when he was alive. He was so serious in the picture, not the way he lived, so they said. She wanted to have that dark strength, Lucas Procópio's mysterious power. The picture was blurred, wine fumes. They always said Lucas Procópio, why did they never say my father, my grandfather? A man much respected, outrageous in behaviour, given to acts of violence. Perhaps Lucas Procópio didn't die completely, was still alive inside her? She was Lucas Procópio's seed. In the darkest corner of her soul, where her own force of darkness sprang from. A force that struggled to be let loose, that wanted air. Lucas Procópio may have had this dark force, but he was one for sun, for greenery, for brightness. She might be like Lucas Procópio. The idea alarmed her somewhat, she was afraid at times. Not now, she was pursuing the thought to its conclusion. Madness, it's the body you inherit, the soul goes to heaven or hell. Lucas Procópio must be in hell, surrounded by his nigger women, whoring, being tormented by a thousand demons. What if there were a little of Lucas Procópio still in her, when the soul frees itself? We always leave our presence in the world, in other people. And what's over, the rest, evaporates. If she were like Lucas Procópio where would she be likely to be now? In Bridge House, said a voice inside her. Maybe somewhere worse, in Mares-Paddock, said another voice. That's where he must be, José Feliciano. Having fun with the whores, lying with them, filthy beast, enjoying himself. Oh

God, why do I get these thoughts? I just loose the reins and away I go all over the place. I know, I'm not Lucas Procópio, definitely not. She was more her father, an upright man, a good citizen. Didn't she copy his manners, his attitude to life? She was coming downstairs, all eyes on her. She went and placed her father's gold hunter right next to the other one, the Independence watch. Just like her father.

I'm like Daddy, not him. Lucas Procópio died a long time ago, I never even knew him. I'm Colonel João Capistrano Honório Cota through and through, she spoke the whole name out loud, pronouncing the words with care. I wonder if Quiquina heard? What does it matter? Nothing mattered. She lives alone in the world, there was no one else. Just herself and Quiquina. The empty glass in her hand, a drop of wine in the bottom, just dregs. She could break the glass between her fingers, cut herself, blood on her hands. Her father only drank on very rare occasions. That madeira was what he liked best. I, João Capistrano Honório Cota. She thought it was funny and started to laugh. She laughed out loud, let Quiquina hear. Then she would come to the drawing room to see how she was. Nearly drunk, thinking aloud, talking nonsense. What if Quiquina came and drank with her? Funny. Quiquina drunk, drunken sign language. She laughed so much her eyes filled with tears. She let her head fall between her arms, her face resting on the table, her eyes closed, her face wet with tears.

She stayed as she was for a while, not thinking what she was doing. Her eyes were full of tears, but she wasn't even aware that she was crying. Her thoughts were floating far away, away in a blue sky, in a dream landscape, she seemed to be dreaming. She lived in another country, she was Margarida, the vicar had long conversations with her. The other man, a real gentleman. Their love was so pure and good, the delicacy of their sentiments. Were there people like that in the world? Only in a village, in

Portugal, many, many years ago. That was where she lived at times, when she closed the book and began to dream. Could that really have happened? Did it exist? She mingled her life with the characters in the book and imagined herself laughing, loving, weeping, weeping for sheer happiness. The clear, pure emotions, the great love. Emanuel could never be like that, even if he wore different clothes. Could it all have happened like that? The writer invented it, they always invent, there are no such creatures in the world.

She had read the book many times, she knew it almost by heart. The three books she had been reading since she was a girl: *The Vicar's Wards, Women of Bronze* and that terrifying one, *The Jew's Revenge.*[8] She read them over and over, in turn, always the same books. The bottle under the table, her glass filled, she would start reading. Everything blurred, in a haze. The characters stepped out of the book and began to live real lives, she could even hear their voices, the ghosts of her solitude. Occasionally Emanuel would be in the book, he would start saying such beautiful things, things he would never really say. She would dress him in a tailcoat and put a tie on him, like the one in the drawing on the cover. He seized her by the waist, lifted her onto the back of his white steed, he was abducting her, off far away to a land where the white snow fell. Then the horse would gallop through the air, they were crossing over a field covered in flowers and she would ask him to stop, she wanted to pick a bunch of flowers. He refused, they had to flee, there were men on their tail.

Dry-eyed again, she looked at the drawing-room furniture, the motionless grandfather clock, the cut-glass chandelier, her own hands lying open on the table, her empty hands. She felt like crying, for some time now she had felt like crying. She who never cried. How could she live there, in that room, in that house, in that hostile town, when there was such a different life out there, in the wide wide world?

Her tears dried up, she opened the book at random. Her eyes fell on a few lines of poetry on the yellowing page. The letters would not keep still, she had to steady her eyes in order to make out the words. The letters were mixed up, she was dizzy, a haze enveloped her. The letters were like wriggling insects. All she managed to read, and that with difficulty, was: 'Tawny girl! Did you but know!' Tawny, she didn't know what tawny was. It sounded as if it meant joyful, fresh. The word played around inside her, repeating itself like the echo which goes on sounding when we shout our name. Tawny, I am tawny, she shouted for Quiquina, for anyone, to hear. Nobody came to the door and she went on repeating quietly, tawny, tawny, until her lips fell quiet and a great silence grew about and within her. With her eyes closed, she was neither asleep nor dreaming. She was just waiting for something, waiting for some sound or other to break the skin of her lake of awful silence.

Outside, the starry night, a distant black sky in which a thin crescent moon drifted like a cut-out boat. A fragrant breeze stirred the curtains, so that they billowed gently like the sails of a ship getting under way with the first breeze after a calm. She couldn't see any sails, but she began to hear a whistling coming from the night outside. A distant whistling, someone was arriving.

José Feliciano was coming back whistling after his nightly pilgrimage. He had started in Italo Brentani's shed, where he looked on while the Italians played a card game he wasn't familiar with (in the evening there was no bowling because of the dreadful din); he got bored with the game and went to watch the younger men playing billiards, his eyes idly following the shots, the dull click of the ivory balls; tiring of that he moved on to the bar and got round them to give him a beer and rum-and-vermouth on tick; he thought of going to see Marie at the Mares-Paddock, despite his empty pockets, she might just feel like a chat. Not a good idea. He went on spinning out his drink in a group of idle natterers, but at least it was conversation; better go back to the house, it was past ten thirty by now, the feeble chatter of those yokels wasn't the least bit interesting.

What a drag, what a piddling life, he said to himself, he hadn't felt bored like this for a long time. What would be really good was a cavy shoot, the night was just right for it. Nobody to go with him, nor did he have a hunting dog; nobody, alone. His fowling piece was no good for shooting cavy, it only did for when he went potting birds with Etelvino. Etelvino as stupid as ever, wasting ammunition, scaring the game. It'd be great if he could find somebody like Major Lindolfo. What a hope, they don't make hunters like him any more, he thought sadly.

Though he was cheerful and talkative by nature, when he had a drop to drink he fell into a quiet sadness and was silent. He took pleasure in that sadness the way one wallows in an unhappy love affair. His body was replete, what he needed now was a woman. More than a week without a bird. Marie in the whorehouse, she was nice, inventive, she had some tricks. In his condition, any woman would do. He started thinking about different ones. They were nice, they always gave a bit of affection. Even if it was paid for, it was affection, love. But without money, without ammunition, what can a hunter, a man like himself do? If he was putting down roots in the town, if he no longer thought of leaving, why didn't he settle down and find himself a nice girl, there's no lack of nice girls, get married? A nice-looking, homely girl. That huge empty house, Dona Rosalina could easily let him take the girl there. No point in dreaming, there was no way Dona Rosalina was going to allow it, she didn't want anything to do with townsfolk in her house. What if he fetched that girl Toni from Guaxupé, the one he got fond of once. Following this line of thought he slowly walked up the street, he was nearly in the square. The houses closed, the street empty, nobody. The street lights far apart, casting a feeble yellow glow. They were yellow and sad, sadder even than he was that night. He could hear his own steps, he was really very lonely, he needed someone like Toni. Toni, her big eyes shining when she doubled up with laughter at the funny things he said. Her even white teeth shone even more than her eyes, which were soft. Her small firm breasts pulling her dress tight, her flesh was firm and smelled of fresh air. The pressure of her breasts on his arm, when he, pretending it was accidental, brushed against them. If he tried, like now, he could bring to mind that pressure, the warmth of those breasts against his arm. She would only let him hold hands, he wasn't allowed any more daring, prolonged endearment. Her long, shiny hair flowing in waves over her shoulders. If Dona Rosalina let her hair down it would be like that. Her hair crackled when he let his fingers play in its silky, live warmth. The smell of her hair, such a good smell that he breathed it deeply, taking its fragrance back home with him. To think about Toni at night, in the hope of dreaming about her. The scent of Toni's hair was still with him, with him now.

He should have stayed back there, got a job of some sort, even heavy work would have done. When a man wants to get married he has to get stuck in. Toni would want him, he could tell that was just what she wanted. She had broad hips, the right woman to get kids on. Lots of children, the first would be a boy. He would make a walking-stick rifle for him, like the one he made for the boy Valdemar. The boy Valdemar burning with fever. Better not think of that, life's cussedness. What's gone by is a bygone, it won't come back. What you start again is always motion. Forward motion, you don't start again from behind, from where you stopped. You never go back home, because the house is never the same. Major Lindolfo dead, Dona Vivinha dead, the child dead. Toni has changed too, no doubt, probably got married, that's all she ever thought about. The world doesn't have stopping-places, you start again all over, from the very beginning. It's not like a school slate, when all you need is a wet cloth to rub out the sums and the writing. When you're far away there's always somebody who carries on writing.

He leaned against the lamppost and rolled a cigarette. He pulled his tinder out of his pocket, made a flame and sucked the smoke in hard, breathing it in. He blew the smoke into the air and watched it rise in the direction of the insects that were flitting around the light. He took another drag. The phlegm in his throat, the bitter taste of beer in his mouth. He had smoked too much, the cigarette was tasteless. He coughed and threw the cigarette away. Then for the first time he looked up at the sky, the starry night, the thin slice of moon above his head. He was just a needle in God's haystack. God certainly wasn't going to bother with him and his tiny sadness, a pinhead stuck in that great, endless world. A starry sky was distressing, it was even sadder in the wilds, in life's outback.

He started walking again, hearing again his own foot-steps. That was when he began to whistle from some-where inside himself a sad melody he had heard someone sing one rainy night. No, it wasn't someone singing, he remembered now. It was that man in Divinópolis who whistled, the linesman, with his coloured lantern bobbing about in the rain, as he disappeared into the night and was lost in the darkness at the bend in the track, and he could still hear his whistle fading away gradually, fading away, then he couldn't hear it any more. All he could hear was the rain drizzling down on the platform roof. He was waiting for the night train, which was late, always late.

In the square the darkness was deeper. Only the lamp of a solitary street light was burning in one corner, over by the church, a blob of light. On the other side, the dark street which led to the cemetery.

The only light was in the manor house. In Dona Rosalina's room and in the drawing room below. She hasn't gone to bed yet, or the light downstairs would be off. She always waited for him to come back, he knew. I wonder why she always waits for me? She says she's not interested in what I do outside the manor, yet she wants to take charge of me, she's always spying on me now. She pretends it's not me, thinks I don't know. Before, when he wasn't living there, did she go to bed early, he wondered. No, she couldn't be tired, all day long sitting still, hardly moving, making her flowers. Such pretty flowers she made. For amusement, she was rich, she didn't need to. Quiquina was very smart. To her share and share alike was more like finding's keeping. Sometimes she gave him some, when she saw the greedy look in his eyes. Quiquina always on guard, a big dog in the dark. The dog smoked, the dog's eyes. The slightest sound, she pricked up her ears, sniffing the air. A pointer. At night she locked the kitchen door, he couldn't get into the main part of the house. If he was thirsty, he had to use the wash tank tap. She slept indoors, in a little room next to the pantry. Dona Rosalina's room was upstairs. Only her room and a sitting room (little used, she preferred the drawing room downstairs) were in use, all the other rooms were locked, a mystery. What was life in the manor house like in other times? In the good times of Colonel Honório Cota, as they said. When the manor was alive, the rooms all open, all the lights blazing. It must have been a sight, cheerful. The big house all lit up. Money flowing, lots of people, the sound of happy voices. After he came back, he knew, (sometimes he went out again, slipping carefully over the wall so as not to make any noise, and, from a distance, in the square, would watch Dona Rosalina's shadow moving behind the curtain in her lighted room) the drawing-room light would be put out. Her bedroom light stayed lit for a long time, he wondered what she could be doing. What a life, hers. All alone.

He knew what she was up to while he was out. Every evening. You start that way and you can't stop. Sometimes he returned stealthily, like a cat, carefully climbed up on a stone he had put underneath the window earlier, for the purpose, and peered inside. Dona Rosalina sitting by the table, the book open, the glass by her side. The occasions he saw her, the book was open but she wasn't reading, her eyes lost somewhere far in the distance. What could she be looking at? What was she thinking about? When she kept still, he could get a better look from his hiding place. Pretty, sad, she was very pretty. She could have been different, someone might have wanted to marry her. Nobody to harvest Dona Rosalina's love. Dona Rosalina was a white lady in her castle. With bated breath he watched Dona Rosalina. She moved. The white lady let her arm drop down, picked up the bottle from under the table. Under the table, no doubt so that Quiquina would not see, so that nobody would see. He winced with annoyance when the spell was broken and that beauty all vanished. She shouldn't move, she should always stay like that. A drinking woman was not his sort, he didn't like to see women drinking.

He pushed open the gate. He was supposed always to go in by the gate. That's what she meant the first time, that day long ago. He went into the garden, the darkness was denser. Leaves and dry twigs cracked under his feet. The air smelled of resin, of the fresh moisture of the bulging mango trees. He went over to the pump. He opened the tap and stood watching the water run, the sound it made falling into the wash tank. Cupping his hands, he raised the water to his mouth. He drank great gulps, repeating the operation several times, he was very thirsty. The taste of warm beer still in his mouth, the taste of tobacco. The water was not very cool, it was nicer when it came from the pitcher, chilled, the cold clay perspiring. The kitchen door must be closed, Quiquina always closed it. He wet his face in the water. Then he stood looking at the dark shape of the mango tree, the darkness was quite solid, just a touch of light glinting on the topmost leaves. He looked up again at the starry sky.

He was on his way to his room, the shack at the bottom of the garden, when he saw that the kitchen door was ajar, a half-circle of light on the ground. Had Quiquina gone out? She never goes out at night. It wasn't a special day, there was no procession or anything like that. He went to have a look. He pushed the door gently, it creaked, he stopped for a moment. Better turn back, go to his room, it was nothing to do with him what went on in that house, Dona Rosalina's business. Wasn't that what she always said? But he didn't want to turn back, his curiosity pushed him forward. Something might have happened, maybe he was needed? He was looking for an excuse. He pushed the door further, more carefully this time, so that it shouldn't creak. He inched his way into the kitchen. Where was Quiquina? Leaning on the table, her head resting on her arms, she was snoring. She got tired of waiting, she was deep in her first sleep. I wonder if she talks in her sleep? he thought, joking to overcome his nervousness. This was what a thief must feel like when he steals into a house at night. If she woke up suddenly, disturbed by his presence, he would say that he saw the door open and came to see what was happening. He'd come to drink water from the pitcher, the pump water was too warm. Would she believe him? If she didn't, so much the better, she'd take more care another time. In any case, why did she lock the door, why couldn't he come into the house at night? He was a servant, a member of the household, he said to himself. Nevertheless he tried not to make any noise. Stopping by the table he bent over to see Quiquina's face as she slept. Sometimes Crosspatch would bark in his sleep. With her mouth open, dribbling a little, she was breathing deeply and snoring. She might bark in her sleep. Watchdogs doze too, then wake up suddenly barking. Toothless, an old dog. Old devil of a nigger, sleep you wretch. That's the best thing you can do.

He moved on to the pantry, ran his eyes over the walls. The print of Our Lady of the Rosary, the pendulum clock showing ten to eleven, the big cupboard with cups hanging from the shelves. The table covered with an oilcloth, the chairs neatly arranged around the table. Order, cleanliness. The silence of things asleep with the light on. Things were clean and cold, but they still had a silent life of their own, a sleep of their own, as if they might suddenly creak. He thought he heard a noise in the kitchen, he stopped in alarm. Nothing, no doubt Quiquina stirring in her sleep, the watchdog growling. Sleep Quiquina, sleep peacefully.

Maybe he'd better go back? Why was he being so rash? Why did he want to know what Dona Rosalina was doing, when he knew only too well what she would be doing? Drinking, she's bound to be drinking. Does she get tipsy? Does she talk nonsense? Dona Rosalina drunk. Tipsy, with none of her pride. She probably laughed. People who are serious and mournful usually laugh when they've had something to drink, people who laugh go all sad, like me. I need to drink, at times I need to drink. Even if I do get sad, it's good to be tipsy, a sort of thick, mumbly numbness. It crumbles life's carapace, shatters life's sharp edges. The effect of the drink he'd had in the bar had worn off by now, he was lucid and unclouded. Drowsiness was better, the mists inside. Motionless in the middle of the pantry, he could not pluck up courage to move forward. Now he got the urge to drink. What if Dona Rosalina offered him a drop? Funny, even when she was drunk, Dona Rosalina would never lower herself, she would never think of inviting him. He was mad even to think of it. Even if she was drunk as an owl, she wouldn't so much as invite him to sit down. Him sitting next to her. She was a very proud woman, pride like that doesn't lower itself. Perhaps it wasn't so much pride, maybe she was just very very unhappy. Laughter turns to tears, tears to laughter. She probably wept in secret, nobody can bear so much sadness and never show it. She was sad, he could see that, very very sad, mortally sad.

Tipsy, she would laugh, laugh properly, not with her lips pursed the way she usually did, but freely, with her whole body. That would be amusing. Except for her pride she was a normal person, nice, quite human. Just like other people, a normal human being. Dona Rosalina talking freely, without constraint. Dona Rosalina relaxed, doubled up with laughter. Showing her white teeth. Sending her memory of her father to the devil, the shadow, the heavy hand that, even in death, kept hold of her from afar. What if she became violent, quarrelsome? Some people get that way, quarrelsome when they've had something to drink. She wasn't like that, didn't look like it. She seemed like a girl at times. Pretty, sometimes she was pretty, very pretty, if you looked closely. If she let her hair down, really pretty, so he imagined. Dona Rosalina with her hair flowing, galloping on her pony Firefly. Rosalina in the clouds, a girl. Firefly galloping. Nice they were, the stories she told. She was like a girl. Once upon a time, a girl in Paracatu. . . .

He halted at the drawing-room door, afraid to continue. The cut-glass chandelier shone brightly. Something out of a dream, that chandelier. He'd never seen the chandelier close to, when it was lit up. The bluish reflexion tinging the edges of the chimneys and the facets of the prisms. A cold sun shining inside a dream. The illuminated castle Dona Vivinha talked about in the stories she told Valdemar. He didn't know what it would be like, but he imagined it. The castle must have been like this, alive with chandeliers, shining with a thousand glass beads.

Ah, there, there she was. Just like he usually saw her from the window. Sitting near the table, her hands resting on the book. Bolt upright, stiff, motionless. Not a movement, a wax model, lifeless. Her face was a livid white, like porcelain. She wasn't thinking, her eyes staring, only the slightest breath of life. She seemed to be looking at the clock stopped at three o'clock. But her gaze somehow didn't reach the clock, caught somewhere between, lost in a void, in a hole in time. He was afraid to wake her, she wasn't asleep, her eyes were open, she was looking. Was she looking inwards rather than outwards? Her fleshy lips were open a little way, moist and shining. They were the only sign of life. How can a person stay like that, be like that? He was afraid, he wanted to go back. He might scare her, she would cry out. Quiquina would come running in, what excuse would he make? That he'd come to see if she needed him? She wouldn't believe him. If that was the reason, he wouldn't be so furtive. The weight of his guilt made him detect something suspicious in his every move. The scandal, he'd be sent away from the house. People might come in from the street, he'd be finished. There was nothing wrong in what he was doing, but for that very reason it was difficult to explain. Now he had to go on, he couldn't turn back any more. What did it matter if she did send him away, he wanted to go on to the end, to see what would happen.

What would happen. He moved a step forward, felt the floorboard creak. Now she knew someone was there, she would cry out. But strangely she did not, she made no sign. She only moved her head slowly in his direction. Her wide open, glassy eyes upon him. As though she didn't see him, she seemed not to see him, or, if she did, as if she didn't recognize him. It's me, he tried to say, but his voice stuck in his throat, he couldn't speak. Me, Dona Rosalina, he said with great difficulty. His voice was thick, husky, it didn't seem to be his. She was very slow coming to her senses, back to the ordinary world, to things about her. Her eyes were still full of shadows, as if she had come from the inner depths of darkness. She blinked, shook her head nervously, struggling to untangle herself from the clinging shreds of her dream state. Now he was expecting her to shout, she didn't. Her eyes began to acquire their normal shine, losing their bewildered glassiness. Like a drooping flower which, as though by magic, suddenly receives a breath of life, rises on its stem and straightens out its petals; or perhaps the reverse: in full bloom, it begins to wither, drooping on its stem, seen in a vision, a dream. He was confused, he couldn't think what to do, he was paralysed. His whole self was a dark core of strength, dazzled by the brilliance of her eyes; strangely lucid, aware of the smallest details, the tiniest gesture, the smallest sound; he was growing. The house was like a tomb, all around a terrible white silence. Deafening sensations. A buzzing in his ears.

Me, Dona Rosalina, he repeated after an endless space of time. Me, he thought, Dona Rosalina, because he knew now that he was himself and that she was the same Dona Rosalina as always, in flesh and blood. The room, the furniture, the clock, the grand piano, everything was returning to the silence, the hardness and density of lifeless things. The house was no longer suspended airily in a dreamlike glow. She lowered her eyes, her eyelids flickered. Yet there was no suggestion of surprise, no alarm, almost as if she had been waiting for him to arrive. Oh, it's you, she said softly, and her voice was husky. Now he was able to speak, he was master of his body, of his feelings. I came because, he began to say. She raised a finger to her lips. Was she asking him not to speak or just to speak quietly? Quiquina might hear. Dona Rosalina, he said quietly, the door was open, I thought . . . Yes, I know, she said, interrupting him before he could finish. They were silent again, she with her eyes lowered, not looking at him, lost in thought. What could she be thinking about? What could she be seeking inside herself? He was nervous, wringing his hands fit to dislocate his finger joints. He wasn't accustomed to silence, he couldn't stand this sickening silence. He looked at the stopped grandfather clock, as if he expected the hand to move. Enough, he thought. I'd better go. He couldn't stand the silence any more. But his feet were glued to the ground, he couldn't move.

Dona Rosalina, I think I'm being a nuisance, he said, more in control of himself. She looked at him, trying to read in his eyes what he had just said. I, he said. Yes, I know it's you, it's you who's here, she said. But you needn't shout. (He hadn't shouted, he spoke more quietly than usual, in fact.) With her eyes she indicated a chair next to her. He didn't understand, or understood but was afraid to move from where he was. She might react unpredictably, he was by now quite accustomed to her sudden changes of mood. Maybe she was just testing him. He was afraid she would go back to being the daytime Dona Rosalina, the ordinary Dona Rosalina. No, she wasn't back to her normal self, though she had lost that bizarre look of someone from the other world, like she was when he came into the room and she stared at him with glassy eyes. Drunk, she must be drunk, he thought suddenly. She wanted him to sit next to her. Where was her pride, the distance between them? Sit next to her was something he never thought possible. He looked at the empty glass, tried to see the bottle under the table. Drunk. I wonder if she knows what she's doing? I made a mistake, she didn't tell me to sit down, she meant something else. He couldn't have been mistaken, she had indicated with her eyes that he was to sit down. He must have read on her moist lips what her eyes had said, sit down. It was an order, not an invitation. Nevertheless he didn't move, waiting for her to speak. This time he wasn't going to be an intruder, he would stay on his own side of the fence. She must speak, he would wait. No pride today, the vindictive thought occurred to him. Not today. She had to see what he was.

And as he didn't move, she said sit down, please. Please, she said, she said please. Her voice was thick, her tongue swollen in her mouth. Did she know what she was doing? He looked around for another chair, rather than the one that had been indicated to him. When she saw what he was going to do, she said no, here, and with her eyes showed him the chair next to her. Then he stirred himself, pulled the chair away from the table and sat down. He felt uncomfortable. He had never been so close to her, he could almost feel the warmth of her body, smell her aroma. He had to keep control of himself, not show any fear. She wanted, he needed to show that he was, a man, the man who was always there inside him, not her daytime servant. But the discomfort, he didn't know where to put his hands.

She wasn't looking at him with her eyes, but he knew that she was looking with her ears, with her body, with her skin. Her white hands on the table, he observed them. Slender hands, beautifully, transparently white. With blue veins standing out beneath the skin. Her fingers trembled slightly, she must be feeling the warmth of his eyes on her hands. Because he was fondling her hands with greedy eyes. She withdrew her hands, clasping them to her body, as if she had actually felt the warmth, the languor, the oily sensuality of his eyes on them. She slipped them under the table. All this without so much as a glance towards him.

Now he observed her face, the delicate profile, the slender fox-like nose, the tip slightly raised, the moist fleshy lips, which had more life in them than the eyes, they seemed to be the only thing that was alive in her doll-like face. Her lips were parted, allowing the tips of her gleaming teeth to show. Her lips quivered softly, as if she were about to whisper something.

All of a sudden another presence in the room. Quiquina in the doorway. He turned swiftly. Nobody, it must be fancy. She wouldn't be so quick that she didn't even cast a shadow as she went. Fancy, emotion. A shudder ran through his body, his heart beat heavily. His knees trembled most of all. It wasn't Quiquina. There was nobody. Fancy, fear. If it was Quiquina, Dona Rosalina would have seen her, she had her face towards the door now. He decided to go on. Doing what? Go on with their silent dialogue, their wordless conversation. He no longer felt the slightest need to talk. A strange pleasure swept through him in waves of warmth.

Her hair was pulled back, held in place by a long-handled comb, dotted with small holes and with patterns made by shiny little gemstones. Her hair was black and shiny. Toni's hair had a warm smell, black like hers, it crackled when he stroked it. What are you doing? Let me. No, not the back of my neck, it tickles. When he tried to kiss her, she slipped away, he was left like an idiot kissing the air. Clever thing, Toni was very artful and clever, smart. Artful, Dona Rosalina. Coyote. He went on. His eyes glued to her lips, her smooth skin, her eyes viewed from the side. Full eyes. She must feel, must be feeling the touch of his eyes. His eyes like electrodes, suckers, a bat sucking her blood in the night. She could see, she couldn't fail to see. His eyes on the nape of her neck, the place where he tried to kiss Toni, where it tickled. She wouldn't let him, it was madness to think about it. Better play it by ear, see what happened. She was not Toni, Dona Rosalina. He mingled the two in the pleasure of observing.

How long had they been like that? He didn't know, had no way of knowing, he didn't care. He could go on like that for longer, he didn't need to talk, it was good like that. The whole night, like that, if she wished, if that warm pleasure didn't urge him to the madness of going further. He had never experienced the pleasure of the subtle quality of things, the small details seen through a magnifying glass. A quiet pleasure, a mixture of fear and expectancy. The pleasure of a draughts player who moves a piece imperceptibly without his opponent seeing. But she was aware, she could see with all her senses, with her body. And she let him go on, without speaking, he went on, kept going forward.

Her well-shaped ear, the thick lobe with a hole pierced for an earring. The doll-like texture of her face, the little blue vein which he looked for beneath the skin. The blood running through it, warm, silent, wild. The blood that he felt in his temples and chest; warm, thick, excited. A momentary quiver of the face, a twitch at the corner of the mouth. The beginning of a laugh, the mouth still closed. Now she was laughing at something that had happened to her, but which he didn't notice. Her body was shaken as if she were sobbing. Her even teeth gleaming. He was afraid that her laughter would spoil the long, patient construction of his dream, of those feelings, his soul.

Quiquina in the doorway. The empty door. Nobody.

He turned towards Rosalina, to her laughter which was now bright and forthright.

I think I'm a bit tipsy, she said, looking for an excuse. He said nothing, just smiled. Their eyes met, they both laughed. He saw that she was looking at his blind eye.

Funny, isn't it? she said; yes, he stammered.

The empty doorway, nobody. Quiquina in the doorway?

He had to go on. Funny, us here like this, he said and wished he hadn't spoken. Yes, she said; aye, he laughed. She was laughing too.

She picked up the empty glass and tipped it towards her. She sat looking at the drop in the bottom.

Do you want some? she asked; yes, he said. There, she said, pointing to the console-table. He understood what she meant. He went over to the cupboard (Quiquina in the doorway) and came back with a glass. While he was crossing the room, she had produced the bottle from under the table. When he came back he saw the bottle with an *R* on the label. The bottle was half empty, a beautiful bottle. He needed a drink now, there was not much wine, not enough for his thirst, for his nervousness, for the empty feeling inside him. Motionless, her eyes on the table top, no longer laughing, she was waiting for him to make the first move. The first move in the direction

of the bottle. He was waiting for her to make the first
move. This hesitation could spoil everything. He couldn't
expect her to serve him, that was too much. He reached
out for the bottle. When his hand reached the bottle, hers
was already there. Their hands touched, he was left holding her hand round the bottle. He felt the chill of her
hand, the smooth whiteness, the warmth of that hand.
She closed her eyes, suddenly smaller, tiny; he felt the
tremor of her body coming through that hand : it was
transmitted to him like an electric current. She laughed
and her laugh was nervous and tinny. He laughed as well,
he laughed a lot, more than was necessary. Outside the
two of them, the touch of their hands was the funniest
thing in the world. Or so their laughter seemed to indi-
cate. Because inside they were serious and earnest, tense,
unsmiling, nervous, waiting for what was going to, what
might be about to happen. Neither of them knew what
was likely to, was going to, happen. They waited. She
waited a little longer, to see, letting him. His big, coarse
hand over hers, covering it completely.

She looked towards the door and quickly removed her
hand. Quiquina in the doorway, he thought immediately.
The door was empty, nobody. He turned back to her,
his face serious as he looked at her pale smile, the gleam
in her eyes.

He helped himself, then her. With the glass in her
hand, she moved back a little, staring at the glass. Then
she touched his glass with her own. The dainty sound of
cut glass clinking. She laughed aloud, too loud. Don't
laugh so loud, he begged with his eyes. Quiquina might
come. Quiquina in the doorway. Nobody. She cut short her
laughter, leaving just a gleam of dark elation in her face.

How it was going to end, he didn't know, he didn't
want it ever to end. A dream, it was all a dream, the
bright haze of a dream, the shadows at the silver edges
of a dream. He couldn't believe what was happening,
couldn't believe his eyes. She couldn't draw back now,

she had taken the first step, she couldn't withdraw again into the dark prison of her pride, of her nunnish silence. She had come out into the light, into an open space bathed in light.

As though this silent communication were not enough, it's good this wine, I'd never tried it before, he said. Is it foreign? More? she asked. This time she helped him. He tipped it back quickly. She drank slowly, too slowly for someone who is already tipsy, savouring the fumes, the perfume of the wine. As if she expected it to be her last drink of wine.

Sitting close to her, he could now smell the warmth of her body, the soft fragrance of her hair. The hair he was touching in his mind, mentally letting it down. Her hair flowing over her shoulders, in waves, like someone else's hair, Toni's. But Toni's hair paled, lost its shine, it was like the hair of a saint's image, dull, compared with the hair on which he now feasted his eyes. He had never seen a woman like her, all the women in his life were mean, petty creatures, pale things in the face of so much light, such sublimity. God, was what he thought, not knowing why he said God, just God. As if he wanted to say that this was a celestial pleasure, a pleasure reserved for the gods. He didn't have such thoughts, it was some dark force inside him, a force that was swelling in him like a great black wave.

The pleasant feeling of the drink, a lasting warmth in his chest. For the first time he experienced happiness without gaiety, a serious happiness, a sort of nervous expectancy. More? she asked. The bottle was almost empty, she looked at the bottom of it with a touch of sadness. He drank quickly, not noticing the sudden sadness in her eyes. What if the wine runs out, he wondered. That happiness was only possible with wine. If the wine ran out, he would be lost, the line of communication would break. She would leave him : alone there in the drawing room, alone in the world. Is there any more? he said, pointing at the bottle. She nodded, yes, one, she said, following the direction of his glance. Quiquina might appear, and then what? Nothing, Quiquina is only a servant, he thought, forgetting his own position. Quiquina, the wolf hound, on guard.

And suddenly she started talking. She talked and talked, and laughed. She talked disconnectedly, he couldn't understand properly. She talked about her life, her pony Firefly, about satin and organdy roses, roses in her hair, parties, balls. From time to time some name or other would turn up as she talked. He once heard her say Emanuel, just Emanuel, not Mr Emanuel, the way she always said it. What had Mr Emanuel to do with it all? And other names he had never heard of. A muddle, all jumbled up. She's not used to talking like this, with her soul, with her heart, he decided. That's what it is. That's why she's not talking to anyone, not to me. Let her go on.

He laid his hand on her shoulder to calm her, as if to tell her not to get excited, to speak more slowly, she didn't need to speak at all. But he didn't say any of this, letting his hand rest, intentionally, on her shoulder. She let him, pretending not to notice. Occasionally she would press her shoulder into the palm of his hand and he would feel the warmth, the vibration, the warm fragrance of Rosalina's body. He moved closer to her, his breathing heavier, his heart beating unevenly. He was on fire, his body, nostrils open, ears, eyes, a cluster of sensations opening out. He gradually worked his knee against her dress until he felt the firmness and warmth of her thigh. She talked more quickly, as if she wanted to separate her speech from her body and divide herself in two; one, sheer voice; the other, the body in flames which spoke to the other body in successive waves of heat. As if her voice didn't come from inside her body. Only Rosalina's dark warm body was alive. He could hear Rosalina's voice, but he didn't know what she was talking about. He only wanted the sound, the melody, the soothing music of that warm voice. It was just as well she was talking. If she stopped suddenly, he might find himself obliged to do something, to take a decision. He was getting more and more daring, he could now feel the warmth of her breath, of her flushed face. He caught a snippet of what she was saying. He heard her say : I thought I was like him, but I'm not like him, I'm like that one, the other. Who was 'he' and who the 'other'? All very confused, very hurried, very heated. He followed her gaze and saw the two portraits on the wall. The pictures of her father and grandfather. She was talking to the portraits, not to him. Her body was his, a vibrant body, the waves of her body. Quiquina in the doorway. Why bother to look, only that body mattered, that body was all that counted. A body that could belong to him, that was already his in his feelings.

His knee was not enough, he wanted to touch her with his hands, feel her with his fingers. He took his hand from her shoulder and raised it slowly and fearfully to her hair. His hand trembled, he could not control the tremor that vibrated right through his body, as if he were an iron bar that has been struck, a bell vibrating. Quiquina in the doorway. His fingers brushed her hair, feeling the electric smoothness of the single hairs. A vacuum, a silence : she had stopped talking for a moment. She turned her face enough to feel the fleshy part of his hand against her skin. A cough caught in his dry throat. He might faint, she might cry out or faint. Anything might happen, all of a sudden, underground. But he had to go on, to keep going on and on. Anything as long as she didn't look at him, as long as their eyes did not meet. He didn't want her to look, their eyes might give the show away, spoil everything. She closed her eyes to feel it, to be able to feel, he thought. Better with the eyes closed. It was like a flower opening inside one's body, in the middle of the night, in the darkness of the body. And his fingers were touching the petals of that flower.

His hand all trembling he clumsily removed the comb which held her hair in place. Unfastened, her hair fell down over her shoulders. He thought he heard the sound of her hair falling onto her shoulders. The soft waves of her hair, the black gleam. As he thought, much more alive even than he thought.

Not only her body, she was now wholly intent on the slightest movements. Her eyes were not on the portraits now, even without looking her eyes followed his slightest move. He could hear her quickened breathing, feel her breath. He was scarcely breathing, he needed little air. He knew that she was watching him. He began to stroke her hair, not now with the tips of fearful fingers, but with the palm of his hand. She let him, she wanted him to, now she wanted him to and let him. I'm not going to think, later he would think about the absurdity of this night.

For the first time she turned her face directly towards him. He saw her eyes were without surprise, they gleamed like live coals, they were aflame. He attempted a bit of a smile, but couldn't manage one. She was serious, deeply, unsmilingly serious. She was a woman without the smallest movement, without the slightest sound, a woman of darkness and heavy silence. Simply a woman.

This was when she made her first movement, as if spirit and body came together and fused into the same substance. As if to tell him that it was not only her body, but all of her that was taking part. She undid the top buttons of her white blouse. What is she going to do? the thought came immediately. No. He saw that she was taking out something that was hidden between her breasts. A filmy white rose, a rose like a spider with petals. A cloth rose, alive. A rose that was more alive than the flesh and blood roses in the garden. A brilliant rose, her life, Rosalive.

Mine, she said. It's for me, she said, but seemed confused and held out the rose to him. She was smiling, he saw that she was smiling. Only with her eyes, her mouth

153

was closed, her face said nothing. He saw the white skin of her breasts, the rise and fall of her gleaming, pulpy flesh. He would think later, afterwards he would have to think. Quiquina. He took the rose in his fingers, expecting the petals to open. He looked at it stupidly, as if he expected it to move. He felt an urge to kiss the rose, to smell the warm fragrance of her breasts. He saw what she wanted, what she meant him to do. He pinned the rose in her hair, my God, she is beautiful. I've never seen a woman like her. What was in store for him? Quiquina in the doorway. Quiquina, the shadow, the fear, the anguish, the nightmare.

He pulled her closer to him and put his arm around her. His lips brushed the smooth skin of her face, he smelled her dense aroma, felt the heat she radiated. With her moist lips parted she looked at him. She was looking at him with the eyes of a woman moist with passion, suddenly with the eyes of a young girl who lets things be done to her without understanding what is happening, letting it happen, motionless, paralysed. His free hand felt beneath her dress for the moist warm flesh. She let him, she let him. A young girl. Her lips close to him, he felt the warmth of her lips, her quickened breathing. She was all aroma, warmth, moisture. He kissed her slowly on the mouth, in the moist warmth of her mouth. He felt her hand on the back of his neck, pressing painfully, as if she wanted to hurt him, bruise him. Her sharp nails on his skin. She could go on, more, on and on.

Quiquina in the doorway, Rosalina saw her. Rosalina freed herself from his embrace and shouted in horror, pointing at the door where she saw Quiquina.

Quiquina was no longer there, the doorway was empty.

When he looked for Rosalina, he saw her half-way up the stairs, running away.

The white rose lay on the floor, a withered spider, dead.

7

The Wheels in Motion

The sun woke her, its glare burning her eyes. The room was a lake of light, the air pink, sparkling with pinpoints of brightness. She kept her eyes closed against the sunny morning outside. Behind her eyelids the glare was pink. She was afraid to open her eyes, afraid of being hurt by the light, split down the middle by the glare like a glass broken by a high note. Like having one's head inside a bell which suddenly started ringing.

She was emerging from a deep sleep, a dreamless sleep, a sleep in which light and shade did not exist, a thick colourless sleep, a sickly sleep. Like someone coming out of a trance, she tried gradually to locate her body, the room. Not the room itself, but where she was: in which room, in which house, in which world she was waking up. She tried to make contact with her silent, motionless, dead body. As if her spirit were returning from the shadows (the white mists, the silent world, before the pain in which her consciousness had sunk for several hours) to take possession of its former abode. The whiteness, the absence of dreams during the night, gave her a terrible painful feeling of rebirth.

Resurrection and pain. The pain, the feeling of being alive. So, with her eyes closed the world was pink, pink and aching. Light and pain, the first encounter with the world. Now her eyes were hurting violently, with the glare, her head was heavy and ached, her whole body was a knot of pain. Pain and heaviness, her body was heavy. The pain and remorse of a body which had lost its equilibrium. She was dizzy, her body certainly knew it couldn't raise itself, the world was spinning round like an infernal machine. Light and motion, pain.

She stayed that way for a long time, until she was able to move her body and open her eyes. Where had she come from, where was she, who in fact was she? I, Rosalina, she succeeded in thinking with some difficulty. I, alive. Instead of the pain of being alive, she would rather be dead, not have woken up again, ever. I – why? Why, as if seeking a connection between individual existence and the world. I, a sort of liturgy, a baptism; to start living, to rid herself of the emptiness, the anguish, the disgust of her body. I, as if summoning someone to take possession of that body shot through with, lit up by, pain. She tried to fill her chest with air, but the pain was so intense that she stopped. Holding her breath, she kept quite still as long as the inhalation lasted. She let the air out slowly. Like someone trying to get accustomed to the dark with eyes open, she kept her eyes closed against the light. She, her room, her bed, she thought slowly, running her hands over the crochet bedspread. Mine, my bed, me. My room, my house. The window is open, the window stayed open all night. How did that happen? A feeling of remorse in her body. She felt her body, mine. Dressed, she had slept in her clothes. How did that come about? What happened? How? Who?

Suddenly they became one : she and her body, herself.

After a while she made another attempt to open her eyes; the sun ached so brightly in her eyes that she closed them immediately, protecting herself. She had slept with the window open, in her clothes. Drunk, I'm still drunk, she thought. No, it's not the drink, I've drunk more on other occasions. Something else happened, she couldn't remember. She opened her eyes again, now it was easier. Except that she couldn't move them, with every movement a searing pain exploded inside each eye, in her head. The lamp was still on, pale, its light useless. The light has been on all night too. When she used her elbows to try and raise her head from the pillow, the room started spinning with a horrible, incredible speed. Nausea, her stomach all churned up. She put her hand to her mouth to hold back the vomit. It didn't come, sticking in her throat. The dry retch, better to have vomited, thrown it all up. A cold sweat on her forehead, her neck. Ill, I'm ill, I shan't get up. Quiquina.

Quiquina's name made her feel a pang of remorse, not in her body any more, in her mind. Quiquina's face all of a sudden. Quiquina in the doorway. Her eyes starting out of their sockets, her eyes saying awful things to her. Him. That other eye, milky, unseeing, white. Quiquina saw me, she saw everything. What did Quiquina see? Quiquina saw what she had done. What did I do, my God? The blind, white eye. Oh, yes, that, him. The milky eye that she had the urge to touch with her fingertips. His hand on her shoulder, hot and trembling. His one eye milky, the other eye gleaming, black, flashing. His voice trembling. With him, did it have to be him? My God, why not someone else? Who else though? The leucoma in that mysterious left eye. Only him, it could only be him, there wasn't anyone else. Emanuel. A glass of wine, Mr Emanuel?

The dry retch again, the painful threat of vomit. No, still not yet. She had to get up, then she could be sick. The bitter, black, acid vomit, like the other times. The disgust, the cold sweat. What about a drop of wine, just a drop? Not on an empty stomach. She would feel better. Just one, Mr Emanuel, won't you take one? He took out my comb, my hair is down. His hand was trembling, his right eye flashed, his bad eye like an egg that went wrong in the hen's ovary. White, jellyish. The urge to touch it. Her hair let down, his hand trembling. It trembled even more when he started to caress her hair. His hot breath on her neck, on the nape of her neck. His eyes aflame, his hot breath, his warm smell. She unbuttoned her blouse, the rose. Why? Why did she do that? Why did she want to? Because she let him. She only had to shout and he would have gone away. The white rose in her hair. Where was the rose? Now. She saw Quiquina in the doorway. Had she been watching from the beginning? Her mouth was warm and moist. On her mouth, she was sure. She wanted him to ask. Untrue, she didn't want that, didn't want to hear his voice at all. When he did it. She was the one who was talking, before, she was nervous. Because his hands were feeling their way forward, trembling. She wanted him to. On her mouth. She wanted it. Why?

If it weren't for Quiquina. What if it didn't really happen? What if she dreamt it? I didn't dream it, I'm sure I didn't dream it. The darkness of her undreaming body. Perhaps I imagined it, a daydream, it happens sometimes, while I was waiting for him to come home. No, it happened all right. She had the memory of moisture and warmth still in her mouth.

Quiquina in the doorway. Quiquina's eyes. The drink, that eye that she felt she wanted to peel. Would it bleed? White, milky, bloodless. If it weren't for Quiquina I would have gone further, my God. How far? Why did Quiquina have to show herself? Not that I wanted to go further. She shouldn't have wanted it, shouldn't have let it go so far, she only had to shout. Why had she come, in the doorway? It was her, no doubt about it. There could be no doubt about it. There could be no doubt: she saw, she saw everything. Why did she have to come? so that I would see that she had seen?

Now she would have to face her. How shall I face her? With him she could fix things, later. But Quiquina. How would she be able to look Quiquina in the eyes, when those eyes had seen it all? If it weren't for her, things would be easier. She would send him away today.

What if he resisted? No matter, *she* wouldn't have seen. She, Quiquina, was the one that mattered. And if Quiquina gave no sign at all, as if she hadn't seen a thing? Like she does with the drink, when the bottle's empty. She doesn't like it, I know she doesn't. But she doesn't say anything, not even with her eyes. It's a good job she's dumb. No, it's worse: dumb, but her eyes were worse, much worse than if she could speak. The first time would be difficult, the first time she saw Quiquina. What if she didn't go downstairs, if she didn't ever go down again? The way she stopped going out of the house. They would still have to meet. Maybe not today, but tomorrow, some day. Not if Quiquina were to die. What if Quiquina left home and she heard nothing more of her? That would be better. Even so, she knew that Quiquina had seen. Her hard, startled eyes. She saw. Why did she have to see? Why had she kept watch on him ever since he arrived? Why does she keep creeping about after him? Did she suspect something? No, she couldn't have suspected what was going to happen. Even I didn't imagine, I didn't want it to happen, I didn't think before what was going to, might, happen. Why did it happen? Why did Quiquina have to see? Quiquina in the doorway. What if she was just agitated, nervous? Just imagination? No, those eyes were real, they were really Quiquina's eyes. It was her, Quiquina. She saw.

She heaved again. Close this time, she couldn't stop it. She mustn't soil the bed. She got up quickly, staggering giddily. She only took a step and fell. Vomit on the floor, black, acid vomit. She cleaned her mouth. The cold sweat, her body was relieved. Now she would feel better, she knew. That's how it was the other times. The acid stench, grains of rice, blood, was it blood? No, it wasn't like that the other times, it was never like this before. The other times she could walk. Not this time. What would she do if the dizziness didn't go? What if she stayed in bed and said she was ill, when Quiquina knocked on the door?

Before she came in. The door was ajar, she had to close the door. The door had been open all night, too. Before she could see her. She wouldn't come all that early, that was for sure. What if she didn't come, never came again? Absurd, she might not come just now, but she would come. She would come later. And if she pretended to be asleep? Some day she would have to open her eyes. His eye was white. She would come, Quiquina wouldn't leave her. Some day she would have to open her eyes and see Quiquina's eyes, those eyes. What if she told? if she told the whole story before Quiquina even looked at her? Would she forgive her? Silly idea, she would belittle herself, make herself a doormat. Wasn't she a doormat? She would feel inferior to Quiquina, she would never be able to give her another order. A slave, she would be a slave to Quiquina. Her pride, her father's pride, the family pride.

If she were Lucas Procópio. People could watch Lucas Procópio, no one had the courage to look him in the eyes. She wasn't Lucas Procópio. I'm just me, all by myself. She will forgive me, she's like a mother to me. That makes it worse, much worse. What if I went out before she could see me? Emanuel, she would go and find Emanuel. She would ask for money, as much as he could give her, my money. The Mogiana train, the eleven o'clock express. She would leave the town, this damned town. They wouldn't hear about me any more. But not Emanuel, she couldn't. Emanuel would find it odd, she had never been there, she never left the house. Since Daddy died. Since that day, I walked down the stairs slowly for them all to see. The gold watch, Daddy's watch next to the other one. Stupid idea, Emanuel wouldn't give me the money, he'd think I'd gone mad. And perhaps I am mad, maybe this is all madness? What if it never happened and I've gone mad? What if I did go mad and started to wave my arms about, make faces, say things that didn't make sense, my hair all unkempt, bedlam. No, why should I do that?

The hard thing will be seeing Quiquina's eyes for the first time. She couldn't avoid it. The first time. Those yellow eyes. Quiquina. Oh God, if only I could die! Die, not think any more, not see Quiquina's eyes. Not see that she knows. Now this stands between us : she knows, she saw. Her eyes, Quiquina's dumb, Quiquina's eyes more terrible still because she's dumb.

Lying on the floor, she wasn't thinking anything now. Her eyes were full of tears and now she was crying. As if she were pouring out, once and for all, a whole life of anguish and unhappiness, all the tears that had been held back by despair, by pride and by fear.

If anyone saw her from a distance, if Quiquina saw her like that, they would feel sorry for that little girl who was crying. For me, she resumed her thoughts.

When she had recovered, she went downstairs. Now she was looking for Quiquina. She looked for her in the pantry, in the kitchen, in the garden. The room where she slept was closed. Should she knock the door, call her? Fear held back her hand. Even knowing that she probably wouldn't be there. Of course she won't be there, she has gone out. She went out so as not to see her, so as not to have to meet her, tell her dumbly that she knew. The locked room magnified the mystery of Quiquina's absence. She never went out in the morning, always busy with the work she kept finding to do in the house. She only went out in the afternoon to deliver the flower orders or to do shopping. At that hour of the morning (it was nine o'clock by the pendulum clock, she couldn't remember ever waking up so late) the door of Quiquina's room was always open, its occupant would be in the kitchen or in the garden, the housework well under way.

From the garden she looked at the window of Quiquina's room : it was also shut. Can she be locked in there in the dark to avoid seeing me? Of course not, she had gone out. But anything is possible, today anything is possible.

He wasn't around either. But that was nothing new, when he had nothing to do he spent his time wandering about the town, listening in on conversations, nattering, minding other people's business. But it wasn't him she was looking for. She would prefer not to see him, but she knew how to deal with him, she had given some thought to the situation and taken a decision. She was a little afraid of meeting him before she saw Quiquina and could know if she really knew, before she met with Quiquina's disapproval or protection. But she knew what he was like, she knew he would only come back later, sulking, checking the lie of the land, whistling. His whistling when he came back late at night. Quiquina was the one she wanted and at the same time didn't want to see.

Now she wanted to see her and satisfy her doubts once and for all; she didn't want, was afraid, to look her straight in the eyes, those eyes that saw it all. Yes, it was Quiquina in the doorway. She saw it, she saw everything from the beginning, from when it started. Maybe she was expecting it to happen one day and was keeping watch, in case it did. If it wasn't her, if she didn't see anything, why is everything different in the house today? She was late getting up and leaving her bedroom, but Quiquina hadn't been to see what was the matter, she hadn't been to call her. Why had she gone out? Where had she gone? She saw it all.

There were signs of Quiquina's presence in the drawing room, in the pantry and in the kitchen. In the drawing room the windows were open, the table clean, the chairs in their places. Everything indicated that she had busied herself there very early. In the pantry the breakfast table was set, the bread basket covered with its chequered cloth; in the kitchen, the coffee-pot was standing in a bain-marie, the stove was alight, but the embers were low – she had gone out some time ago. Where has she got to? Where can she have gone? She might be a long time, the strain was unbearable. She now needed Quiquina urgently, she wanted to know, to know if it had been her, to know if she knew. She could no longer stand the uncertainty, now she wanted everything to happen, wanted her to say, without even a nod of her head, just with her eyes: I know, I saw. She wanted to see it in Quiquina's eyes, wanted to see if they were the same eyes as the previous night. Quiquina standing in the doorway, her startled yellow eyes. What if it was all an illusion, a delusion, and nothing happened? She had to see Quiquina, she needed proof from Quiquina's eyes. It had happened, she was sure. The house tidied, the table set, the room locked, the house empty.

In her nervous state the absurdest ideas occurred to her. What if she had gone. . . . No, impossible, she wouldn't have the courage, the nerve. Quiquina would never do that across her. They had to sort out their problems between the two of them, as they had always done. What if she had gone to Emanuel? Nonsense, idiotic. Even if she wanted to, she wouldn't be able to tell him, it was difficult for her. Even if she did try to tell him, he wouldn't understand. Quiquina's gone mad, he would think, so absurd was the story she was trying to tell in gestures. When Quiquina was nervous or upset, it was hard to understand her signs. She was the only one who understood what Quiquina was trying to say in her dumbness, with her pathetic sign language. If he couldn't understand, though, seeing Quiquina's desperation he would come to find out what had happened. Although he seldom came to see her, he was so helpful, he took such care of her interests since her godfather, Quincas Ciríaco, died. Oh God, how could she explain, how would she have the courage to say it was all untrue, that Quiquina had invented it, Quiquina's silly ideas? There would always be a seed of doubt though. She would never be able to see him again, when he came she would hide in her room,

163

say she was ill. He would suspect, he would know as well.

She went to the window and looked up and down the street, from end to end. What if Quiquina brought him back with her? She was very muddled, her head ached, it was heavy. Nothing like that could happen, it was absurd. She badly wanted something to happen, but was so afraid. But not him, not Emanuel. She preferred Quiquina's eyes, dreadful though they might be. No, she went out on some errand, she went out just to avoid seeing me, to prepare herself.

What if she had gone away for good, if she had left her? Wasn't that what she had hoped for to start with, when her physical distress, the agony of waking up, was greater? Quiquina wouldn't do that to her, her heart was not like that. Quiquina was like a mother to her. Quiquina wouldn't leave her in that state, alone in the world. Quiquina was the only person she could rely on, the only person she had in the world.

In front of the locked room again, with her hand raised. Locked inside there in the dark with her grief, her shame. She had hidden in the dark so as not to see her. Her heart thumping uncontrollably, she stood there waiting without the courage to knock. What if she shouted Quiquina? Shouting would be worse, speaking was worse. She knocked gently, so that Quiquina wouldn't hear. No answer, no sign of life inside. She knocked harder, once, twice, three times. When she could see there was no one inside she called out Quiquina, Quiquina! She's not there, she sighed with relief; at that moment she no longer wanted to see Quiquina. The silence in the house was massive.

In the drawing room she saw the irons, the wires and the materials for her flowers. She saw to everything, so that nothing should be missing. She saw to everything, as if she planned to leave me. Alone in this house, without a soul in the world. Her eyes swam with tears, she was going to cry again. If Quiquina saw her crying perhaps she would be sorry, perhaps she wouldn't say anything with her eyes. There was no point in crying any more, it was useless. She thought she had wept all the tears she had.

The grandfather clock stopped at three o'clock. The three o'clock when Mummy died. It all started with them, damned clocks. The Independence watch was the first. Then the grandfather clock. Then it was my turn to hang the gold watch on the wall. What was it for? Why those actions repeated so meticulously, like someone preparing a well thought-out crime? That pride, that silence, those unmoving hands. They must be waiting, patiently and silently, for the hour of vengeance, the final hour, the hour of death. The old boy's pride and crankiness, he thought he could be a match for time, and for them. But they beat us, old fellow. There was she, stifled by time, defeated by the world. The silent language of the clocks, she too had spoken through them once. Out loud, in silence, at the top of the stairs, for all to see. Why had she let herself be carried along by her father's pride and insanity? Damned clocks, she said, clenching her fists. As if she were threatening to destroy them, as if she meant to destroy the past hours they had recorded one by one, uncaring, storing them behind their hands in the bottomless depths of time. The hours of her life, of the life of João Capistrano Honório Cota.

She let her arms fall to her sides, there was no point in venting her anger on the clocks and watches. She could not destroy what was already in the past, in time's seedbed. They were a part of her life, of a life that she had made consciously, if unwillingly, had shaped patiently and with the same fastidious care as her father. That was her life, her light; that her duty, her silence. Not the shapeless nebula of the previous night, the dark force that had carried her down into the maelstrom of muddy waters. Not those treacherous waters that had lain hidden for so long, so long buried inside her.

She was strangely calmer now, suddenly tranquil. The confusion caused by Quiquina's absence gave way to a cold certainty. She had gone out for some different reason, nothing to do with her, she wouldn't bring him back with her. Quiquina would soon be back. She would wait to see what happened, she wouldn't make the first step. Quiquina must do what she saw fit, she would endure it all in silence. Nothing further could happen to her. She was certain now : Emanuel would never know a thing, no one in the town would know anything. He, the other one, wouldn't tell anything either, it was in his own interest not to tell : no doubt he'll want it to happen again. After today she would go on with her life as usual.

In the pantry once more, sitting at table, looking at the cup of white coffee, the bread, the green glass butter dish in the shape of a hen sitting on her eggs, she drew lines on the oilcloth with her nail, writing her name. She had to eat, her stomach was empty, she thought she would now be able to eat. She had to eat before Quiquina came back and saw that she had only just got up. She mustn't see her at table. Why did she have to hide everything from Quiquina? She didn't want to think about Quiquina, didn't want to think again about those yellow eyes because she knew that the same distress was at work in her, deep down in her anxious heart. When she put the bread in her mouth and caught the smell of the butter, a violent, painful heave shook her whole body. She couldn't eat, if she tried she would make matters worse, vomit on the pantry floor, like in the bedroom. Fortunately she brought nothing up. She emptied the cup in the sink, wrapped the bread in some paper and put it in her pocket. She would throw it away later.

In the drawing room once more, she spread her materials on the table, the irons, the scissors, the pot of starch. She would pretend she was working when Quiquina arrived. Her hands trembled, her mind was restless, she was no longer interested in her flowers. To while away

166

the time she could, for instance, make a rose. Where was the white rose she had concealed in her bosom yesterday? He fastened it in her untied hair. Was that after he took out the comb? Mine, she remembered saying to him as she offered him the rose. The shame of it, my God, it was she who gave him the rose to put in her hair. How would she face him? He wasn't the problem, the problem was Quiquina. She didn't want to remember what happened last night, she ought to forget it. Quiquina there in the doorway. She turned in alarm to see if she was there, repeating the terror of the previous night. But Quiquina took a long time, she only came at about ten o'clock. Quiet as always, trying not to make any noise. This time she seemed to be taking more care. But Rosalina, listening in the direction where she must be, could just catch the flip-flop of her loose slippers. Now she's in the kitchen, poking the fire, handling the saucepans, she could hear the noise; now she's in the pantry, she saw the empty cup, the open butter dish, the breadcrumbs on the tablecloth, she can see the signs of my presence in the pantry; now she's in the kitchen again, at the sink, she has turned on the tap, the noise of the water running; now silence, I wonder is she in the garden? The creak of a door, she's in her room; when is she going to come? Had she seen her in the drawing room perhaps? Come Quiquina, for God's sake, come and be done with it, don't keep me waiting in this nerve-racking way.

Quiquina still didn't come, she was waiting. She must be avoiding her. Was it going to be like that all day long? She wouldn't be able to bear it, she would call Quiquina, would shout Quiquina. Oh God, why? She must be as upset as I am, she won't want to see me, she won't know how to look at me the first time. Quiquina will understand. But she saw, she saw it all with those yellow eyes. Saw what? No, she didn't want to remember.

Suddenly she was aware of Quiquina in the drawing room. With eyes downcast she tried to see whereabouts in the room she was. Near the door, standing in the doorway like yesterday? Not like yesterday, yesterday she stood there in the doorway watching me. Now she's moving: she can hear her steps right behind her. She wouldn't turn round, she wouldn't even show surprise. Let Quiquina take the first step. Quiquina was now in her field of vision. At the window. She pulled back the curtain, the sunlight flooded into the room. She saw Quiquina's back. Quiquina was standing looking out into the square. She leant out of the window, looking for something. Him, she's looking for him. They can't have met, he went out before her. What is she going to do now? And then she turned round. When she caught Rosalina's eyes, she shrank back a step, startled, as if she had not expected to see her. Stock-still, open-mouthed, her eyes motionless, her face like stone, ashen.

Then their eyes met, without moving their eyes met and spoke. And Rosalina saw, although Quiquina gave no sign, not a pucker of the lips, no twitch of her facial muscles, no quiver of her eyes, Rosalina saw that she had seen everything, she was trying to say I saw everything last night. Without a sign she said she knew, she had seen everything. So Rosalina knew now that it was all too awfully true: it was her in the doorway. She had seen everything, she knew all about it. And Rosalina knew that Quiquina knew she knew. They both knew, but one knowing what the other knew made it that much less bearable. They both knew, it was terrible. If Quiquina had made a sign, any sign, she might still be in doubt. But in their dumb confrontation, just through the eyes, they had told one another that they knew; now it was impossible to hide or to escape. Quiquina had perhaps said more than she intended. Perhaps she didn't mean to let on and that was why she stepped back, startled. But their eyes met and the one had to tell the other what she knew. Now they could never be the same again, a barrier between them. Because they both knew.

What are you going to do now, Quiquina, she asked with her eyes. And Quiquina's eyes said I saw, I saw you, I saw him, I saw the two of you together. Quiquina, but I, she tried to say. Quiquina's eyes could only keep on saying that they knew. Quiquina, hit me, slap my face, she wanted to say, but Quiquina's eyes were on the floor now, she wasn't looking. Looking at the floor, Quiquina was a sad, dejected figure, like when a cloud suddenly hides the sun. In the cloud, the sudden darkness, Quiquina's silence and stillness hurt more than a slap in the face. Then Quiquina stirred and went over to the console-table. Quiquina's fingers stroked the cold white marble of the table top. As if she were trying to read something in its blotches and streaks. She who could neither read nor speak. Who, unable to speak, needed no sign to say I saw. The moment was too long, it dragged on too much for Rosalina. Now she wanted to talk to Quiquina, she wanted to say something to her to break the silence. Quiquina looked at her again. This time her eyes said nothing, didn't say whether she had seen or not: they were empty.

Quiquina, I wanted . . . she said eventually, painfully breaking the cocoon of silence. But she was unable to go on. Quiquina raised two fingers to her lips, begging her to stay silent. She didn't need to say a word.

He only appeared at lunch time. He came back sullen-faced, whistling aloud to cover up his uncertainty. When he saw Quiquina at the kitchen door he stopped whistling. He didn't look at her. He couldn't make up his mind whether to go to his room or go into the house.

He had gone out at the crack of dawn, with the day just showing in a cold grey sky. Quiquina woke early and he didn't want to run into her before he knew what he was going to do. He wanted to give it time, see what they would do. Particularly what Dona Rosalina would do. He could never be sure of her behaviour, she was always strange and unpredictable to him. But today is different, he thought. After what happened yesterday. Now there was something between them and Quiquina had no part in it. She saw everything, she had been watching from the beginning. A ghost in the doorway. At the beginning only he had sensed the other presence in the room, though he hadn't once seen Quiquina in the doorway. Not even when Rosalina shouted out : when he looked the doorway was empty as before. It wasn't an illusion, she saw it as well. Quiquina had been spying on them from the beginning, he was sure. But he wasn't too bothered about Quiquina's reaction. He just didn't want to meet up with her alone. He wanted the two of them to be together, he wanted to meet Dona Rosalina first. Depending on her behaviour he would decide how to deal with the other. Quiquina made no difference to his plans (his head was full of plans now). Yet he was afraid the two of them might have worked something out with regard to him. The two of them were very close, a silent understanding from which he was excluded. A deep understanding going back to long before his arrival. They were like mother and daughter. No, Quiquina was not like him, he knew that. Quiquina was now no better than him. Now there was a night of tenderness between him and Dona Rosalina, a night of love, he thought, afraid of the word love, because it might seem ridiculous, depending on the attitude she decided to take. No, it wasn't love, it was something very different, something strange, something bizarre which he didn't know what to call. Something so strong, yet so fragile, that he could barely encompass it in thought. It couldn't be love, she could never love him. He knew his position, he was aware of his inferiority in relation to Dona Rosalina. It wasn't love, it was something else, something he couldn't put a name to.

When he left his room the kitchen door was still shut. He went to the wash tank and gave his face a good wash, as if he meant to wash from his eyes the thick dough of the dreams he had rolled in all night. He had slept badly, a restless, disturbed sleep, waking up from one moment to the next. Only half of his body seemed to be sleeping. His mind was cool and lucid, he was aware when dream interfered with his line of thought, while he kept trying, a thousand times over, to recollect what he had just been through. His dream carried on from where his endearment was cut short. He saw Rosalina lying next to him; naked, passionate, speaking words he couldn't properly understand. In the darkness her body gleamed white, illuminated by dim light. His hands felt for her breasts and they were firm, warm and heavy. His hands ran over her hips, following the curve of their outline. And she was talking passionately, pleading. His hands reached the soft mass of hair in the hottest part of her body. An open flower, throbbing. He never finished, waking up suddenly, his heart thumping, he could hear his heart-beats in his throat. It was a strange mixture of happiness, of fear, of panic.

He started once again to think over what had happened, going over in his memory the details of his sensations, to be sure he had not been mistaken. His body was listless, his legs felt limp, his eyelids were heavy, and, unaware of the dividing line, he slipped back into the land of dream. At the beginning he could still tell that it was a dream. As if he were both himself there with her and another person watching him, seeing the two of them naked, in each other's arms, in the bed. He wanted the new dream to take up the previous one at the point where he had woken up. But it was impossible, now he was in a different place. On the Little Stone Ranch she talked about so much. The two of them were running about in the field : she was a girl, he was a man and a boy at the same time. On the verandah of the ranch house Dona Vivinha was watching them from a distance. He could see that Dona Vivinha was trying to tell him something, but he was afraid to hear what she might say. Major Lindolfo, my godfather, might come out onto the verandah at any moment, his shotgun glinting in the sun, loaded with buckshot. Better pull Rosalina behind some bushes, where Dona Vivinha couldn't see them. He tried to turn round to tell Dona Vivinha that they weren't doing anything wrong, they were only looking for Firefly the pony, which had strayed. The sweet dewy grass wet his bur-covered trousers. She lifted her skirt so as not to wet the hem of her dress and he saw her long girlish legs. He wasn't going to do anything to her, he wanted to tell Dona Vivinha who was on the verandah, but seemed to be watching them through binoculars, right close to them. He wouldn't do anything to her, she was just a girl. A young girl laughing happily for no reason at all. But Rosalina's eyes shone like live coals, with the fire of a grown woman. If he wanted to, she would let him, like a young girl does in bewilderment. But Dona Vivinha's eyes were on them, something told him. He pulled Rosalina in the direction of the stream, saying Firefly is down here. The cold clear water gurgled amongst the pebbles on the sandbanks and became frothy. She picked up a round pebble and started playing with it, then she threw it up in the air and he caught it. The smooth shiny pebble was like a polished stone. He put it in his pocket as a souvenir. Rosalina continued to play in the stream, her bare feet in the clear, glittering water, her hands cupped against the current. Then she threw water over him and it was nice and cold; he washed his face and everything was suddenly all clear and bright. His bad eye began to see and he saw that the world was more beautiful than he supposed. I'm better, he shouted to her, I can see you with both my eyes. She laughed, pleased with the miracle she had worked. He kissed her slender, ladylike hands, looked up at her broad smile and Rosalina was shimmering behind a curtain of water, river water and tears.

He washed his face in the wash tank. He closed his good eye, trying to see out of his wall-eye. Maybe it could happen. All he saw was the usual milky glare, the white cloud. His useless eye. He wanted another eye, he wanted to be different. Perhaps she wouldn't receive him unless she'd been drinking. Drunk. Not too much, she was aware of what she was doing. If it wasn't for Quiquina. Her hot breath, the taste of wine in her mouth. Her warm, moist lips, her hot panting breath. He put some soap on his finger and rubbed his teeth. The nasty taste of the soap was difficult to get rid of, however much he rinsed his mouth. He shouldn't have cleaned his teeth, better have kept the sticky taste of sleep in his mouth. Now the taste of the kiss had gone, the taste of her moist lips, the taste of his dream. When he remembered the kiss now it was a cold feeling, as if it hadn't happened. The taste of soap still in his mouth. He rinsed again. He raised his hand to the back of his neck, where she had gripped him. The skin was broken, the mark of her nails. True, it was all true. Cheerful and contented, he squeezed the skin as if his hands were hers, squeezing, pressing painfully, the way one picks up a cat by the neck.

The kitchen door was shut. Quiquina was not yet awake. He went to the bottom of the garden and chopped some wood. He put the firewood near the door. When she opened the door she would realize that he had got up before her, done his work and gone off. He had never done this before, he didn't know why he was doing it now. It was always Quiquina who asked him to chop wood for the fire. Perhaps it was his way of showing her he was smarter than she was. Maybe he was just trying to please her. Nonsense, she saw, she did see, a bit of firewood wasn't going to make Quiquina change her mind.

Everything will depend on Rosalina, Dona Rosalina. On the way the two women worked things out between them. Dona Rosalina was smart, a will-o'-the-wisp. Like a coyote. She was well able to look after herself, she didn't need his help. He was in her hands. What if she changed her mind and didn't want it to go any further? Impossible after what happened last night. Before, she was a will-o'-the-wisp, he could never pin her down. When he tried to get on familiar terms with her by means of conversations. When he thought he'd caught her, she would cut him short sharply, with a frown, she wouldn't be the same person. A will-o'-the-wisp, like lightning, she would always be in a different neck of the wood, not where he thought she was. Not now, he held her in his arms, he kissed her on the mouth. She couldn't retreat now. If she did try to pull back, return to her former coldness, he would be there to remind her. He had only to look at her, wink his eye. If she pretended not to understand, he would remind her. Wasn't that what he had a tongue for? Nonsense, she liked it, she wanted it. The only reason we didn't go further was because Quiquina turned up just in time to mess things up. She'll want to go on. Or maybe she won't, but I'll make her want to. He had his weapons, she knew, she ought to know. He only needed to hint that the secret might not stay with the three of them. If he were to tell, would the townsfolk believe him? They were dying to believe, they wanted to believe anything about the manor. In the beginning hadn't they been for ever making guesses? He would only need to say that riffraff is going to find out, for her to change her mind. Now she was in his hands. No will-o'-the-wisp with me, he said triumphantly. He was a good hunter, she would see. She'll do what I want now. We shall see, we shall see, he repeated, a cruel smile on his lips, as he opened the gate and made for the street.

In the square he rolled a cigarette, lit up, took a couple of drags. On an empty stomach and after the wine of the previous evening he felt queasy and threw the cigarette away. He took a deep breath, filling his chest. The thin fresh air of the grey morning (the sky gradually turning blue with the approach of the sun) had a good, cold smell, like new. A fresh smell of earth damp with dew. He took deep breaths, inhaling the air with his nostrils wide open, trying to fill out his lungs with the fragrant breath of the morning. He shivered and a thrill of new life ran right through his body. What a night, what a morning! A morning new like himself, a night black with surprises and nightmares.

He looked at the manor house, the open window of Rosalina's room, the whitish colour of the light bulb. She didn't bother to close the window and switch off the light. Drunk, she must have gone to sleep drunk and slept through. The heavy sleep of a child, a girl asleep. A young girl, he continued to think, serious, his eyes saddened by the recollection. An innocent girl sleeping. A girl who lets you do things to her. Not at all innocent: she'd been active (he raised his hand to his neck), she kissed hungrily. She was no girl, she was a woman, her needs were different. On fire, she had fire inside her. He thought of Rosalina as a young girl because he wanted to feel tender, tinge his memory with sadness. That other one, Esmeralda, she was a young girl. On the farm back in Paracatu. Ten years old, a mad thing. If he'd not heard the footsteps and the booming voice of Major Lindolfo, he would have. She was letting him, with round startled eyes, she was not resisting. Like a girl letting the dentist fiddle in her mouth or the doctor examine her. Rosalina was not a girl: a grown woman, a passionate woman. After that, he would never stay alone with Esmeralda. But the imp was always near him, her round eyes shining, egging him on. Did she really know what she was doing? He was a grown man, he was afraid of what might happen. It was madness what she was doing. Ten years old, she was a member of the household, the apple of Dona Vivinha's eye. The major would put a bullet into him, the major was not to be trifled with, he liked to administer justice himself. Later, when she was thirteen, she went bad, turned whore and went to live in a brothel in Paracatu. At first he sometimes passed beneath the window of her room. The other girls made fun of him, hey Joey Bird, is your rifle jammed? And they laughed. She didn't, she stayed serious, watching him with sad, longing eyes, but always with a hint of a smile. Like she was trying to tell him that he had been the first. He wasn't the first; my godfather, the major, with his booming voice and his boots thick with mud, turned up just in time to save me. Nor was he the second, he'd never been alone with her after that day. One of the cowboys, Romão, a bloke without scruples, was the first. He hopped it, for fear of the major's buckshot. He was never heard of again. In his godfather's presence he heaped abuse on Romão, it's just not done! Doing that to a child, an insult to you and your family! Thirteen, a child, it's just not done! he said earnestly. The major approved, clearing his throat, unsuspecting. He was afraid, she might tell about that time the two of them nearly ended up doing it. She said nothing, the smart brat, he sighed with relief. Afterwards, he avoided going past the brothel so as not to see Esmeralda's longing eyes and sad smile. Life was so topsy-turvy. He didn't want to think about that business, he seldom remembered it. When the thought came to him, he would brush it aside the way one drives away a fly. A child, he couldn't understand.

Dona Rosalina was not a child, she was a woman, mistress of her own life. A woman such as he had never seen before. Such fire, such excitement. Why had he been the one it happened with? Thinking about it got him no further, he couldn't understand. The best thing was to wait and see what would happen, let time pass, time takes care of everything. Like lying in wait on a shoot. The game might come, or it might not. It always does come. Sometimes.

The houses were all shut, there was nobody out of doors, the life of the town had not yet begun. The first swallows were settling on the telegraph wires, flying down from the eaves of the houses. Soon the wires would be black with swallows. A cock crowed in a yard, a horse neighed. The first signs of day, of life beginning again. The sky was clear, greyish blue. Not a cloud, a cold, fragrant brightness. The sun was showing behind the mango trees in the garden. Soon it would be higher, it would dry the dew drops on the leaves. Then it would be day.

Before the town began its daily life and the people came out into the street, he decided to take a longer walk than usual. He didn't know why, but his steps took him in the direction of the road which led on from the street towards the cemetery. The way he had come when he first arrived in the town. Silvino and the boy Manny who was so scared of the big hole. The way he had been startled, was it fear? When he saw the gaping jaws of the craters. Their rabid greed for earth to devour. Silvino was funny, he'd only seen him a few times since then. Silvino asked him how things were going at the manor. So-so, he told him, not bad. Didn't I tell you it might work out, friend Joey? I'm pleased to have been of help. Life's like that, like helps like. What about her, the madam? She's all right, friend Silvino. I quite like her manner, her seriousness. You know, Silvino, I never met a madam like her. She's got her oddities, but then who hasn't? That's just what I told you, said Silvino. And the town, has she made it up with the town? No, that she has not, Silvino, she won't forgive them. Well, she's got her reasons, said Silvino and he called out, whoa there, to the oxen, setting the cart in motion.

Now he was on the road, the houses were behind him. The lime-washed walls of the cemetery were whiter in the fresh light of morning. The air was thin, pure and light, no mystery. That's where we all go, sooner or later, he said, but without really thinking about death: life was teeming bright inside him. We have to live life properly, to the full, so that death don't come like a ghost, all of a sudden. If you're afraid of life you won't find peace in death, he said, in answer to a thought that was forming deep down inside him – Rosalina, always Rosalina. He'd not been able to think about anything else since yesterday. He could not exactly distinguish what had happened from what he had been thinking, from what he had been dreaming.

A goldfinch came flying down and settled on the barbed-wire fence. It started with a long trill, then burst into song; and seeing the goldfinch he suddenly felt happy, as if he had met an old acquaintance. He whistled in imitation of the bird, accompanying it in a duet. Wee birds were the best things there were. As for a goldfinch, none better. When he was a kid he used to love catching small birds with a branch coated in birdlime. In bamboo cages they would sing a treat. He used to spend hours watching and listening. The goldfinch stopped singing and hopped about on the wire. Then a hawfinch perched a little further on. It sat preening its damp feathers with its beak. A bird's life is an easy life, he thought, as he walked on. He carried in his ear the dainty notes of the birdsongs. He stopped at the craters. They didn't frighten him any more, he was so accustomed to them by now from going past them every time he went hunting with Etelvino. Yet he never failed to look at them, he was held by their secret, their mystery, their lure. Once he even went down inside, right down to the bottom of the valley. Etelvino stayed up top watching him from a distance, like an idiot, why was he doing that, there wasn't any game down there. Sorry to hold you up, Etelvino, he said, but I'd never been down a crater, I wanted to see what it was like inside. Nothing to it, is there Joey? said Etelvino. Aye, he said, nothing at all. The ground at the bottom is really quite firm, there's even a stream running down there. Etelvino laughed, he thought he was very funny, every time he opened his mouth Etelvino gawked and grinned oafishly. A bit of a dolt, that Etelvino, with his new rifle and all.

Nonsense what he thought the first time, when he arrived in the town. We get fancies, superstitions. See something glowing in the dark, think it's a ghost, when all the time it's your old dad smoking his pipe. So they say. Silliness, your mind wandering, someone walking over your grave. When he had the bad dream about the child and the major shooting him; when he saw the cemetery, the craters, the dust devil in Carmo Square; when he heard what Silvino had to say about the people at the manor house. It all seemed to be a warning for him. There was no point in running away, what had to happen would happen, wasn't that what Dona Vivinha said about the story of the father and the daughter? Nothing did happen, nothing bad happened. Nonsense, fancy. It all vanished into air, like the shades of night fading away in the new light of morning. The sun was half-way up the sky, a ball of blinding fire, he could hardly look at it. The world was bright with clean, pure colours; the song of the sunlit morning.

Nothing happened? What about yesterday? Yesterday, he started thinking, with a hint of alarm. Maybe it was all a warning to him after all? Maybe he should get away, turn his back on the manor and the town, be on his travels, keep a-moving. No. Why should he? When it was so good yesterday. And Quiquina? What could happen? Nothing. He wanted to finish what he had started, what Quiquina disturbed. What could happen was that he would sleep with a woman like that, a woman he'd never known the likes of before. But what if the danger was just that, in the pleasure, in the satisfaction of desire? What if she had inside her the lure of those craters? The worst that could happen was if she didn't want it again. If she dismissed him. This she couldn't do, he knew that. Not now, not after what happened. All he need do was drop a hint about the townsfolk, just a word. Fancy, temptation. Better not think about it. The more you pray, the more temptation comes your way. Life is ahead,

what's behind is darkness, just dust, memory. He looked
again at the craters, jagged wounds. The sun's light laid
bare their red innards. All clear, no mystery, no hint of
bad omens. Life was as clear as water trickling from a
spring. He could be happy. He carried on walking, leaving
the craters behind. At the cemetery gate he stopped. He
sat down on the stone step and took his knife out of
his pocket. To while away the time he began to clean his
nails with the tip of the blade.

He heard a muffled sound of hoofbeats, a horse was
approaching. It was Ismael on his splendid, caparisoned
piebald, coming in early from the ranch. Good morning,
Mr Ismael, sir, he said. What, you here at this time of
day, Joey Bird? said Ismael. He slackened his pace, then
stopped. You're not going to tell me you're here for a
funeral, he said. Funeral be blowed, Mr Ismael, me I'm
trying to clear my head, had a damn awful night, nightmare after nightmare, he said. And the cemetery's a good
place to cure that? asked Ismael, with a laugh. Aye, I
hadn't rightly thought of that, said Joey Bird. He crossed
himself exaggeratedly. Only you could get an idea like
that, Joey Bird, come to the cemetery to clear your head,
he said. Well maybe the cemetery is a good place, said
Joey Bird. When you see the dead, you remember you're
alive and feel still more alive. Ismael guffawed. Go on,
Joey, you don't change a bit, do you? I'm going to be
in town for a few days, see you come round and tell me
some tales, I feel like a bit of entertainment, he said. I
don't feel like laughing today, Mr Ismael, he said. But
I'm laughing, said Ismael. You're laughing because you
like to laugh, I haven't said anything funny, I'm really
down in the dumps, said Joey Bird. It will pass, Joey,
you're never sad for long. I'll be going, I'm in a hurry,
good day to you. Good day to you, Mr Ismael, sir, said
Joey Bird, watching him spur on his horse and ride off,
then disappear at the end of the street.

He stayed there, killing time, trying to spin out time.

He always liked to be with people, but now he wanted to be alone. He wasn't thinking about anything in particular, just letting his thoughts wander. Every so often, like the long, slow swing of the pendulum of a grandfather clock, Rosalina. He allowed his memories and dreams to take shape gradually, fat lazy clouds in the sky. A dull drowsiness, lethargy, a pleasurable idleness took control of his mind. Underneath, the anxiety, which he was trying to forget.

When the men arrived with their shovels, he got up. Well, look who's here, said one of them. No mourners for your funeral? joked another. He looked at them moodily. They were so used to seeing him make fun, that he felt obliged to be amusing. My time's not come yet, he said. You'll not get your hands on this precious body so soon either, you skulking vultures. They laughed. Your day will come, said the first man. Just see it ain't too long coming, Joey Bird, I mean to render you this service, said the second. Aye, he said, briefly, to shorten the conversation. I'll be getting along, g'morning. It's early yet, said a third man. Wait a bit, there'll be a funeral along soon, that's what we're here for. No, I'm off, he said and went on his way.

Life had got under way again in the town. The stores were opening, the small shops, people coming from mass, others on their way to work; there were people at the chemist's shop already; at the post office, the buggy was ready to fetch the mail from the railway station, Cassiano sitting up front, puffing on a maize-stalk cigarette, nodded him a friendly invitation to get up alongside, but he shook his head, saying nothing, he wasn't talking to anybody; at the meeting place there was already a good group, he could have stayed there, they called him over, but he went on. He sauntered on aimlessly. Time was passing so slowly and he didn't want to go back to the house any sooner then he had to. He would go back, he had to. If only to get some odds and ends, his gun. Because he was beginning to think of going away, of leaving town. Might be best. No, it's not, the best thing'll be to go back and see what's going to happen. Then he would set his course. Everywhere, on his way, people buttonholed him, inviting him to stay for a chat. He kept refusing. You're not very talkative today, are you, Joey Bird? they said, surprised at his silence and strange manner. He shrugged his shoulders and went on his aimless way.

He stopped at Emanuel's warehouse. Mr Emanuel was giving orders to some men who were about to unload coffee from a lorry. A well-built, good-looking man, Mr Emanuel. His face set in a frown, a pair of pale grey eyes. Hard working, serious, Mr Emanuel. An honest man, like his father, Quincas Ciríaco, he'd not known him, that's what they said. Emanuel, yesterday she said Emanuel. Is it possible there was something between them? He hardly ever goes there, he's only been once since I've been there. He only stayed a little while, with me watching behind the door. He was embarrassed in her company, twisting his hat round by the brim, head down, eyes on the ground. What if he was embarrassed because of something that had happened a long time ago? A married man, upright, respectable, so they said. He wasn't like the others who spent their time with the whores at Bridge House. If there was something between them, did he go all the way? No, couldn't be. She kissed hungrily, she didn't know how to kiss. That don't mean anything, it might have been just once. He might not have gone all the way. Like with him yesterday. Then she stopped it and didn't want anything more to do with him. Some women never learn to kiss properly, to do it. Lumps of cold flesh. It depends on the man. Like with a guitar, it only makes music when it's handled by someone who knows how to play. He knew how to play, ask Marie at the Mares-Paddock, and the others. Virgin, she was still a virgin. Mr Emanuel didn't look the sort who would do anything, bashful, always got his eyes on the ground. If

she wasn't a virgin, it'd be better for him, easier. And her
excitement when she kissed, her passion? He raised his
hand to his neck. Her sharp nails. The mark was still
there. Virgins aren't like that, a virgin lets you. The girls
he knew, not one of them like her. With Esmeralda he
didn't do it, it was Romão, the cowboy, who finally
serviced her. Esmeralda, a kid, crazy. Just as well he didn't
do it, the major turned up just in time. Nonsense, Romão
did it later anyway. It came to the same thing, it had to
happen. Some women are born whores, nothing you can
do about it.

But she was no child, she wasn't like Esmeralda. At
times there was something of the child about her, her
eyes were like a young girl's. She said Emanuel, he remembered her eyes when she said Emanuel. She said other
names as well, he couldn't remember. None that he knew.
If they were people he knew he would have remembered.
What if there were others before Mr Emanuel? Of course
not, she was very young when her father died, so they
said. Like Esmeralda when Romão did it? No, older,
Esmeralda was still a kid. Afterwards she never went out
and nobody went inside the manor house, except Emanuel.
Even he went very rarely. If it was anybody, it was him.
Wasn't him, did he look the type? Serious, honourable
man, they said. Like his father. Married, with children,
a good man. What if it was before he got married? If it
was before, why didn't he marry her? God knows, she's
odd. . . .

Seeing himself observed so closely, Emanuel turned towards him. What is it, Joey Bird, do you want anything?
No, nothing, he said, I was just watching. Anything for
the manor? Did Dona Rosalina send an order? No,
nothing, Mr Emanuel. She don't need anything. Mr
Emanuel was puzzled by Joey Bird's silence, him so
talkative, a proper chatterbox. Joey Bird's eyes, that blind
white eye. Joey Bird didn't take his eyes off him. What
can he want, what is he up to? Why on earth did Rosa-

lina need to stick a stranger like him in the house? It couldn't be anyone from the town, he'd tried hard enough to find someone to help her, but Rosalina just wouldn't have anything to do with anyone from the town, except himself. He was the only one who could go inside the manor house. She's getting worse by the day. When he did go, she dressed herself all up, put perfume on, dolled herself up for him. The way she looked at him. The only thing was to avoid going there. He went sc seldom now. . . . He couldn't understand those Honório Cotas. His father did, understand them. Well, Joey Bird, if you have nothing to do, I have, he said roughly. He went back to his work. Giving orders, harshly. Joey Bird didn't say goodbye and went off furious with Mr Emanuel. He was no dog for people to treat that way. Thinks he's somebody. Nobody treats me like that, only him. Thinks I don't know. . . .

He went to the station and stood watching a goods wagon being loaded with coffee. There was a youngster selling coffee and cakes. He ate some. Now he could smoke a cigarette. He sat down on the bench on the platform, near the telegraphist's window. The whirring of the machine sounded like a clock, except that it sometimes went faster, then slower, sometimes clattered away, then fell silent. Not the clock, the pendulum clock, Dona Rosalina wound it up. Only the clocks and watches in the drawing room were stopped. Quiquina would be getting on with her work. He didn't want to get there before lunch. When the two of them were together. Or just Rosalina. . . . He got up, went over to the ticket office and asked the fare to Tuiuti. Planning to travel, Joey Bird? asked the ticket clerk. Could be, he said mysteriously. The man laughed. Everybody laughed at him, it wasn't nice, he thought for the first time. Sad. He couldn't remember ever feeling so sad and quiet before. What happened isn't the sort of thing to make a person sad. It's because I'm nervous, I don't know what's going to hap-

pen. Maybe nothing will happen. The fare was dear, his
pockets were empty, if he decided to leave town he would
have to walk, the same way he had arrived. Why run
away? Wasn't he a man? Him afraid of Dona Rosalina,
a woman, that was funny. He tried to laugh, he didn't
manage. He walked up and down the empty platform.
As if he were waiting for a train that was late. The station
clock showed half past nine. Might as well get moving,
lunch at the manor was at ten.

He stopped opposite the manor house. Maybe it would
be better not to go in? He looked at the house as if he
were seeing it for the first time. Like the first time, when
he couldn't make up his mind whether to knock on the
door or not. She told him to go in by the garden gate,
where servants were supposed to go in, people like him.
Proud, haughty creature. Then see what happened, last
night. He laughed a nasty, vindictive laugh. He looked at
the manor house, trying to puzzle out its enigma. He
opened the gate and went in. He whistled aloud to cover
up his nervousness. At the kitchen door Quiquina pretended not to see him. Should he go to his room or
straight into the house? He hesitated a moment and
stopped whistling. Let's get it over with, he said to himself.

Morning, he said to Quiquina. You were late this morning. I was off out bright and early. (His voice quivered.
He stuck his hand in his pocket, so that Quiquina should
not see he was trembling.) I left some wood ready
chopped, so's you wouldn't have the trouble. . . . She
kept her eyes on the ground, avoiding looking at him.
Nonsense what he'd said. He was furious with himself,
he couldn't keep his tongue still when he was nervous.
Quiquina, he said, trying to see if she was looking at him.
She shrugged her shoulders, turned her back on him and
went into the kitchen. He followed her. She poked the fire,
took the lid off a saucepan and sniffed the steaming food.
He stood close to her, not knowing what to do.

Suddenly she turned round. Quiquina's eyes were hard with silent hatred. She saw us with those eyes, she saw us. A cold shudder went right through his body, his legs felt weak. But she made not a single gesture, not a movement. Her eyes fixed on him. As if she wanted to kill him. He lowered his head, avoiding Quiquina's eyes.

Quiquina, I wanted . . . he began, but was unable to finish what he was trying to say : she turned her head in the direction of the drawing room, telling him it's up to her, talk to her, we shall see. At the drawing-room door he stopped. She was sitting at the table surrounded by materials, wires, scissors, irons. Her hands motionless, her eyes staring into space, Rosalina wasn't really looking at anything. He cleared his throat to announce his presence. She turned her eyes towards him.

For a brief moment she appeared to hesitate and lowered her eyes, blushing. He took two steps towards the table. He felt Quiquina behind him. His heart raced. The grandfather clock. He looked from her to the silent clock. Suddenly she raised her eyes towards him. Her eyes were cold and empty. The flush had left her face, giving way to its customary pallor. Her face was still, not a tremor. She was hard, she could control herself, not like him. Her eyes now looked at him questioningly, surprised by his presence there. Her former eyes, not as they were last night : her daytime eyes. Could she be intending to go back to the way she was before? Does she think it can just be forgotten? Maybe it was because Quiquina was there behind him?

A long silence. He didn't know where to put his hands, where to look. He lowered his eyes, afraid to look her in the face. He felt small in her presence. That is no way to behave, she began – her voice was firm, no hesitation, not a quiver. You went out early without telling anyone. Today of all days, when I needed you to do something for me. What a woman, my God, like stone. She even had the courage to tell him off, after what happened.

Maybe she was putting it on, because of Quiquina she was pretending. Ah, if he could be like that!

Well, I . . . he stammered, fishing for an excuse. I wasn't feeling well, a bit off colour, after yesterday. . . .

Idiot, he was an idiot! He always managed to say something he ought not to.

What? she said.

Quiquina was close to him, he could hear her breathing, her eyes were fixed on Dona Rosalina. Cornered like an animal completely surrounded by dogs. His time had come.

Rosalina, I . . . he said floundering, looking for support in her eyes. They were cold and empty, expressionless.

What! she shouted. Rosalina? Watch your tongue! Mind your place!

His arms sagged to his sides and he looked at Quiquina. She had a satisfied smile on her face.

And so they did not speak for the whole of that day. They were worlds gravitating around the same dark centre, the same secret. There was no possible meeting point, no communication. If the house was naturally silent, that day the silence became even heavier, aggressive, stifling. Of the three, it was he who could least endure the dense atmosphere of the manor. Because the two women were accustomed to it, they had no alternative. They understood one another, they understood one another in silence. They didn't need words, they understood one another the way they had always done. Strangely (he noted) Quiquina even treated her with affection, paying more careful attention to her: like somebody taking broth or medicine to a sick person. As though she wanted to tell Rosalina not to talk, the doctor had recommended peace and quiet. Although she didn't go to her very often, she was always somewhere at hand. At the slightest sign or hint that she needed anything, Quiquina would be there. Eyes lowered, she didn't dare look her in the eyes.

The two women's eyes rarely met and they spoke little. Rosalina tried to complete her interrupted sentence, the explanation Quiquina would not let her give. On these fleeting occasions Quiquina's eyes would say you don't need to say anything, she understood and forgave. Immediately she would lower her eyes, as if she were the one who had been caught, the guilty one : she would disappear quickly into the back of the house. Then she would return and watch Rosalina from a distance; there was distress, tenderness and love in her eyes. Like someone waiting anxiously for a sick child to get over the danger point and the fever to abate. This tacit agreement between them, the silence, the wordless gestures, the absence of speech in their manner of communicating, left Joey Bird even more cut off. He couldn't understand, never would understand Rosalina, wouldn't ever understand Quiquina. They understood one another, they were in league; they're against me, he said to himself. They'll see, I'll show them who I am!

But he didn't know what to do. All his threats, all his imagined acts of vengeance seemed useless and childish. The world of the manor house was so alien to him now, more so than when he first crossed the threshold (the world of the manor house was governed by its own laws, from which normal reason and understanding had withdrawn), that all he could do was writhe in impotent hatred. What use would it be going and telling the town, when they (Rosalina especially) did not care what happened in the town or what the townsfolk might think? He would be considered a fool, they already knew him for a story-teller. Nobody would believe him. And if they did, what good would it do him? What could the town do to Rosalina, shut away in her manor, other than mutter curses and feel that they were now quit of their remorse and resentment? What would he gain, what good would it do him to talk? Who would have the courage to knock at the manor door to say anything? Mr Emanuel? Not him, Mr Emanuel was reserved but short-tempered, he didn't encourage familiarity. Mr Emanuel didn't allow anyone to talk to him about matters concerning the manor. Didn't he give him a hard look that morning and send him on his way? The only thing to do was wait and see.

He waited. He waited all day long for Rosalina to speak to him, or at least to look at him, so that he would know what she was thinking. She didn't look at him. Or if she did, her eyes were so empty and remote, so cold, that she might just as well not be looking. Her eyes told him nothing, not one moment did she hesitate : nothing had taken place, yesterday did not exist. At first he thought it was because Quiquina was there, she didn't want Quiquina to see there was something between them. But no, even when they were alone, on the two occasions when he managed to be near Rosalina without the black woman being there too, her eyes were just the same, the same distance, the same indifference. Maybe he was mistaken, perhaps she didn't remember a thing? It wasn't possible, when he saw her the first time she was embarrassed, she lowered her eyes, red in the face. Afterwards she controlled herself, became again the way she had always been : worse than before, now he couldn't even talk to her, his voice stuck in his throat, fear in his breast. Dona Rosalina was unpredictable. Let's see at night, he thought. Maybe she's thinking that at night . . .

He tried to talk to Quiquina. He talked about household matters, everyday things. She didn't answer, he stammered. He avoided mentioning Dona Rosalina's name as if it were a forbidden word. She didn't even look at him, pretending to be busy with her work. He would give up, go out into the garden, then come back again. Quiquina couldn't hide her feelings, she wasn't like Dona Rosalina. With her heavy, hostile silence and her lowered eyes she was telling him that she knew, she saw everything last night. And that she hated him; out of my sight, you devil! Eventually he couldn't stand it. Quiquina, do you need me for anything? And when she didn't even raise her eyes, he prodded her with his fingertips. She whipped round with an angry scowl and looked at him with hate in her eyes.

He turned away and left the house. With his gun over his shoulder, he didn't know which way to go. He wanted to get out into the countryside, away from that house, away from that town. When he passed by Etelvino's house, Etelvino was at the window, he pretended not to see him. Hey Joey, Etelvino called. He couldn't pretend he hadn't heard, he turned round. Where are you going at this time of day, Joey, rifle and all? Not far, he said abruptly. Why didn't you call me? It's not the best time for hunting, but I'd have come just for a natter, said Etelvino. I'm not going hunting, he said. I'm just going to take a few pot shots, somewhere here, see if I can get things off my chest with a few shots, I'm like a bear with a sore head today. Seeing Joey Bird's gloomy face, Etelvino said what's happened man, tell me, it's better to talk about things. It's nothing, friend Etelvino, just me, not anything I could talk about. You wouldn't understand, I don't even understand myself what's happening. We'll talk later. Etelvino looked at him, curious, he had never seen Joey Bird like that. Aye, he said, you go on then, it'll do you good. Good day to you. Good day to you, friend Etelvino. He walked on quickly, for fear that Etelvino might insist on going with him.

He followed the road. He passed the craters, unloading his gun in the direction of the open jaws and listening to the explosion which echoed like thunder. Damn you, you bitches, he yelled. He didn't know who he was swearing at, he cursed to get it off his chest. The same way he shot into the air without aiming at a target. He went past the cemetery without stopping. He wanted to walk until he tired himself out completely and then, when night fell, limp back, worn out, numb with tiredness, not thinking. Blasted life, crazy damned idea, why didn't I stay in my own place? Mind your place! that's what she said.

Night was falling, the first stars were twinkling in the vast sky of the bush. More than the approaching darkness, punctured already by the cries of crickets and other nocturnal animals, his night was that of the spirit, the blackness of despair, unrelieved melancholy. Only the hope that the night would be different shed a faint light in his weary spirit, like the bright chirp of an insect in the darkness.

And he returned to the town : his powder horn empty, still sore at heart.

And he passed by the square, looked at the manor house, went on his aimless way.

And he walked the streets of the town : he did not even answer the greetings he received, didn't respond to the jokes they made about his gun. I'm not a clown, I'll show them.

He stopped at the railway station. Worn out, weak at the knees, he slumped onto one of the benches on the platform. The platform was empty, mosquitoes hovered around the lighted lamps, the rails disappeared into the night. No train at that hour, the ticket office closed, the telegraphist's room closed, the warehouse doors closed. Only himself on the empty, lighted platform in the stillness of night. He would go back to the house later, the same time as last night. His stomach was empty, he thought they must be wondering where I am. Let them wonder! They can go to hell! He would go back later. She knew what time he returned. He heard steps in the dark, somebody was coming along the sleepers. The linesman was taking a lighted lantern to his hut. He shut his eyes, pretending to be asleep. The linesman stopped and looked in astonishment at seeing Joey Bird in the station at that time of night. He shrugged his shoulders and went on. The red light of his lantern bobbed about and disappeared in the darkness.

Later on he went back home. It must be the same time

as yesterday, he gauged, from the houses being shut and the lights going out one by one in the windows. He stopped in Carmo Square, afraid to approach the manor. The light was on in the drawing room, the light was on in the bedroom. Like yesterday, everything the same as yesterday, he thought. She must be waiting. Like yesterday? Everything the same. He opened the gate and went in. He went to put his gun in his room. He took a bottle of hooch from under the bed and pulled the cork out with his teeth. He drank a few swigs from the bottle. He needed to be ready when the time came. The drink burned in his empty stomach, his belly rumbled. But it gave him a pleasant, comforting feeling, filled his chest, he felt sure of himself. He would take the bottle with him, they weren't going to stick to that drink that took so long to work.

He expected everything to be the same, but contrary to his expectations the kitchen door was shut. She was smarter this time, was Quiquina. The light was off. No doubt with her ear to the door, listening to his footsteps. Damn you, old woman, he said. He pushed open the gate and went out into the square. The drawing-room windows were closed, the light switched off. She's skipped it, she don't want it again. Only her bedroom light was still on, the window closed. The bedroom light stayed on for some time. He didn't know what to do, standing there bottle in hand, his eyes glued on her bedroom window, in the absurd hope that it would be opened. The window was not opened, the light went out.

He tipped the bottle to his mouth greedily, furiously. Tipsy, he ground his teeth and shook his fists at the closed window. Powerless in his hatred, he went on drinking. He staggered over to the centre of the square, near the cross. He hurled the empty bottle away, wanting to hit the manor house. The breaking glass shattered the silence of the night. With the effort of throwing the bottle he fell down. He stayed motionless, his ear close to the ground as if he were trying to hear the dark sounds of the earth.

The next day everything was as normal, life repeated itself as monotonously as the passing hours. Exhibiting self-assurance and indifference, Rosalina showed not the slightest sign of embarrassment: she returned to her normal occupations, to her fabric flowers, she talked to Quiquina, she gave him orders. Bewildered, he obeyed. Never once did it occur to him to question Dona Rosalina; humbled, dominated, he accepted the situation as final.

He waited for the night without the anxiety of the previous day.

And night came. When he came back he found the manor in darkness.

He was despondent, nothing more was going to happen. He wanted to have done with it for good. He wanted to go, he wanted to stay. He should destroy Rosalina, but she was stronger than him, she was holding out; he waited.

He went on waiting. If he had not waited, he would have gone to see Marie at the Mares-Paddock. He would have sunk into the swamp of that cheap flesh. He would leave.

He didn't leave, he waited for the third night.

The third night, when he came back, he saw the light on in the drawing room, the windows wide open. She was waiting for him, she wanted to go back to the moment before Quiquina had appeared in the doorway. His heart beating wildly (it wasn't joy, he expected anything from Rosalina) he approached the window and saw her at the table, book open in front of her, the half-empty glass within reach of her hand. Everything like the first night, he thought suddenly, quivering with excitement. He opened the gate and went to the kitchen door. It was not like the other times, Quiquina had taken her precautions. He returned to his post under the window. He had to act quickly or the light would be switched off and he would lose his last opportunity. He pulled back the curtain and stuck his head in through the window. She seemed not to notice him framed in the window. His heart leaping in his throat and with an unbearable trembling in his knees, he waited for her to turn and see him. She might shout, startled by his face at the window. Nothing mattered now, he would call her.

Pst! he called. Now she knows I'm here, he thought; she didn't turn, but he saw Rosalina's body shudder. She was still again. What's the matter with her? Rosalina, he said aloud, louder than he intended, his voice like a broken flute. Then she turned and saw him. Her eyes wide-open and shining, her lips parted, startled by his presence. Her eyes were emerging from a dream, trying to become accustomed to the real world. She didn't shout or make any sign; without moving, she looked at him as if she didn't know him. Rosalina, it's me, he said huskily.

Then the white stony face stirred, the eyelids quivered. He thought he saw a fleeting smile on her lips. She went away and he stood waiting for her to come to the window. He waited some time, but she didn't come. Then he heard a noise and saw a slit of light appear between the two halves of the door. Glued to the ground, he couldn't pluck up courage to move. He couldn't stay there like that, he would lose that opportunity. Without a word she was calling him. He went to the door, pushed it, it creaked. The dark corridor, the door of the lighted drawing room where she had gone.

He stopped at the drawing-room door. She was standing by the table. She was smiling at him, there couldn't be any doubt. She's smiling at me, she wants it. His heart filled with a fierce joy. His eyes watered, he was almost weeping. His heart was bursting. Come, he said, without taking his eyes off the door where Quiquina might appear at any moment. She made a move as if to pick something up from beneath the table, but he showed her the bottle in his hand.

And she came, with faltering steps, adrift in space, as if she were hovering on the edge of a precipice.

8

The Seed in the Body, in the Earth

That was how he had Rosalina. Had her white body,
explored its every secret. A full glowing body, the opposite
of what he was expecting. Some women are deceptive,
they look thin, yet they're not. What a piece of leg, he
said to himself, remembering her firm heavy thighs. Her
breasts were the only part of her body that was small,
small and fragrant, contained wholly within the hollow
of his hands. In the daytime, away from her, his hands
retained the warm living perfume of her flesh. A young
girl's breasts, like Esmeralda's were when Romão had her.
Esmeralda was well-developed for her age, afterwards her
breasts became large and heavy at the window of the
brothel.

Rosalina was not a young girl, though at times there
was something girlish in her eyes. He would stare down
into her eyes, trying to understand her. The eyes, moist,
shining, sultry, would follow his nervous movements. She
was excited as she watched him. She was not a young
girl, not like Esmeralda; she didn't let him do things, she
took an active part, she was passionate and violent. Eyes
aflame, lips moist with passion, her mouth hungry for his.
The hot breath of her dilated nostrils. Her breathing
quickened, she gasped incoherent things. She seemed
to be talking to someone else, not to him, he didn't know
who she was talking to. Sometimes he was sure he dis-

tinctly heard the name Emanuel. In the beginning, when they first started. He took no notice, or pretended to take no notice : he wanted her feverish, tumid body, he craved for her body.

Her body, he was the first. He gloried in the thought. She was a virgin before. He'd never had a woman for the first time. Maybe she didn't know the sort of tricks Marie and the other tarts used, but her passion, her moans and her violence often intimidated him. That waiting body, that body burning with passion, that body full of mystery might engulf him like the dark jaws of the craters. That woman might be the end of him; he could think only of disasters. He didn't know what might happen, he was afraid even to think. In the dark of night he made his way into a tunnel not knowing how or when he would escape.

Although her body was his, her spirit hovered somewhere far off. Her spirit belonged to the dead, or perhaps to Emanuel. But why should Emanuel bother him, when Emanuel had never touched her, never would touch her? Their meetings, the aloofness of their contact when they did meet, he timid and reserved, his eyes lowered, afraid to look at her, this he saw from behind the door when Emanuel visited her. Why should their contact bother him, when her body belonged to him for the time being? How long would her body belong to him, he wondered, afraid that it might all come to a sudden end. He lived in suspense, in darkness, it might all end suddenly. She might suddenly change her mind and refuse him her body, as she now denied him access to her mind and her eyes. Her eyes, like her spirit, perhaps belonged to the dead, perhaps to Emanuel. When they finished making love and she lay exhausted, her naked body limp and subdued, she would look at him, but her eyes had a glazed look and she seemed not to recognize him. She looked at him as if he were a stranger, lying there next to her. She's drunk, he thought, striving to grasp the vision which inhabited the depths of her eyes. But Rosalina's eyes evaded him, telling him with their transparent listlessness that only her body was his; only her body, and as long as it was heavy with passion.

When he became tired of gazing into her eyes and lay looking down on her body, like from up on a mountain looking back at the sea of mounds he had ploughed, she would suddenly seem distressed, molested, and would pull up the bedspread, covering her nakedness and her shame. He would still attempt a caress, running his hands gently over her flowing hair (every night, as a sort of ritual, when they went upstairs the first thing he did was let her hair down), stroking her shoulders, reaching the swell of her breasts where they were covered by the bedspread, and she would close her eyes. With his own eyes closed, he would kiss her face, whispering sweet words and repeating her name (Rosalina, Rosalina, Rosalina) as if she were asleep and he wanted to wake her. She wasn't asleep. Her lips were closed and she ignored his pleas. If he tried to kiss her lips, her mouth would shut fast, her body contract convulsively, her hands clutching the bedspread. If he persisted, she would get impatient. Then he would realize that her silent refusal was her way of sending him away. He would close the window, put out the light, take a farewell look at her body against the pale darkness of the bed, then go away without a word. He would go downstairs slowly not knowing what to make of the life he had been leading for these days and months.

When she wanted him, when in the grip of passion she covered him with anguished kisses, clutching his body violently, murmuring passionate words and names he did not know and could not make out, it didn't seem to bother him because he wanted her too, with an ever stronger desire to worm his way into her intimacy; but when, afterwards, he went downstairs feeling desperately hurt and rejected, he would promise himself that he would not go back again. He could not go on with this silent struggle, striving to achieve the complete possession which was denied him. For him only the feverish body. When the waters of that body were at peace and the body fatigued, he was dispensed with. He was to go on his way, down to the lonely room where he struggled through the nights in anguish. He would go to his room and lie thinking about the meaningless absurdity of his days and nights. He was living a life that was not for him, experiencing a love that was not meant for him. Who was Rosalina's love meant for? – if you could call it love. Although she sometimes spoke Emanuel's name (she no longer concealed it, at times she would actually shout his name out loud), he could see that she did so not as if pretending that his body was Emanuel's, but as if she herself were divided and were calling to someone far away, infinitely far away. His body was simply a body to her. They conversed only with their bodies, only their silent bodies were in tune. Because her mind and her eyes were denied him. They belonged to the dead.

He couldn't make it out, he would never understand it. She was way above him, he knew that. He was too small for her, his usefulness ceased the moment her body found peace and untroubled silence. He didn't think of it in these terms : he remembered the women he knew and compared them with Rosalina, totally different from them all, a different sort of creature; he remembered the happy life he'd led before and thought how sad and with-drawn his life was now, sufficiently so as to be commented on. He pondered over the life he led by day, and that he led by night : at night, before he possessed her, when he was kept at a distance. It reminded him of a dog who gets used to being petted by its owner and when it comes expecting the same treatment, finds its owner in a bad temper, is sent packing and can't understand why, so keeps its distance, its tail between its legs, its eyes watering.

Because after he began to visit her in her room every

night and they indulged in drinking and love-making, his daytime existence became even more of an absurdity. By day she was different. By day she was the same Dona Rosalina as before, his employer. He treated her with respect, as though they had made a tacit agreement. When he said Dona Rosalina, do you need me for anything? he looked at her with such humility that he hated himself. Yet it never occurred to him to alter the situation, to remind her that the whole business was false, absurd. Because he didn't know how to put an end to it. It was not just the presence of Quiquina that made him behave in that way. Even when she was not there, he said Dona Rosalina, as if she were a different person, not the one he knew by night, he never tried to remind her that the two of them had a different relationship at night. She saves herself for night-time, he thought to himself, when he saw her distant and aloof, occupied with her fabric flowers.

How can she, how can she? he wondered, in the day-time, when she looked at him placidly as if nothing had happened between them at night. She's not pretending, he told himself. She's not pretending, someone who's pretending has a different look in their eyes. Because not for a moment did she hesitate, never once did she show emotion nor did she ever appear to recognize him as the man who came to her at night in different circumstances. Since she disconnected her eyes and mind from her body, she led different lives by day and by night. In the day-time she was so placid it almost frightened him. In the first few days it made him feel resentful, he felt he was involved in a game, a ridiculous pantomime, a revolting puppet show. Afterwards, when he became aware that she was concealing nothing, that she was utterly sincere and straightforward and that he had to resign himself to accepting her as she was, that she really was like that, he began to feel more at ease. He would even ask permission to stay in the room and watch her work at her flowers.

She would let him and even seemed pleased. She would look at him placidly, smiling occasionally. In her eyes and her smile he could see no hint that she had any recollection of what went on between them at night. She was a young girl after all, a pure innocent young girl.

Once he gave up trying to work it out, he accepted his double life : the nights and the days. By night Rosalina, in the daytime Dona Rosalina. He no longer attempted to fit the two of them into one person, join the two halves together. He came to the conclusion that they never came together : each one followed its own course, never to meet except perhaps in death. Would the death of one mean the end of the other? No, only the death of the body – like the motion of the pendulum in the grandfather clock (now stopped), which created the illusion of a series of pendulums in succession (like the old image of the arrow in flight as several stationary arrows), momentarily becoming just two outer pendulums, extreme left and extreme right, if one stares hard enough, and when the pendulum stops the succession of pendulums ceases to exist (because he couldn't see the slow-moving sequence of figures going on inside her to take the form of two Rosalinas; or perhaps there was not one or two Rosalinas but an endless number, not one of them motionless like the pendulum of the stopped clock, and one wouldn't know until the end of time, until she died and one could add it all up, joining them together, fusing them in one, like the other old image, apparently opposite in meaning, whereby nobody steps into the same river twice), like with the motion of the pendulum the death of the body would destroy the two Rosalinas at the same moment. Yet the body was the same, he could see that, though with difficulty – the same body in which the two Rosalinas took turns. Did the body still exist without the night? Was it possible to have just light, or just total darkness?

He would lose himself in absurd trains of thought, not

along abstract lines though, but in the form of concrete images, the people and things he was familiar with, which somehow represented thoughts of this sort, in his endless but futile struggle to try to understand her, so that he could take refuge in two Rosalinas (how, for God's sake, could he take refuge in the frenzy, the black depths of the nocturnal Rosalina? At night the intense perfume of the jasmine in the gardens, in the daytime it fades and disappears), whose common ground, whose link, was the body. . . . Yet her body was undergoing great changes (time was passing), her body was not the same, he could see that. When he was near her, his eyes focused on her pale delicate hands fashioning a white organdy rose (when that first time, in this very room, Quiquina appeared in the doorway and she fled leaving a white rose lying on the floor, that's where it lay until I picked it up and took it with me to my room, I shall take it with me wherever I go), he watched in silence as she worked patiently, peacefully, her eyes serene and tranquil (before it all began she was hard and tense, moody and restive), her eyes pure and gentle, playful as a young girl's, and he tried to look unthinkingly at those eyes, those hands, that body.

But suddenly, to his amazement, he discovered that she was three, not two. The Dona Rosalina who existed before his arrival at the manor house and who continued to exist until that night (when he killed her for the first time, because she had ceased to live, like a navel cord which shrivels up and falls off); the Rosalina of those feverish nights of delirious passion; and this daytime Dona Rosalina, at whose side he meekly spent the quiet unhurried hours, savouring a modest new pleasure he'd never known before. Such distinctions were too much for a simple fellow like him.

Dona Rosalina, he said to her one day, excuse the comparison, but you sometimes remind me of a coyote. A coyote? she said, not knowing what he was talking about.

You won't know what it's like, I doubt you've ever seen one. No, she said, she didn't know, and he said it's an animal that's sort of always on the move, you can never be sure where he is, keeps vanishing into thin air. Major Lindolfo, my godfather, I think I told you about him, he used to go hunting coyote. I went with him once, out in the bush, way beyond Paracatu, where we used to go. There, in the undergrowth there, he said, look, he saw it first. Then there was a rush, us running, the dogs running with us on their heels, guns loaded and at the ready. And do you think we could find the coyote? The coyote's like that, Dona Rosalina, a sort of will-o'-the-wisp. When you think he's in one place, he's in t'other, and when you get there, he's far away, the wily critter, just like he was making fun of us, playing hide-and-seek with us. He's a right will-o'-the-wisp. . . .

A will-o'-the-wisp, me? she said, seeming not to follow him. I'm always the same, I'm always in the same place. I don't change, José Feliciano, if anything my life is too unchanging. Day follows day just the same for me, not a bit of difference. I even find it hard to remember when things happened. Today, yesterday, the day before yesterday, the day before that, the same thing all the time. Unless I ticked things off on the calendar, but there isn't a calendar in the house. In any case what is there to tick, José Feliciano? I don't see how you can call me a will-o'-the-wisp, or a coyote as you call it.

He studied her voice, the expression in her eyes, her smallest gesture. No shadow crossed her eyes, there was no quiver of the hands. Her eyes were clear and bright, limpid. Nothing to suggest she was lying. Does she really just forget, after she's had it she just forgets? Perhaps she didn't remember the things the two of them did at night? Impossible. He just couldn't make it out, she seemed so innocent, so sincere.

Since he found he couldn't understand, he started to accept her as she was. He would hang around her, basking in her languid gentle silence (her eyes wandering, lost in the clouds), savouring her leisurely inconsequential talk, broken by long spells of easy silence which no longer made him nervous, her stories about the past, about her family, her childhood on Little Stone Ranch which he now felt himself somehow part of (not just in imagination like before when he would follow her in his dreams, seeing her as a young girl romping in the woods in pursuit of the pony Firefly who had run off, and Dona Vivinha would be watching what they were doing from the verandah, watching what he was up to with her behind that thicket), having heard so much about it, and when she told a story about Little Stone he would close his eyes and he seemed to remember (not the episode she was retelling and her words as she told it, but a flesh and blood memory, his own remembrance, as if the incident had happened to him, not to her), he remembered his own life, himself as a child playing with her on Little Stone Ranch (just as he believed he had replaced Emanuel's body with Rosalina by night, when she moaned his name in the agony of her ecstasy, as though she were calling for him way back in time), and where she had mentioned another boy's name (Emanuel) he substituted his own name, his own body, his memory of himself as a child, in that pleasurable daydream, and he followed when she capered around up on the piled up sacks of coffee, darting up and down the dark corridors between the walls of sacks like castle walls in Mr Emanuel's warehouse (in reality she was talking about the warehouse when it belonged to her father and Quincas Ciríaco), he would visualize the scene which she had actually taken part in, in reality, and he in imagination, in Emanuel's coffee warehouse as it was now (not with its appearance though, but coloured by his own childhood in Paracatu on Major Lindolfo's ranch, his way of life and the picture of himself as a boy riding bareback with reins made from creepers, or himself in the paddock, making no noise, smelling the steaming cowpats, while he aimed at a pigeon nibbling a grain of corn with his walking-stick rifle like the one he once made for the sick child who kept pointing at Our Lady and saying that she was talking to him and it was driving Dona Vivinha out of her mind, until Major Lindolfo told him to throw the toy rifle away in the woods), when she told him these different stories (different because he now experienced them in his mind and because she told them differently, with a different voice, in different words), so different from the same stories as she told them to him before, when he first came to the manor house and was groping in the dark because he didn't know which topics were forbidden territory for him (she'd told him so more than once, before, when he was slily trying to establish a familiarity which was being denied him; and she like a will-o'-the-wisp, with her unexpected reactions, never still in one place, a pendulum), nearly everything about her past life was forbidden territory for him (like the portraits, the stopped clocks, that Lucas Procópio the townsfolk told so many stories about, that João Capistrano Honório Cota, colonel, leading citizen, a man of bearing, social standing and breeding), because the stories were different now not just because he experienced them in his imagination but because the teller seemed to be a different person, it was as if she were recounting *his* life, and sitting near Dona Rosalina with his eyes closed he was conscious of the passing hours only because of the clock striking in the pantry (now the exclusive domain of Quiquina who didn't venture into the drawing room when he was in conversation with Dona Rosalina), the striking of the clock reminding him that there was another life, rousing him to reality, so that waking from his dream the mists of illusion would disperse and give way to the hard, bare, black, heavy furniture, and even the flowers she was making lost their sheen and their freshness and went back to being just fabric flowers, the flowers which were ready for him to go and deliver, this being one of his duties now, no longer performed by Quiquina, who kept very much to herself.

Once he began to accept her as she was and to take pleasure in her quiet gentleness and the stories she told him of times gone by, in the afternoons after he'd done the chores, watching her fashion her flowers, his eyes glued to her pale slender hands, her placid motionless eyes, her quiet body which was held in readiness for the night, the dark waters and burning waves confined deep down inside, her body now at peace, with none of the tenseness and rigidity of those early days when she was still the Dona Rosalina who now no longer existed for him, that body of hers which though slender gave the impression of being plump because of the sense of peace and softness he experienced from her calm movements (like – with due respect because of what they did together at night – the way we remember our mother as warm, plump, good, unhurried, when we're away from her or she's died or when we didn't really know her but remember her in our heart and imagine the insignificant things), he was happy during the daytime while he waited for the clock to chime for him to leave Dona Rosalina and go out to deliver the flowers, and he found himself trying to compare the daytime hours with the night-time hours, with the silent hostility of their frenzied copulation, and he came to the conclusion that he was happy during the day, while at night it was the lure of the craters, the darkness of those red jaws from which he could not draw back, and he became aware that those nocturnal meetings were a vice, a sentence, though pleasurable : he was condemned to stay with this woman, this house, this life (till when, for God's sake?), he would never be able to get away, unless some violent occurrence (he shuddered with foreboding) put an end both to his dream of peace and to his nightmare; though he'd frequently promised himself (when he was savouring the peacefulness of those afternoons with Dona Rosalina) to let a few days go by without going to her at night, when he came back from wandering around and found the light on in the drawing room, the door no longer locked, Rosalina waiting for him, he could not resist, a powerful force drew him to her arms and they came together in a frenzy, after which she fell quiet and he would withdraw, going sadly downstairs to the tormented silence of sleepless or fitful nights, with nightmares of Major Lindolfo with the shotgun (Dona Vivinha watching it all from the verandah, calling his godfather to come and see as well), the shining new shotgun aimed straight at him, because at last he'd seen him having it off with Esmeralda (all of a sudden it wasn't Esmeralda, it was Rosalina) in the field, and he would be hit in the chest by the bullet and slowly bleed to death.

This was when he discovered, not by means of analysis or any similar logical mode of comprehension (of which he wasn't capable, being the person he was and because of his rough simple life), but through remembering and comparing what he'd seen and experienced, because remembering and seeing are ways of learning, this was when he discovered that there were not two but three separate persons in one, or rather : two Dona Rosalinas who were different though they looked the same, but if you looked carefully you could see the first, the earlier one, tense and severe, the second comely and relaxed, with a peace of mind that showed in the tranquillity of her gestures, and a solitary Rosalina who could only be reached through shock, by being taken sexually, through the body, not through the eyes or the mind, an anguished nocturnal Rosalina who was totally unlike the other two though they existed in the same body (even the body, taken in isolation, seen and remembered in separate circumstances, seemed to be three separate bodies according to the spirit which moved within it, then, now or before), that same body which acted as point of contact and resting place (and there might be many more, if he were perceptive enough to see them, as with the image of the sequence of

many pendulums or that earlier one of the arrow —
though for that one he would have to have, out of the
question for him, a capacity for sophistry and a power of
rational analysis — or yet another one, not mentioned
before but easy to foresee between the lines, the fertilized
egg that divides into 2, 4, 8, 16 . . . an infinite number
of cells which form into groups before achieving eventual
unity, that's if they do, when the moment of birth arrives),
this was when he discovered and was able to distinguish
the three (for each one of them he too was different, depending on his readiness to get close enough to know
them); he too divided and changed : oh, he was never
conscious of it, he only became aware of the division in
her, despite the fact that he sometimes wondered when
they mentioned it (you've changed a lot, Joey Bird, for
some time now you've been so different you don't seem
like the same person, even Etelvino, who was a bit thick
and not very observant, said to him one day), because
he was so gloomy and depressed, stopped telling stories,
stopped cracking jokes and fooling about, kept to himself,
not even poking his nose into other people's business; it's
true, I have changed, he would say and try to find a
suitable excuse (not for Etelvino, he didn't matter) so that
they wouldn't speculate about the profound change he
himself was aware of : they were beginning to suspect and
gossip, townsfolk are always gossiping, always suspicious;
I have changed, I've had a piece of bad luck, he said, to
their astonishment adding : I got a letter from Paracatu
telling me my mother has died, his eyes full of tears; but
wasn't your mother already dead? I mean my foster
mother, he lied : but wasn't Dona Vivinha your foster
mother? I had another, it's a very sad story, I can't bear
to think about it; and from then on he began to receive
condolences, and when he didn't go back to being his old
cheery self, didn't get back his skittish birdlike manner
(since she died I'm not the same man), they went along
with his explanation, because they liked him a lot, only

a few carried on suspecting, speculating; three Rosalinas, then, and the first was dead now, just a memory when he tried to remember what she was like before, while the second, by whose side he spent the afternoons (she was filling out before his very eyes – as the saying goes, putting on weight), would never merge with the third one, the night-time one in the bedroom, the blood pounding in searing waves until she became quiet, and afterwards in bed, still naked and pulling the bedspread over her white naked body (he didn't want, really didn't want the two to come together and merge, he was happy with her in the daytime, as he later realized, when she was attending to her fabric flowers and would ask him to tell her some of his hunting stories, about his people back in Paracatu, in fact he didn't want the daytime Rosalina ever to change, wanted her to be like a mother always, and wanted the night-time one to fade away gradually, not too quickly, because his desire for her, the habit of her body, was still too strong to stop from one moment to the next, even though in the daytime he swore to give her up), like the saying about parallel lines never meeting.

And so with the passing of time he gradually became aware that the third Rosalina, or rather the second, the daytime one – because as has been said the first no longer existed, the place of the first was now taken by the night-time Rosalina – the second was becoming so soft and gentle, with such an air of serenity (her eyes radiated a soft glow of contentment, her movements became slower and more relaxed all the time as if she were taking sedatives or was too awake to sleep at nights), so placid and maternal (she no longer had that girlish look he used sometimes to glimpse in her eyes or in the way she smiled, which made him follow the long road back to Esmeralda's body, which in turn merged in his repeated dreams with the other girl, the young Rosalina of Little Stone Ranch), so placid, maternal, unhurried, like a cow in the meadow chewing its cud, that he quite felt like opening his heart to her and telling her what he did with the other, her sinister replica at night in the bedroom, as if he did it with some other woman, the way you might confess a shocking sin (he restrained himself, it would be madness, the revelation would destroy the two of them at a stroke, and he didn't want that, for God's sake, the last thing he wanted was for this Dona Rosalina ever to change), or – an even more secret, impossible desire – laying his head on her bosom and asking her to stroke it soothingly (it was ridiculous, he wasn't a child any more, but he wanted to be one), such was the love he now felt, his tenderness, and that while the second Rosalina filled out, slowly increased in size and changed in appearance though she otherwise stayed the same except for the gentleness becoming more marked in her, at the same time the first Rosalina, the one he knew in bed, was fading in strength and she too was becoming softer (oh God, what if the first one becomes so tranquil that she eventually merges with the second, the one in the drawing room, with the fabric flowers, standing in front of the stopped grandfather clock, who when he asked why would now tell him the story but in the third person as though it had not really happened to her and her father?), because there were times now when she didn't want to make love any more, because she was tired, and just wanted to sit drinking until she passed out next to him or threw up – now she would only make love in the dark, if he insisted.

And sometimes during the day Dona Rosalina would get peculiar attacks of nausea which he couldn't understand, because she'd always been in such good health, and she would go pale, white as a sheet, and run out of the room making for the nearest place to retch, and he would be left wondering what if she's sickening for something, what would they do about it (she wouldn't let them call a doctor, no one, not even the doctor, entered the manor house, with the exception of Mr Emanuel who now came less even than before, fortunately for him, because he was jealous of Dona Rosalina, of Rosalina, now, and he would cover her mouth not letting her speak Emanuel's name when they were making love), no, she wasn't ill, if she were Quiquina would be worried and Quiquina took no notice at all of her nausea, he couldn't think why she didn't prepare a special diet or make her special teas, instead of which she was always making her snacks and titbits (she was eating ravenously these days, behind Quiquina's back, she was for ever eating) and she actually asked him to go to the woods with Etelvino and shoot some quail, she was so fond of quail (forgetting she'd once refused some and he had been offended, she had meant to offend him, but that was the first Rosalina, who didn't exist any more) which she ate greedily, neglecting her good manners and ladylike upbringing.

. . . and then, suddenly, he began to find the drawing-room light off every night. The door locked, no matter how much he knocked she didn't open it. And he stood in the middle of the square, hopelessly watching the lighted bedroom window, until eventually the light went out and everything was swallowed up in darkness and silence.

. . . at hourly intervals. The pains coming at hourly intervals. It will be a long time yet. Sometimes it's like that all night long. More than a day. They're lucky when the pains are sharp and come closer and closer together. Bad when they're sluggish, don't do one thing or another. Two days. That's what happened with Dona Sebastiana. First child, Dona Sebastiana was terrified. She never saw a woman so afraid. Had to call Dona Aristina to finish the job. Plenty of experience, she didn't need Dona Aristina now. They wanted her, what was she supposed to do? Dona Sebastiana was scared, she never saw such fear. Pain and fear. Like Rosalina now. She writhed (Dona Sebastiana) and shouted and moaned, grinding her teeth

enough to break them. Now she couldn't call Dona
Aristina to help her. Nobody, even if things went wrong.
She couldn't call anyone. Nobody could come into the
manor, know what was happening to Rosalina. Now she
was the one who wouldn't allow it. She had to go through
it all alone, even if things went wrong. If Rosalina was
in danger of dying. She wouldn't call Dona Aristina then,
she'd call Dr Viriato. Dr Viriato's startled face. His small
eyes blinking behind the thick glasses. Sometimes she
had to call Dr Viriato. When the bleeding got worse and
there was no way of stopping it. The fever afterwards.
The fever that goes on for days and the poor thing starts
going delirious. Fever sends a woman off her rocker, sends
them mad. If the fever started or the bleeding got too
much and she couldn't make it stop, she would call Dr
Viriato. Better not, she wouldn't call Dr Viriato for anything. Only if she absolutely had to, if she couldn't find
a way to stop the bleeding, the fever. Rosalina gets delirious with only a bit of a temperature. Since she was a
child. In Dona Genu's days, poor thing. If she'd suspected
that this would happen to her daughter, she'd die. She'd
died in good time so as not to see what is happening,
what has happened. After the birth, Rosalina getting
fever. Dr Viriato would come at the drop of a hat, she
only had to call him. Dr Viriato was a great friend of
the late Colonel Honório. But he fell in with that bunch
of traitors. At the time of the elections, when he went
crazy. The colonel never forgave him, he wasn't the sort
to forgive. The more they'd been friends before, the
greater his hatred, unforgiving. Crazy, fever after child-
birth usually sends them crazy. The Honório Cotas are
all a bit touched. What about that there Lucas Procópio,
his excesses, his outrageous behaviour. Her mother hated
him, everybody hated him. But they respected him, that
they did. Her mother said once he tried to have her by
force. He pushed her up against the wall, his thing out,
tore her dress in his fury. Didn't bother whether anybody

was watching, even his own wife. He took no notice of anybody, didn't care a damn for anybody. Only he counted, only he gave orders. Not the colonel, he was different. If he was soft in the head, he was a gentle loony, the harmless sort. Not like boss Lucas: grabbing black women, getting them with child, spawning kids all over the place. Blessin', godfather, they would say, respectfully. You never knew when they were really his and when they were godchildren. It came to the same thing. But Colonel Honório was right to go that way afterwards. These people are no good, he used to say. They are no good, Rosalina would say. Now she's not saying anything, the pain won't let her.

The pains again. Stronger now. The waters haven't broken yet. The pains are still far apart. How many hours still? Ten at the most. This one will take time. Looks as though it won't come before two o'clock. If it goes on like this. Some kids are lazy. Breaking the waters would help. Better to wait, always better to wait. That's what Dona Aristina says, she taught me. Perhaps the pains will come quicker, stronger and stronger, closer together. Then it's nearly over. You never know how it will be. Sometimes the pains start coming regular and then they stop. Sometimes they come strong all of a sudden and the kid shoots out like a bullet, tears everything. Looks like it'll take some time yet. She felt around, had a look. Just a bit back she had a look down below, the opening was still small. No point trying to help, telling her to push. Her belly's fallen, but not very much, not far enough yet. Hard, smooth as a drum. Her navel's flat, hardly has a navel any more. Like an ox bladder, blown up for kids to play ball with. Makes you feel like sticking a knife into it, just to be wicked. An odd sort of hankering. The belly hard, like a carbuncle. When she was a child she asked her mother what it was women had in their swollen bellies, she would say it's a carbuncle. And her mother would laugh, thought she knew it all and was asking just for asking's sake. She did know, Mother was right. She'd known since she was a nipper. It was the first thing she learnt. Except she didn't know how a man and woman did it. She imagined, vaguely. She was revolted by what they did in bed, in the woods. Even now she didn't rightly know, she was a virgin. She's always been disgusted by men. She was dumb, they tried to take advantage of her in the past. There was one who tried to force her, like her mother said Lucas Procópio tried to do with her. She couldn't shout, being dumb, she just squawked and nobody came to her assistance, she had to bite his neck until she drew blood. Then he punched her in the face, she got a face this size. She couldn't manage with her hands to tell what had happened. She could only cry, her mother didn't understand. Whenever she saw a pregnant woman, she stopped to look. Where did it come out? The first time she assisted Dona Aristina, that was when she really understood how it happened. She was scared of fainting because of the woman's yells. The belly hard, the thing wriggling about inside like a piglet in a sack, you never know where the head will be. Sometimes they come out bottom first, that's bad, the woman has a bad time. Too bad, nobody made them do it. Funny thing, she wasn't much bothered by the shouts, the hullabaloo some of them made. Never again, never again, they would shout. Then they'd turn up pregnant again. The really amazing thing is the skin tight as a drum. Their thing open down below, the kid filthy with the yellow slime of the placenta, like potter's clay. After, she got used to it, didn't take any notice, she was quite good at it, copied Dona Aristina. Dona Aristina, now she's calm, doesn't worry. Sometimes she'd go to the sitting room and do some crochet. When the time comes, give me a shout, she'd say, crocheting a bootee. Sometimes she had time to finish the bootee. When the child was born, the bootee would be the first present it got. She didn't make a bootee, she no doubt thought it was never going to be born. Did

she ever think it could happen? Of course not. That mad
streak again, Rosalina was a bit crazy. Drunk night after
night, every night the two of them upstairs in the bedroom. To start with, until she was pregnant, until she knew
she was pregnant. After, she didn't want anything more
to do with him. She never said a word, just once she tried
to say something. The first time, that time. But then she
wouldn't let her, felt sorry for her. Rosalina didn't need
to explain, she pretended she understood. Then she found
that way of being two. One at night, with him in the
bedroom, drinking, doing that; another by day, with her
and him. How did Rosalina manage it? He wanted it the
same way in the daytime as at night. Rosalina put him
in his place. Gave him a lesson. See, clever dick! He
learned. He was as rotten as they come, a liar and a
cheat. If she let him he'd take charge of the house like he
owned it. She didn't let him, just as well. It was only
at night, that awful business, that frenzy. He would even
be wanting to order her about. No good with her, he
didn't know what she was like. Even if Rosalina hadn't
done what she did, he wouldn't have the courage. She
was quite capable of bashing his head in with an axe,
when he was asleep in bed. She had often wanted to finish
him off, get him out of Rosalina's life; have done once
and for all with that frenzy every night. Ant poison in
his food, ground glass, a little bit every day, the way she
heard her mother say that a woman once killed her husband. Afterwards she gave up the idea. What use was
there in her taking up the cudgels for Rosalina, if she
was the one who wanted it, wanted that frenzy every
night? Even so she didn't like to see the two of them
together in the drawing room in the daytime. Though
she knew that Rosalina didn't let him near her during
the day. In the daytime she was the madam, he the
servant. At night that shameful business. He had come
and taken her place in Rosalina's heart.

This time the pain was stronger, it hurt. Look at her

215

grinding her teeth. She doesn't cry out, she's pretending she's tough. When the time comes, then we'll see. She won't cry out so as not to attract attention, she might be heard in the street. She's not shouting, so as not to lose face, poor dear. She didn't need to hide it from her. As long as she didn't yell too much, didn't attract attention. Only her body was crying out, her mouth clamped shut, her teeth grinding away. Her eyes glassy. She doesn't seem to see anything. Even when the pain goes away. When the pain goes she shuts her eyes, so as not to see. She didn't need to do that. She only had to put her head on her shoulder, open her heart and cry, she would understand. Didn't she always understand? Had she ever said anything? Wasn't she there to help? How would Rosalina manage without her? He wouldn't be any use, that one-eyed devil out there. He's outside waiting now, the beast. Once she went out to fetch hot water, he kept watching her. His eyes showed distress. Eyes no, his good eye. The other was like a milky marble. That eye, she'd always been suspicious of that eye. The salesman who liked to tease her had a glass eye. Silly, but it was more horrible than no eye at all. Since the first day when he arrived. She could already see something bad would happen to them with him at the manor. That face doesn't deceive anybody, that white eye. Beware those who bear my mark, they say Jesus said. Who told her that? She couldn't remember, there were so many who pestered her, somebody said it behind her back. It was for her, she was dumb, they meant it for her. Sheer nastiness. Cruelty, they were always being cruel to her. Not just the kids in the garden, throwing stones. Grown-ups too. The same as touching a hunchback's hump, for luck, they say. Because she was dumb, she'd been born dumb. But she wasn't deaf, she could hear everything they said about her. Because she was dumb they didn't think. They should be more careful. A person's got feelings, however lowly. They didn't need to beware of her because she was marked by Jesus. Does

216

Jesus really mark people before he knows them, when they are born? Just for amusement? Strike me dead, heaven forbid! St Benedict save me. St Benedict was black. Our Lady of the Rosary of the black people. Blacks don't go to heaven, not even preachers. St Benedict is there, like a rock. Because of their stiff hair. Lady of the Rosary. It stabs Our Lord. Anyone can be born black, dumb, blind, deaf, lame, even with water on the brain. Why does He do that? God's will is just. Monsters must tear the mother bad. She had never seen one born. Dona Aristina had, Daft Tommy. He goes about like an idiot, dribbling, he says silly things, dirty things, the others teach him and he repeats things, innocently, just an idiot. So that others will keep away from dangers? A warning from Jesus, and He knows the pattern of things, life's destinies. She didn't harm anybody, only did good. Like poor Daft Tommy, with his big head wobbling about. Only good. Wasn't that what she was doing now to Rosalina? What if it was born with water on the brain? Wasn't she like that to everybody? Dona Quiquina is a good soul, they said, when they needed her. When Dona Aristina got too old to attend, didn't she go along willingly? He was marked as well. Joey Bird was different, she knew. The devil. That milky white eye. Behind it, inside the eye, his wickedness was hiding. Hobgoblin. Two of them, both marked, in one house was too much. What if Jesus was right and Rosalina was suffering because of the two of them? Not because of her, she did no harm. It was all him. She certainly tried to avoid it, she did everything she could so it wouldn't happen. She only happened to leave the kitchen door open, and that was that. She always locked the door, put the bar across every night. Shutting the stable door after the horse has bolted. After, there was no point, Rosalina went and started opening the front door for him. The two of them sat there drinking, then went upstairs to wallow in filth. Let her get on with it. You make your bed and you lie on it. If that was what Rosalina wanted, she wasn't going to teach her grandmother to suck eggs. Before he arrived, it was all so different. She was marked, but nothing bad ever happened at the manor because of her. Weren't the two of them happy before he came? Damn the day she opened the door to him. She did send him away though. It was Rosalina who called hey, young fellow, come over here. We saw what happened afterwards. This is the result.

She doesn't shout, only moans at times. We'll see when the time comes. Whether she can stand it, some women can, those that are built for childbearing. She's not built for it, you can see from her pelvis. She has a pelvis like a young girl, couldn't know how she would be when the time came. Women with a broad pelvis, comes out like it goes in, so they say. Yeast in the dough, bread from the oven. That's what they say to their niggers. Men say that, they always hop it when the time comes, so as not to see. That's why people say that it's good for a husband to see his wife giving birth, then they know what the pain is like. The pain from what they've forgotten. It's them that say it, women don't joke about these things, they know what it's like. They forget, though, so Dona Aristina says. A clever woman, Dona Aristina. Well, she's helped plenty into the world. If only there was some way she could send for Dona Aristina. But no, Dona Aristina sometimes lets her tongue run away with her. She would beg on her knees, point up at heaven, pray to Our Lady of Pregnant Women, she'd beg Dona Aristina for everything she held dear. She might promise she'd say nothing, then she'd get an itchy tongue and everybody would get to know. She had to sort it out by herself. Not that she didn't know how to do it, she knew it all. She was just afraid of getting nervous when the time came, because Rosalina was like a daughter to her. What can you do anyway? The body does it, when the time comes, out it comes. The woman suffers, but it comes out. She may die, it still comes out. A midwife does very little, just gives a helping hand. But when we're not there, it seems as if it's more painful, very painful. Perhaps because they're afraid? She helped a lot, she had a clever knack of squeezing the bump down, she made the woman take a deep breath and push as if she was relieving herself behind a bush. Or like pushing on the lavatory. What would it be like inside? Right there in the guts? She was a virgin, she felt her own belly. When the time comes, it always comes out. Nobody dies before their time comes, they say. Only a turkey dies the night before. Or so say those that gobble like one. There was no point in stopping the clocks. Just as well they left the pendulum clock in the pantry. With two round pieces, like a figure-eight; there are nicer ones, shaped like a prayer cabinet. Figure-eight clocks are very common, you get tired of them. Prayer cabinet clocks are nicer. But anything like the grandfather clock (when he came downstairs, walked across and stopped, looking them in the face slowly one by one, was it him did that or was it Rosalina? on the day of the funeral, he went across and stopped the grandfather clock), there was nothing like the drawing-room clock, nobody ever saw anything so splendid, so very old. The pantry clock, when the time comes, she's the one who would stop it. She liked to listen to its chimes, the pleasant tick-tock of the pendulum swinging to and fro. Funny, like when it rains and there's a leak drip-dropping. The hours striking, tinkling music. Rosalina's music box, it was the colonel gave it to her as a birthday present. Every time you open it, it plays a piece of music. A minuet, Rosalina says it's a minuet. When you close the lid the music stops. There must be a pin that makes it play. Rosalina probably didn't stop the pendulum clock because she's expecting something else bad to happen. Who would be the one to stop the pendulum clock? Like it was with the grandfather clock, the silver watch, the gold hunter. The colonel was the one who started the craze. Crazy, these Honório Cotas. Gentry, upper crust, so they said. Gentry, and she went and did it with a bum of an odd-job man like that one-eyed Joey Bird, just imagine. Enough to make you spit, his name makes your mouth dirty. He looked at her like he was waiting to know how Rosalina was getting on. As if she would have any truck with a louse like him! Hadn't he done enough already? A swine, a louse. A bug, tumblebug, turtle-dove, little bird. He should have gone away back to that place of his. After Rosalina didn't want him any more at night. After he saw that her belly was growing. But he didn't go because she encouraged him, chatting to him during the daytime. She even enjoyed it, that quiet mother-to-son talk. What if he was really bewitched by her? Because he should have gone away when she stopped opening the door to him. Can he be expecting that once she's pushed the kid out it'll start all over again? But she wouldn't allow that, she would even take the axe to both of them while they were asleep.

This time the pain was worse, she contorted herself. It's taking longer than other times. She's in a cold sweat, she's vomited. She has learnt, she grips the bedhead like she showed her to do before. She does grind her teeth so, she should bite on a piece of cloth so as not to cut her lips and tongue. She'll make them bleed. She can't carry on like that. She wiped the sweat from Rosalina's face. Her hair was soaked in sweat. Looked as if she'd come out of the bath. She patted her, timidly. Rosalina looked at her, she seemed to recognize her now, her eyes were not glassy like before. She tried to smile so that Rosalina would see she was not angry. Console Rosalina, console her to let her know she understood everything and forgave her. But only her eyes smiled. Did she understand? She did, now she's looking at her with the eyes of a suffering madonna. A little girl, sometimes she's just like a little girl. To her she'd always be a little girl, she shouldn't have grown up, ever, so's that wouldn't have happened. Ah, to lay her head on her shoulder and rock her. Like she did

220

on Little Stone Ranch when she was fretting because she didn't want to go to sleep. Those were the good times. Little Stone Ranch, Dona Genu alive, Colonel Honório before he got that craze for politics, just on the farm looking after the coffee, or at the warehouse with Quincas Ciríaco, that good-man-for-ever. After Dona Genu died only Quincas Ciríaco could come inside the manor house. He and his son, Mr Emanuel, so good-looking. She should have overcome her fear and told Mr Emanuel everything. When it started to happen. Before they went to bed the first time. When she came that night and saw the two of them locked together and Rosalina ran out of the room and up the stairs. Why did she carry on waiting, why didn't she tell him everything right away? Mr Emanuel was quiet and conscientious, he wouldn't tell anybody. He was fond of her once, he wanted to marry her. The colonel was very happy with the idea. But she wouldn't, because of that crazy business of staying with her father, joining in that rage against everybody, nursing such a hatred, it's a sin, even. She didn't tell, but not for fear of Rosalina. The next day she got as far as the warehouse door. What's happened Quiquina, what are you doing here at this time of the morning? Should she tell or not? She started to join her hands the way she did when she meant Joey Bird, stopped half-way, then made the sign she used to ask for money. He thought it was funny, she didn't know why he was amused, perhaps because of her goggling eyes. If she didn't tell, it wasn't because she was afraid he would tell the others, he was a very honest man, conscientious, the old fashioned stick-to-his-word sort, as they say, the sort you don't find nowadays, just like Quincas Ciríaco. And he would probably, that's the way he is, not say a word to Rosalina. He would just send Joey Bird on his way. He was the devil, the bugger. The bugger will go and tell the others, spread it around the town, that and all sorts of lies. Rosalina done for, humiliated, disgraced. That was why she turned back and stopped the sign that meant Joey Bird and said money, like that, with her fingers. It would be much better if Mr Emanuel was married to her. None of this would have happened, they would be happy. But she wouldn't, in the bitterness of her hatred. She wanted to do just the same as her father. The stopped clocks, the grandfather clock was so lovely, everybody oohed and ahed when they brought it, with its dainty, resonant chimes like music. The silver watch on the wall, covered in pictures, there was one of the king on horseback and lots of people behind him on the bank of a river. The gold hunter, the chain across his waistcoat. When he died, Rosalina came downstairs with her face painted white like a soul from the next world and without a word went over and put the watch on the wall next to the other one. Now only the pendulum clock kept time in the manor. No doubt waiting for one of them to die. But she wouldn't die before Rosalina. Rosalina might die now. If she died, she would stop the pendulum clock. Her belly sticking out, the muffled drum beat, a clock striking in the memory. If that happens it will be the end of all the clocks and watches in this house.

Every quarter of an hour. She knew, she saw the pendulum clock when she went downstairs to fetch more hot water. He looked at her, kept watching her from a distance. She pretended not to see. Quiquina, he said. She pretended she hadn't heard. Suddenly she rounded on him and her eyes blazed. To let him see that she hated him fit to kill. When it was all over, they would be settling their scores. Old and new. He'd see. He was like an anxious father, the one-eyed cur. He wasn't going to be anybody's father. It wasn't his child, wasn't anybody's, she wouldn't allow it. He took advantage of her innocence. No, she wanted it herself, she wasn't a child any more. But she was drunk, she wasn't in her right mind. She could, couldn't she? Rosalina would never notice. All she had to do was not shake it, if it was born blue, not smack it, if it was born gasping for breath. Sometimes a baby dies because the midwife isn't smart, doesn't start it breathing. When it bellows, you know the air's gone in, it's alive. A wee little creature, so easy. After, she would be grateful. Now she's going to yell, the pains are getting too strong and lasting too long. Doesn't look like it'll be long. Her belly's hard and low down. The drum roll in that story Dona Genu liked to tell Rosalina when she was a child. Low and hard. She had a feel just now and could tell the baby was in the right position. Hard, her belly was all smooth. A man beat the drum and the rats, or was it a flute? She was mixed up, couldn't remember, the rats ran after him and left the city. Nice and hard, moving about, alive. A cat's litter, all those kittens. Some people prefer to drown them, so as not to have thousands of blasted cats all over the house. Alive, is it? Sometimes it isn't alive, it's just the movement inside. She's pushing, she's helping. No point in pushing too hard, it's not quite time yet. When it's really time then she needs to push. When the time came, she would help her. Not yet though, it might turn, complicate things. Not for the baby, for her. For the baby it would be better, she didn't need it. No, my God, she couldn't do that, it was a sin. An awful sin, without forgiveness. Wasn't it a sin the same to let it live? How was she going to manage with that child in the house? How long could she hide it from the town, as the child grew up? How had they hidden Rosalina's pregnancy? Nobody got to know. The worst is that he would be wanting to play the father, be master of the house, he would have the right. That wasn't the worst, the worst was that the town would know. No, that child couldn't live.

And God willing . . . Another little angel. Better that way. Like Dona Genu, her fate. She might be like Dona Genu. No, she's not, it stuck first time. Dona Genu never went the nine months. Or if she did, the child was born dead. Rosalina was the only one that survived. The miscarriages, the little angels. The colonel walking back and forth in his nervousness. When Dona Aristina came and told him it was another little angel, he would lower his head. There were people who said they'd once seen him weep. That was a lie, he didn't cry, he was hardened by pride. Poor Colonel Honório, he so wanted a boy. Long after, after many miscarriages, stillbirths and little angels, came Rosalina. If only God had answered the wish for a male child. Then she wouldn't be here now going through that trouble, that humiliation. She, Quiquina, that was. The colonel would go on for days on end suffering in deathly silence. He didn't go along to the cemetery with the little angels. Nobody did, except her. Damião carried them. Sometimes, when it was a miscarriage, it would be in a shoebox. If it was one of those wrinkled little corpses, a big wooden box would do. They never bothered to have a coffin made. So pretty a little coffin. A coffin for a little angel. The gilt fittings. All white, the children carried it. Grown-ups carrying it would be odd. Damião with the box under his arm like somebody carrying a parcel. It meant nothing to him, he was so used to it. A shallow grave, they didn't dig a big hole. They had to dig the grave at the time, the colonel didn't even bother to send word. Sometimes Damião did it himself. Some fate, that. It was almost like a curse. Maybe that fate has been passed on to Rosalina? That would be her salvation, she wouldn't need to do anything. Another little angel. Oh Lord, call this one. A little angel for the Lord. The Lord needs little angels, one more won't be missed in the world. To Damião miscarriage or little angel made no difference. It came to the same thing. All he had to do was carry the box and dig the grave. Wasn't the same at all for her. She believed that even little angels were people, even when they weren't whole. When he started shovelling earth on top she would cross herself. Once it gets going it's a person, that was what Dona Aristina used to say. It would be like a crime. It's a crime, she once heard the public prosecutor say to Dona Aristina. He didn't need to warn Dona Aristina, she never did it. She didn't know of a single case. She could have done it to Rosalina. Not even for the whores at Bridge House and the Mares-Paddock. He spent his nights there now. Since she shut the door on him. Like animals, the female doesn't receive the male once she's pregnant. Poor thing, comparing her to a cow or a mare. Not even for the poor creatures at the Mares-Paddock, the poorest ones. Poor creatures nonsense, it's probably just sheer lewdness. Couldn't she see? That pig wallowing in it every night after she didn't want it any more. They had to see to it themselves, if they wanted to get rid of one. They weren't to rely on Dona Aristina. Nor on her. Didn't one once ask her if she had a strong medicine to get rid of it? Imagine who it was. Dona Fúlvia, the prosecutor's wife. A crime, that was what he said. His wife did it by herself. Or did someone else do it? She didn't know. All she knew was that afterwards she appeared with a flat tummy and no baby in her arms. His wife did it. She could have done it for Rosalina. She did think about it. She was scared, she didn't want to. She wouldn't be going through this worry, not knowing what to do. What she had to do now was much worse. In any case, a crime. That was what he said, the prosecutor. And his own wife did it. She did think about it. She even prepared a special tea. How was she going to get Rosalina to drink the tea, though, when Rosalina hadn't said anything? She never said a word, kept hiding it. She felt sorry for her, seeing what she did to hide it. From the very beginning, she could see. In her eyes, her manner. Her eyes were gentle, soft, dull: a haziness, a startled gleam sometimes. When, without meaning to, their eyes met. Her movements were slow and gentle. Her gluttony, her vomiting. She thought she didn't notice, poor dear. She ate in secret, then went down the garden to throw up. She bent her body forward to hide her tummy when it started to show. Dona Genu's rubber girdle on the chair. She saw it once, when Rosalina was asleep. She didn't need to do any of that, she only had to say the word. They would have dealt with it before.

Phew, this time it was really strong. Bite the cloth, dear, or you'll cut your lips and your tongue, you'll hurt yourself. That's it, grip the bed, push. You can start pushing to see if it'll come out. It's gone, not ready yet. Another couple of times, she thought. Now she's panting like a dog, she's learnt. It's good, it relaxes, then it doesn't hurt so much. She's learnt. Dona Aristina told them to pant like a puppy dog. Comes out anyway, but it helps. The skin as taut as a drum. Rum-ti-tum. You can see it moving about inside. There are his feet sticking out, like an egg inside her belly, poking. He's turning over and back again. Like a piglet in a sack. What a big belly, unless there's a lot of water she's going to have a big baby. Water on the brain, like Daft Tommy. It'll tear her apart. Don't think of it. Boy or girl? That's silly, like a father. It was all the same. All she had to do was let it suffocate, if it was born not breathing. If it was born breathing, she'd have to do something else. She didn't know how she would manage, she was scared. Not of Rosalina, she won't even notice. All she'd have to do was make a sign with her hands: it was born dead. Would Rosalina cry? No, she must know that the child would complicate her life. It would be doing her a favour. Fear again. Not of Rosalina. Of somebody hidden somewhere, in the room there. Inside herself. A voice, an eye. A crime, the prosecutor said. And his own wife did it. Didn't he know? Or did he say it's a crime just to sound out Dona Aristina, to see if she would do it for his wife? He knew. It's hard to hide these things. As long as she could, Rosalina hid it. Then, when there was no other way, she let her belly show. It made you feel sorry for her. Only once she seemed ashamed, went all red. Afterwards she found a way of pretending. The way she did with one-eye, like she was two. One in the daytime, the madam. At night in bed, a bitch. She didn't mix the two. As if to say the belly isn't mine, as if hers was a flat tummy, a girl's tummy, she pretended, silly thing. Silliness, she should have said something, they would have done something about it. She wouldn't need to do anything now. She was afraid to do it, but she would, for her she would do it. She would do anything for Rosalina. After Dona Genu died she took her place. A child, the child she never had. Always sitting down, hiding her belly under the table. She didn't get drunk at night any more. She still drank, only a little, but she did drink. Better if she had been drunk every night. She might have got rid of it then, before its time. She should have made Rosalina drink that tea. Worked like a shot, they said. Now she ought to give it up, her vice. It was her vice that made her take leave of her senses. At times he seemed to be amused looking at Rosalina's belly, the job he'd done. She pretended not to notice, but from time to time she would catch him looking. The rotter would act innocent, the one-eyed devil. He would sit near her, looking as if butter wouldn't melt in his mouth, enjoying the pleasant tranquillity that Rosalina had when she was making flowers. An angel next to Our Lady, to put it crudely. Our Lady was expecting too. But from God, not from a pig, a louse like him, in the Mares-Paddock every night with women of his sort. She didn't hide her big belly from him even. She wasn't ashamed any more. Had the two of them ever talked about it? No, she found a way of being two people : one at night, another by day. Now she's suffering, the time is close. No point stopping the clocks, the hour will come. It was easy to hide it, nobody ever knew. Rosalina won't know, if she does it. She never went out, so nobody found out. Unless some peeping tom pushed his face in at the window. No, she took her precautions without letting on. When Rosalina was not sitting with her belly under the table, she would always go to the window to check that there was no snooper about. Once she had a narrow escape. My God, he nearly saw. When she went to the window, there was Mr Emanuel on his way over. She stood there pop-eyed, not knowing what to do. Mr

Emanuel knocked at the door, should she open or not? Rosalina was at the table making flowers. Better open. First she had to get rid of Rosalina, hide her in a corner. He mustn't see her, he must never see her. Quiquina, he said to her as she stood motionless at the window. She signalled to him to wait with her hand, like this. She took hold of Rosalina and started pushing her up the stairs. She looked in surprise, letting herself be taken, not knowing why she was being pushed upstairs. She understood when she heard Mr Emanuel's voice. Quiquina, will you call Dona Rosalina, he said. She stopped to think a moment. Then she made a face as if in pain, pointed to her chest and put her open hand on her head, as her way of saying that Rosalina was in bed. Oh, she's ill, he said. She stopped to think a moment. He twisted his hat round, the embarrassment he always showed when he was near Rosalina. Rosalina was upstairs, he didn't see her. Is it serious Quiquina? Maybe we'd better call Dr Viriato. She shook her head, no. A crazy idea, to call Dr Viriato. She had to get rid of Mr Emanuel somehow and quick. That was when that nosey one-eyed blighter came in. Listening behind the door, always eavesdropping. It's nothing serious Mr Emanuel, he had the cheek to say. Woman's upset, you know what they are. To say that! His manner, his swagger, his master-of-the-house act. In front of her, in front of Mr Emanuel. Mr Emanuel red in the face, not knowing which way to look, twisting his hat round faster. Well, he said, after a while, stammering, with his eyes on the ground, I'll be getting along. Just tell her I came (at least he spoke to her, he never so much as looked at one-eye, he didn't encourage him). I'm going to leave some papers, if she wants to talk to me later, just to send for me. He left, and didn't come back. Never. Did he perhaps suspect something? She didn't send for him, she wasn't stupid enough to do that. Of course he didn't suspect, he was just timid. He probably thought she didn't want to see him. Afraid of making himself a nuisance, tight-lipped like his father. The fact is he didn't come again. Thank God. How would she have found another excuse, an illness like one-eye invented couldn't be used again. Mr Emanuel would send for Dr Viriato. He wouldn't believe that it was woman's trouble again. One-eye had a cheek saying a thing like that! A disaster, the shame of it, everything down the drain.

My God, she's suffering though. The more afraid a woman is, the more she suffers. Women who are made for childbearing are relaxed, they're much better, they push it out in a flash. Only hurts a bit. She's seen many like that. There are some that like a bit of sympathy, when it gets tough. Sometimes it helps. Like people on their deathbed who don't seem to want to die. There are people who make a hard job of dying. Because of their sins, their remorse. Lucas Procópio was like that, she remembered. Very young, she was, but she remembered. All those people in the drawing room, night after night, waiting. And he wouldn't make up his mind to go. Hard in death even, rotten beast, even in death. Her mother said it was because of his sins, the wicked things he'd done to others, to the niggers, all sorts of people, even animals suffered at his hands, rotten devil. Balking like a mule at death's door, on account of his sins, his eternal hatred, that fury that took control of him at times. When they thought he was fading away, the old bugger would come up again blustering, gasping, puffing and blowing. Once he tried to do it with her mother, even tore her dress, had his thing out of his trousers, couldn't care if anybody was watching. He took no notice of anybody, threw it in their faces. What he had to do, he did in front of everybody, they could skedaddle if they wanted to. The whip lashing their legs. Jump nigger, wriggle nigger gal, piddle nigger wench! When he appeared, her mother said the niggers set about making themselves scarce. He was quite capable of walking arm in arm with a nigger woman. Rosalina was like him, she had confronted the town. Lucas Procópio would parade the nigger woman and her swollen belly round the town, couldn't care, just for the townsfolk to see. Not her though, she's more like Colonel Honório. The pride, the injured silence of Colonel João Capistrano Honório Cota. The way they liked to say it. He liked to say his whole name, it was a mouthful. He was like his father in that. But Mr Lucas was different, they said. No, he wasn't like him, he did everything not to be like Lucas Procópio. Sometimes he would say he honoured his father very much, but you could see it was just lip service. He had the manor built on top of Lucas Procópio's old house. Me and him together for always, he said to the mason and the mason went around repeating it to all and sundry, like a refrain. She takes more after João Capistrano Honório Cota. Colonel Honório might have made a decision like that : to be one person by day and another at night. Yes, that's it. In the daytime she was João Capistrano Honório Cota – the haughtiness, the pride, sins condemned by God. At night, in bed with that one-eyed pig, she was Mr Lucas, rutting like a stallion. Me and him together for always, in the manor, in the person of Rosalina. She was an unhappy creature suffering here. Lucas Procópio suffering and couldn't die, couldn't find his journey's end. On account of his wickedness, his sins. They were all paying for Lucas Procópio's sins. The fate of the manor. The little angels. The craters she saw when she went to the cemetery. God didn't want Lucas Procópio with Him not for a moment, because he was a jinx. He wouldn't call him. If He called him it would be to send him to the bowels of hell. Seems God was taking His time to despatch him. One-eye and his rifle. Made a bang like a thunderclap. But God was all eyes. He could see everything, He could even see that scrap of cloud that went through her mind, her wanting to put an end to the child who was as firm as a piglet in a sack. She's suffering too much. Can't make its mind up. Lucas Procópio couldn't make up his mind to leave this life. Or was it those who had suffered at his hands who didn't want him to go? On account of this he couldn't die, suffered the agony of not dying. Then his enemies, those people he'd offended, sent word that they forgave him, so that he'd die quickly, but he still wouldn't die. The cross in the square looked like one huge candle. Her mother went and prayed too and said that she forgave him. Nobody could stand it any longer, the suffering of that man who was alive and who was dying. One day he died, but they said he only died when he wanted to, when he gave up wanting to keep death at bay any longer. He even refused a priest, swore at them, his last insult. And he reckoned he was a Catholic, they said. It was him, after all, who gave the land to build the church on.

Now the waters have burst, she's soaked. What a time she's having! She had seen lots already, helped with so many births, but it's as if this is the first time. It's because she felt for Rosalina, it hurt inside her, churned her up deep down inside. The pains were stronger and stronger, more and more prolonged. Nearly following on without a pause. When they came one after another, it would be time. Sometimes it happens all of a sudden, she had to be ready. She was helping now by pushing the bump downwards, getting her legs in position. It would all come out right, please God. As for the child she'd have to see what was to be done. We'll decide at the time, no point in dwelling on it before. If there were time, before Rosalina saw the child. She wouldn't even suspect. Just show her the little dead creature afterwards. God is great, we'll manage something. It might well be the case that Our Lord will make it come out dead, another little angel given birth by the manor, Dona Genu every time, the destiny of these Honório Cotas. Maybe she inherited her insides from Dona Genu. This fate weighing on the house, suffocating it. Then she wouldn't need to do anything, her hands would be clean, except for the filth of the placenta. The worst is afterwards, when all the blood comes and she's between life and death. Or else she'll get the fever, then she'd start going out of her mind. She knew of such cases. The fever after the birth. The woman starts going crazy, delirious, nothing you can do about it, loses her reason, goes mad. Occasionally one doesn't come back to normal, stays daft for the rest of her life. She was already a bit touched, like Colonel Honório Cota, that craze of his. In the family, there are cases like that. That cranky idea of being one person by day and another at night, was that being right in the head? Foolishness, oddness. A bit dotty, that's what Rosalina was. But then who could stand living the way she did after those deaths one after another, shut up in the manor all her life?

Phew, now it's coming. That's it, push! Grab hold of the bed! Push! There he comes. Just a wee bit more, keep it up. Just a wee bit and it's done. There he is! Yellow, the colour of potter's clay.

Lying on his back on the bed, with his hands clasped under his head, motionless except for the slow rise and fall of his chest as he breathed, his eyes still, fixed on the open door and beyond into the silvery green of the garden – the moonlight was as gentle as the wind – he was waiting for daybreak. In the dark, his room lit only by the moonlight coming in from the garden, he was waiting for the first light of day so that he could be on his way. The moonlight filtering through the foliage – the leaves seemed to be coated in a glittering dust – mottled the ground with whitish patches, which danced when the breeze blew softly, swaying the branches.

The moon was high in the sky, white, small and round; no longer that huge, round moon like a Minas cheese, when night began and he had to go out with the bundle which Quiquina gave him: he only took one brief glance at the moon now, not caring about anything that was happening outside himself, his eyes were looking inwards, he was inside the darkness of his body, in the billowing mists of his thoughts and recollections of that terrible night which was so long ending, recollections and thoughts which he was trying to get sorted out. Only on the odd occasion, as if he left his own body and was able to see himself from outside, and to escape from the dark night, the nocturnal world within, did he look out at the garden bathed in moonlight, smelling its moist aroma. With his eyes staring into the emptiness of the open door, he hardly saw the patches of moonlight on the ground now, and the world of the garden. At first he still watched with interest the silvery gleam of the moonlight on the leaves, making them all look like pumpwood leaves, the gentle dance of the patches of moonlight on the ground when the wind swayed the foliage of the mango tree more roughly. Now his eyes were barely enough for the darkness inside himself, he was trying to see a light, put his recollections in order.

At the bottom of the garden a toad started another round of his intermittent gruff croaking. When the toad, which, with eyes popping out of its head, was basking rapturously in the moonlight, fell silent, the song of the cricket broke in splendidly, as if the two of them had made a wager to see who could sing longer, the arrangement being to spend the whole night taking it in turns. Now it was a gentle duet, a peaceful, leisurely, monotonous song, instead of that restless, teeming world of chirps, birdsongs and noises he had heard along the road before he got to the first trees and before he reached the craters : towards which he was walking unthinkingly.

He continued to listen to the cricket and the toad taking it in turns, but without interest, the way you listen to distant music before going to sleep and the music blends with the first waves of sleep. But he didn't go to sleep, sleeplessly he waited, taking leave of the noises, of the garden in the moonlight, turning back to his waking sleep in an absurd world of recollections that made up that night; not only this one, but the other, the previous one, when, with his ears straining in the direction of the upstairs room, he could hear Rosalina's muffled moans, when Quiquina opened the door, closing it again carefully, and came down to fetch the kettle from the stove. Now he was waiting, indifferent, limp, apathetic, for the daylight to come and that night of nightmares and agitation to end, so that he could leave.

It was better to go, there was nothing more for him to do in that house, he was being expelled. That was what he saw in Quiquina's eyes when he ran back and found her waiting for him at the kitchen door; after she heard what she wanted, she stood motionless and gave him a long, slow look, then told him, with her hands and eyes, go away from this house for good, get out of my sight, and slammed the door shut. He couldn't see her face properly, make out her features, only the gleam in her eyes, that final mute order that he had to obey. With her back to the kitchen, blocking the light, she stood in the doorway, her body arched over him in a giant shadow, as if she meant to embrace him. He was looking up at her, she was on the step of the stairs, barring the way. She thought he would want to go in. Silly idea, he had no desire to go into that house again, he'd made up his mind on that, she didn't need to stand there showing him dumbly, with her body in the doorway, blocking the way, like a guard, a watchdog, hunting dog. He was afraid of Quiquina, of what she had done, of what she might still do.

The two of them motionless, unspeaking. She without a gesture, just the anxiety, in her silence, of a person waiting for an answer which, being dumb, she could not ask for; he was panting, the words stuck in his throat. She waited impatiently for him to recover from rushing back in (he tore into the garden without even bothering to close the gate, as if someone or some thing were pursuing him) and be able to speak. He was panting like a boy who had come running to report the outcome of an errand. Inside he was boiling with violent hatred, but he was powerless against the manor, against Quiquina, against destiny. Faced with that absurd world, he could only obey. He felt small as he looked up at Quiquina standing motionless in front of him, hands on hips, waiting. Small, he could only obey. Quiquina's silence mesmerized him, he was no longer master of his own will. One glance from Quiquina was enough to move his feet, he obeyed without a word, and yet he hated her more than anything in the world. Like a bird going, cheeping and struggling, unwillingly, straight into the snake's mouth.

This was why, since he had no power, there was nothing more for him to do in that house and he was waiting for day to break so that he could leave. The day that was taking so long to wake him from his sleepless night.

A stronger gust of wind shook the crown of the mango tree and he smelt the damp scent of the foliage, the sharp smell of resin. The grove of mango trees in the garden behind the farm house, where he first saw Esmeralda tempting him and called her with his eyes, a twist of his head, in the direction of the meadow, where the two of them then made for, he in front, she sneaking along behind, at some distance. Afterwards, the major nearly saw them, he came just in time to save him. Dona Vivinha on the verandah pointing at him and Rosalina, close by as if she were looking through binoculars. Major Lindolfo's shotgun, the buckshot, the shot in his chest. There was a buzzing in his ear, the whining sound came nearer. He was waiting for a cart, any sort of ride, he was very tired. That was when he saw the ox-cart in the distance, the guide boy coming on ahead. Then Silvino was chatting to him. The cemetery with its wrought-iron gate. The craters. The boy Mannie was as scared as he was. When he went that way he turned his face away, went past like the wind. He should have gone past the manor in a hurry, gone on his way, never gone into that crater. There were all sorts of portents in the air that day. His dream, the craters and the dust devil in the square; a warning to him. The major, on horseback, shotgun and all, was behind him with a great clatter of hoofs : he expected a shot in the back at any moment. On the road, after he threw the last spadeful of soil and his fear grew, he jumped over the fence, tearing his trousers on the barbed-wire. He came running back with his heart in his mouth, hearing the hoofs of the major's horse right behind him. When he got to the square, where it was lighter, his fear began to subside; even so he carried on running, pushed open the half closed gate with his chest, then saw Quiquina standing facing him, and stopped. Quiquina's presence, although it scared him, was a real presence saving him from the shadow of that awful world that was galloping behind him.

Quiquina was waiting for him to speak. Quiquina's eyes were gleaming. Without a gesture or a sign, she was asking her question. Still trembling, panting for breath, but sure that Major Lindolfo had vanished, he had returned to the real world and was now looking fearfully at Quiquina. But it was a fear he could bear, not that madness, the nightmare back there on the road after he jumped over the fence and came running back.

He caught once more the smell of resin from the mango tree, the scent moist with moonlight. In a way he was happy to be there now. The scent of the mango tree was real, he was there in the garden, not back on the farm in Paracatu, in the mango grove behind the farm house, running along the road. He was safe there, in his bed, waiting for daylight so that he could leave.

Now he remembered how things had started that night. He was in the kitchen, slumped on a bench, looking into the ashes of the stove. Like the previous night when he waited for Quiquina to come and fetch the kettle of water. He didn't know what was going on up there in the bedroom. Once (he was up on the stairs, he couldn't stand waiting) he was aware that Rosalina's muffled moans had stopped altogether and he thought he heard a baby's cry; it was followed by a vast, still silence the rest of that night, and the whole of the next day, in Rosalina's room. He didn't know what was going on up there, the two of them shut in there all day long. Only once during the day he saw Quiquina come down : she fetched something from the stove, from the kitchen cupboard. He watched her from a distance, followed her movements, not daring to approach her, unable to pluck up courage to ask her what had happened, how Rosalina was. At that moment he was thinking about Rosalina, his heart heavy with fear, guilt and pity. He didn't know what to do, like a child he waited for an order from Quiquina. All day long, waiting there for Quiquina.

When night fell she came. She was carrying a parcel under her arm, like a bundle of clothes. From where he was he had the feeling that the parcel was damp, as if it were daubed with mud. It was a long parcel, sewn up with string : so that he wouldn't open it. In a flash he saw what it was. The parcel was more like a ham or a salami, sewn up in a sack. She didn't need to say anything, she handed him the parcel. He tried to back away, a cold shudder ran through his body. Rooted by the expression in Quiquina's eyes, he no longer had a will of his own, he put his arms out and took the parcel. It had a strange sort of weight, an unpleasant dampness and a nauseating stench that even now reeked in his nose and on his fingers. A feeling of disgust, a desire to vomit. Like once in the poorhouse. . . .

He took the parcel and stood looking at Quiquina stupidly, not knowing what to do with that damp, dirty bundle. His eyes were asking what he was to do, although he knew, because he could not get a single word out, as if he were the dumb one. Quiquina did like this with her hands, her nails, like a dog nimbly digging a hole in the ground. Then she turned and looked under the bench where he had been sitting, and he saw the spade; he knew now what she meant. With the parcel under his arm, the soggy, slimy bundle wetting his shirt, he picked up the spade as if he were sleepwalking; without a glance, without a word, he turned his back on Quiquina and went out towards the bottom of the garden. That was when he heard Quiquina's piercing grunt behind him. He turned round. She was gesticulating wildly, at first he couldn't make out why. She pointed to the gate and he realized that it couldn't be in the garden, she didn't want that. In her confusion she was inventing signs, grunting. She made a cross with her arms, then opened her mouth, adding to the size of the hole with her hands, a big open hole. She meant cemetery, craters. Oh God no, he hadn't the courage. He stood on the spot, waiting. Quiquina grunted again and his fear was such that he could not resist; he ran out, opened the gate and went out into the street.

Now he was running along the road, the slimy parcel under his arm, the spade in his right hand. His heart was in his mouth. He ran. The moonlight shone on the gravel, glinting on the mica in the stone chips with which the road was paved. The moonlight on the road made it like a dream vision, full of mystery and fear. He could see the silvery road ahead of him like a long carpet leading him to the black abyss of the craters. Suddenly, seeing the open jaws, the innards which the moon licked with light, like a deep red gum, almost black, seeing the gloom of the craters barely lit by the moonlight, he stopped. A fear, greater than the other fear which had driven him this far, gripped his body, shackled his legs. His first reaction was to throw the repulsive parcel away, get rid of that nauseating damp smell and run all the way back. But the idea of Quiquina waiting for him to come back stopped him in the act. He couldn't go on, he couldn't go past the craters. Not once did he think what he was going to do, from the moment when Quiquina ordered him to go out, when she told him cemetery, craters. He didn't intend to bury the parcel in the cemetery, in the craters. He just obeyed. Now he stopped. He could neither go on further nor tear himself away. He couldn't leave the parcel on the roadside. The fence, the meadow. He threw the parcel and the spade over the fence and jumped over. A little further on, between two clumps of trees, he began to dig hurriedly, as fast as he could. It had to be good and deep. Because of the armadillos, he said to himself. Armadillos root up everything.

The crickets, the toads, a longer call – sounded like a curassow. A long whistle followed by a short one, at intervals, like a rat or a bat squeaking. Everything was humming, everything going round, everything mingled together in his ears.

It was after the last spadeful of earth that he started to hear in the depths of the night the clatter of Major Lindolfo's horse's hoofs. The major was behind him with a loaded shotgun. I'll fill you full of lead, you devil! He had to run, he couldn't stay there, the major had seen it all, he was coming closer.

His heart started to beat fast, just remembering made his heart beat fast, as if he was running again. Raising his body from the bed, he leaned on his elbows and dropped onto his knees on the floor. He didn't know why he felt an overwhelming desire to talk to somebody, to say a prayer that Dona Vivinha used to like. But inside him there was a great void, a bottomless abyss . . . (Quiquina's image appeared to him again. She was asking, demanding to know with one gesture, just with her eyes, her hands were silent. Quiquina barring his way. Quiquina in the doorway, like a hunting dog. Done it, he managed to say eventually. I've done it just the way you said, he spat out the words.) . . . and as he couldn't remember Dona Vivinha's prayer (Quiquina's image grew, like a ghost in front of him), he raised his fists in the air. Damned house! Damned life! Damn her! Damn everybody! Damn me too! He shouted as if he wanted to tear his heart out. In his room dimly lit by the moonlight, his eyes glistened moistly. And he started to cry.

9

Rosalina's Song

Suddenly we found ourselves back in the manor house. We crossed the bridge at last, the manor opened its doors to us. It was like those other occasions, when Dona Genu died, when Colonel João Capistrano Honório Cota left us for good. In that house everything tended to repeat itself. Like a clock, one of those stopped clocks – we saw the other times how it happened, how and why those clocks began to stop.

The manor was filling up with people, just like a party. But it was a feast of speculation, everyone wanted to know what would happen, though many people said – with a semblance of sadness in their downcast eyes and contrite faces – that they were there to pay a last respect, show their love and respect for Rosalina and for the memory of Colonel João Capistrano Honório Cota: the wound in our hearts ached at times, when we remembered.

There were people all over the house. At first they spoke in whispers, then the buzz of voices began to grow louder and louder, from time to time someone had to clear his throat and ask for silence. It was showing scant respect, the way they talked, conjectured, rooted around in the drawing room, the pantry, the kitchen; surreptitiously, pretending not to be interested. There were even some in the garden amusing themselves sucking jaboticabas (the bushes were skinned in a flash) while they waited.

The upper floor of the manor was the only place we couldn't go, on account of the soldier they stationed at the bottom of the staircase. Everybody wanted to know what was happening, somebody was always coming with a fresh piece of news. Then the hubbub would increase as the comments went from mouth to mouth, the murmur of voices would grow. What happened, what was it? Emanuel has just arrived, said one. No he's not, said another, Emanuel was first here. I saw him arrive. The soldier actually tried to stop him, the judge had to come to the top of the stairs and order him to be let through. How ridiculous! said another, dying with curiosity. This police lot go too far! Even Mr Emanuel, who's one of the family, like a brother to her, not able to go in! They should let some in, the more respected citizens, the most important. Not everybody though, or it'll end up in a rabble.

No one was to go up, that was the order the soldier was carrying out to the letter. Except for the authorities and Mr Emanuel, they only made one exception, which we considered quite correct. That was when Colonel Sigismundo arrived. A surprise, his arrival. He came in a shiny new car. We heard the noisy hooter from far away, he had it sounded at every corner. We got a kick out of that brand new car, it was gorgeous and beautifully finished. The driver was Zico, a sort of godchild, protégé and bodyguard of the colonel's. It was a pleasure to see Zico at the wheel, he had even unearthed a chauffeur's cap from somewhere. And he sounded the hooter with gusto, seeing that Colonel Sigismundo liked to do things in style.

The car stopped right outside the door, Colonel Sigismundo jumped out. The crowd of kids on the pavement went over to the car. In a flash they were climbing all over it, threatening to spoil the gorgeous red paintwork. Every so often Zico had to shoo them off, or they would make a mess. Let me show you what it's for, he would say when a more daring one had got inside the car and was trying to pull one of the knobs. We expected Colonel Sigismundo to come back down with the news. He didn't come, he stayed upstairs. Some people got angry and reckoned Colonel Sigismundo had been given special treatment, if not worse, even taking into account his car and all that. People talk too much, they have to have their say. As if it was the right moment for such arguments. When they ought to be feeling sorry.

At one stage someone did come with a piece of news. Some days ago Joey Bird had been seen slipping out of town. Who saw him, nobody saw him, all lies. It was Donga Novais who saw him, said the one who had brought the news. You know how he spends the nights awake, suffers from insomnia he does, stands by the window. At the mention of Donga Novais, no one put his evidence in doubt, he wasn't an untruthful person, quite the reverse. They believed it, they would believe anything. They wanted to know, they were dying to know. They believed it, it seemed a reasonable probability. No one had seen Joey Bird yet, and recently he hadn't been around much in any case.

All this idle talk made you edgy, got on your nerves. The women were whispering, the men sucked their long home-rolled cigarettes, even when they had gone out, and they spat and nattered. The women, who were more in the know, even so sent one of the children, surreptitiously, to find out from the men if there was any more news. Everybody knew something and something more was always added on, so that the story kept growing just like that swarm of buzzing voices without respect, the lack of good manners. Some even came close to messing with the clocks and watches, wanting to wind them up, pull the weights. If the soldier hadn't been there, they would have. Needs a soldier to impose respect, when a lot of people come together like that, a uniform's the only way.

Just when we were more or less losing hope of any

243

worthwhile piece of news, somebody came with the information that Quiquina had come downstairs, gone to the pantry and stopped the pendulum clock. But no one saw her, when did they see her? Because suddenly the pendulum clock was still. We had expected things to be repeated, but not so completely, like a repeater watch. It wasn't just now, it was at the beginning, when there weren't many people here, somebody said. Did you see? were you here? No, I wasn't, but Ramiro was, he was first to arrive, he saw. He was telling the others outside there. It all seemed true, it was true, we believed it, there was no other explanation for the pendulum clock having stopped.

In any case the first person to let on what was going on at the manor was Donga Novais, whose evidence, because he was awake throughout the night, was always called upon and no one doubted his word. If Donga Novais said it, it must be true. He was the first to give a reasonable explanation for the singing we suddenly started to hear, coming out of the depths of the night, from the bowels of the dark. It was a weepy sort of singsong, high-pitched like the Veronica in Holy Week (that's what it sounded like to us), when Dona Auta, who always took the part of St Veronica, got up on a chair and started singing that lovely hymn that goes like this, oh ye sinners, etc. Because some people had the wildest theories, we didn't believe them. They talked about headless mules,[9] spirits from the other world, those things people invent out of fear. But the song was very strange, just hearing it gave you the creeps. A song that no one had ever heard before : we couldn't catch the words, all we could hear was the tune. It was Donga Novais, too, who got to the bottom of the mystery of the nocturnal singsong. He went himself, in person, to see Mr Emanuel in order to avoid misunderstandings and sort matters out properly. Emanuel was the one who should take some measure, it was up to him. Because there were people wicked enough to be thinking of going out at night with sticks and guns to unbind the spell on that spirit-from-the-other-world or teach a lesson to the joker who was playing tricks with our nerves.

It's her all right, said Donga Novais. And since they were in doubt, he said I saw her with my own eyes, God help me. I saw Dona Rosalina once all in white coming from the direction of the cemetery in the middle of the night. When he mentioned the cemetery, nobody could believe him, people thought that not sleeping for so long had affected his reason and that he had started talking nonsense. Listen, Mr Emanuel began, frowning, courteous, as was his way. Listen, I don't like to be fooled about with, you know that, I like to have respect, I don't go in for silly behaviour. If you've got nothing better to do, friend Donga, look about you, there's plenty of work to do. If you are making fun of me, you're wasting your time, you might even come off worst. Old Donga was ready to quarrel, they said. He didn't, the two of them came out of the warehouse deep in conversation. At first the conversation was just between the two of them, later we got to know about it. It was Donga Novais himself who decided to tell people. You come with me, Donga Novais said earnestly. I'll show you, I don't joke about things, I am respectable, you know that, you have no right to doubt my word. Any night you wish, I never sleep, as you know. . . . And that's how we discovered that every night, for many nights, late at night, when everyone was asleep, Rosalina would leave the manor and go singing her song in the dark of night. What her song said, no one ever knew. Some repeated the words, but you could tell they were just making them up. At times like this, we imagine things and make up a lot. Anyway, Mr Emanuel called together the judge, the prosecutor and the police inspector. They held a private conversation and took all the necessary steps.

Now we were back in the manor house, waiting. In a

way, everybody was at home in the house. It wasn't like the other times, the funeral of Dona Genu, the death of our unforgettable Colonel João Capistrano Honório Cota, whose memory we praise and exalt as an example of rectitude and character. Character is a good thing.

The confusion and the chaos were general. People were now into the cupboards, meddling with pots and pans; some were making coffee. If it went on any longer, if Mr Emanuel didn't give the signal for the procession, they would end up cleaning out the house, there were already some people eyeing the gold hunter. At that point there was a commotion in the drawing room. The buzz of voices got louder, then there was an astonished silence. No one ventured to open his mouth to speak, all eyes were turned upwards.

At the top of the stairs, this is what we saw :

First came the judge, unhurried, with his gold-topped cane, his ruby ring with the diamond cluster, his striped trousers, his felt spats. The judge was whispering something, Colonel Sigismundo was next to him, rather clumsy, but making an effort to be as serious and composed as possible, so as not to contrast too much with the polite, well-educated bearing of Judge Saturnino Bezerra. They walked with their heads lowered, not looking at anybody, as if they were at a ceremony where no familiarity was allowed. With bated breath and unblinking eyes, we waited for more, we wanted the main reason for our presence in the manor house. There was a stir, someone let out a cry, which was immediately stifled, but which still vibrated in the air after everyone fell silent with amazement.

All in white, with a long dress trimmed with lace and a full white rose in her hair, there she came. There came Rosalina, descending the staircase on Mr Emanuel's arm. They came down slowly, step by step. He kept turning towards her attentively, as if he were afraid that she might suddenly fall. Head held high, her bearing erect and stately, she was more like a queen descending a palace staircase, a bride floating heavenwards. And she was smiling, my God, we saw Rosalina smile for the first time in many years. She seemed to be smiling at us. But we knew she wasn't smiling at us : it was a dotty sort of smile, meant for no one. She didn't seem to recognize us, yet she was smiling, her eyes were glassy and didn't really see, though it was at us that she was looking and smiling.

When Rosalina reached the bottom step of the staircase, she stopped and whispered something in Emanuel's ear; no one heard, just a faint motion of her lips. He nodded a yes. And they continued their wedding march. We moved aside instinctively, opening a path for them. She looked at us, lowering her head a little, as if shyly acknowledging our greetings, which we muttered with difficulty, silent and fearful. They were not for us, those gestures, the expression in her eyes, we knew that inside ourselves.

We made a circle around the car, even the children behaved with respect. Emanuel opened the car door for her to step in. He gave her his hand and helped her. We saw that he made a bow to her, like a vassal addressing his queen. She sat between him and the police inspector. On the front seat, the soldier, with Zico at the wheel. Colonel Sigismundo didn't go, he stayed with us and watched the car move off.

The car made a noisy start and left behind it a cloud of dust. There went Rosalina, off to distant lands. There went Rosalina, our thorn, our grief.